★

"I suppose you plan on standing around until I hazard a guess?"

"We've nothing else to go on."

"I'm marking it as possible asphyxiation."

"Accidental, then."

"Possibly, but unlikely. I'd say her face had been pressed into a muddy surface and held there until she suffocated. And in case you hadn't noticed when they took her out—she was pregnant."

"What?"

Not one murder, but two.

★

"The tale is told in short takes that move swiftly from scene to scene, and from character to character, with high-level suspense..."

—*Kirkus Reviews*

Previously published Worldwide Mystery titles by
KAY MITCHELL

IN STONY PLACES
A LIVELY FORM OF DEATH
ROOTS OF EVIL
A PORTION FOR FOXES

A Rage of Innocents

Kay Mitchell

WORLDWIDE®

TORONTO • NEW YORK • LONDON
AMSTERDAM • PARIS • SYDNEY • HAMBURG
STOCKHOLM • ATHENS • TOKYO • MILAN
MADRID • WARSAW • BUDAPEST • AUCKLAND

A RAGE OF INNOCENTS

A Worldwide Mystery/August 1999

First published by St. Martin's Press, Incorporated.

ISBN 0-373-26318-X

Visit us at www.worldwidemystery.com

Printed in U.S.A.

With grateful thanks to Nathan Potechin
for wisdom, words, and unfailing humour.

ONE

THE BODY slipped into the ditch quietly and without fuss, folding like a marionette into a foot of mud and water, its open-eyed presence unremarked except by the small scavengers that would later test its sanctity.

When rigor mortis ended, the hands gave up their hold on torn-out grass, and above, on the rim of the high bank, heavy rain casually obliterated the imprint of heavy feet.

THE WARM and greasy smell of fish and chips washed down the street from Brooks' chippy along with the rain, seeping through gaps in the windows of bedsits and wafting through air vents at the corner cinema. Halfway down the street, hunkered cold in a shop doorway, Lucy Walton told herself that if she waited, timed it right, looked hungry enough at closing time, Brooksie'd feed her for free. The thought of it moistened her mouth and sent a spurt of acid into her stomach. Arms clasped round knees, she tucked her head down and tried to block out the smell.

Across the road a Panda turned out of a facing street, headlights sweeping dark shop fronts, the chippy a regular Friday-night call. Two bags of chips well laced with salt and vinegar. Dandelion and burdock to wash it down with.

Except that night, having seen the girl huddled there, they couldn't ignore her.

Jeans tight and bulging, top button undone, she got bundled unceremoniously into the patrol car's back seat where she sat with folded arms and tight lips, refusing to give anything but her name. Philosophically she told herself a cell would be warm and dry, but she wasn't taken to the police station. Instead, because she was young and pregnant, she was taken to St Ursula's Women's Shelter.

Given a free choice, she would have chosen the cell.

Do-gooders were a pain!

All of them.

Wasn't anybody's business but hers where she went, or what she did. Except for Rollo—and he wasn't around, was he?

Handed over from one custodian to another, like a delinquent runaway to a headmaster, she stuck out her jaw and raised two fingers at the departing uniformed backs.

As they went back out into the rain the heavy ex-vicarage door thudded shut behind them, and she shifted her eyes to the do-gooder they'd left her with. His beaky nose and white dog collar were added irritants. She disconnected her mind, a trick she'd learned to do a long time ago, and let the syrupy voice flow out through the prissy mouth and past her own thoughts, paying him no attention.

Transvestite wearing a woman's dress!

That's what Rollo would have said.

Thinking that made her smile, paper-pale face animating. Wet blonde hair lay flat against her scalp except where bits tufted up like bird feathers.

The catechism of sound from the rosebud mouth stopped. The final words, *Come and eat,* Lucy heard. Her eyes, gone from blue to grey-blue with fatigue, drifted past the dog collar towards the inner door. Her nose picked up the warm scent of cooked food. She shifted her feet, undecided. Father Donnelly said remotely, 'This is a refuge not a prison. Leave now if you want. The door is unlocked.'

She turned a deaf ear to that too, strolling past him like she had all the time in the world, making out he wasn't even there, the caramel smell of fried onions more attractive by far than either his voice, or the rain.

Inside her head she listened to Rollo's whisper, a soft,

subversive voice telling her, *'You can't trust the devils—no—that you can't, Lucy-Locket. Bastards every one. Judas priests.'*

'Yeah, right,' she muttered. 'So I'll eat his food and *stuff* him!' She knuckled her right hand and jerked it, middle finger upright, then worried if she'd said the words too loud and let herself be caught talking to angels, squinting sideways at her escort to see, but Donnelly was looking past her with a silly little smile on his face, and eyes that reminded her of a brothel keeper's.

When he took her to the dining room she ate what she was given, swallowing it down hungrily and without ceremony like a dog that had missed being fed. A beefburger, meat thin enough to have been through a mangle and the bun toasted to mask it being stale, onions caramelised and scenting the place out. Thick mustard on the burger, chips swimming in ketchup.

All the time she ate, her eyes moved around, sizing up the women and taking in the kids. Had to be a proper refuge she supposed. Not just a place to dump strays like her for rehab. For some reason the thought made her feel better, and when she'd done eating and pushed the plate away she folded her arms on the table and laid her head on them, almost asleep when Donnelly came back and offered her a bed, pointing out stiffly it would just be for the one night. She accepted for the baby's sake—but did it grudgingly just the same—telling herself the poor little sod could do with an easy night.

Never trust a Judas Priest. Rollo's voice created itself again, and this time Lucy ignored it. Come morning she'd be gone and out of the place. Free to go where she wanted. Lying in bed, naked between the sheets, asleep almost before her body reached horizontal, she slept until her nose woke her at seven-thirty with the smell of frying bacon.

Her mouth filled up with saliva again, and the baby kicked and shifted.

Stomach rumbling, she pulled on her clothes and almost ran into the dining room, waiting to be fed much as Oliver had waited for porridge, and coming away from the counter with more food on her plate than she could normally beg or scavenge in a whole day.

She told herself if it hadn't been for the baby she would have stuck with her plan to eat and be gone, sullen when she faced Donnelly and asked if she could stay on, eyes watching the carpet and not the priest's face.

'A week,' he said, eyes on her belly. 'And that's stretching rules more than I should.'

Lucy shrugged.

Here today and gone tomorrow, that's what charity was all about. Do-gooders needed people like her to look down on, else they wouldn't be happy. Her eyes moved to the window and the thudding rain. Then the baby shifted again and she smiled, crossing her hands over her belly.

Seven days was seven days.

SATURDAY MORNING, the shopping mall was packed close to solid with shoppers keen to get out of the rain. Shoals of them dripping in from bus station and rail terminus, bedraggled, shaking wet out of their hair and steaming gently in over-warm shops, while at the north end, where cars fed into massive multistorey car parks and queued bumper to bumper, tempers frayed at the thought of wasted journeys if the FULL sign showed before they got past the sentinel arm.

Darren and Skeeter had missed all that, setting off early, with Skeeter, still half asleep, driving the once-white Transit Darren had picked up cheap, and feeling good because Darren let him do that. Blue exhaust trailed them down the motorway, belching foully at each incline. Skeeter watched it hover in his rear-view mirror and grinned, slack-mouthed as drivers gave him a wide berth. Poxy little wimps worried about their frigging lungs. Needed a good kicking.

In the Mall before nine, they made a beeline for the American Bar, and when it opened paid over the odds for a couple of Budweisers, nursing them, making the one beer last until the crowds got thick enough for them to get busy. By eleven they'd emptied a dozen purses and netted six hundred and eleven pounds forty-seven in cash, plus a couple of dozen assorted plastic cards. Like Darren said, purses were easy pickings, a baby could do it the way some silly cows left bags hanging open.

In the basement gents, both of them cramped up in one cubicle, they shared out the money, Skeeter having to shove the plastics down inside his Y-fronts, feeling the cards slip against his skin and nip uncomfortably at his cock when he walked. He didn't complain. If he had, Darren would have replied with physical swiftness—which was why Skeeter had been doing everything Darren told him to do since he was ten.

Dawdling back to the van they'd seen the shop with the monkey masks. Pliable vinyl with synthetic fur, fitting snug, but expensive. Skeeter saw the label and picked up something cheaper, hard plastic and no hair. Darren gave him a shove, hard, so he near knocked over a display, and made him get the hairy vinyl, snapping it on over Skeeter's head and sneering, 'Tough!' when Skeeter complained, then sorting out its twin and scratching at his armpits when he'd got it over his face, the both of them laughing raucously as they gibbered and grunted in front of the checkout girl sitting at the till with her long red nails. She snapped at them sniffily, and said not to be so sodding daft, impatient to put the sale through the till and get the queue moving.

Darren hadn't liked that, couldn't stand cocky women.

When she handed him his bagged monkey face and change, he leaned across the counter and made her blush.

Crossing over the car park with the rain down to a sticky drizzle, Skeeter, never less than two jacks short of a pack, pulled on his mask again and capered, scaring a blonde piece into dropping her shopping and snapping a heel.

Darren watched the woman bend, taking in the heavy jerk of breasts as her leather jacket hiked up, and felt tempted to take the joke a little further—like the back of the Transit.

Recompense for the snooty bitch at the novelty shop.

He was monkey-faced up to match, hands out to grab her, and the blonde still picking up the shopping when the Mall doors spilled out a bunch of nosies, and forced him to be content with a lewd gesture. The blonde's mouth opened and let out a string of obscenities that stopped the nosies dead in their tracks. Under the monkey mask Skeeter's jaw dropped in admiration. Darren snarled, 'Bloody move yourself,' and gave him another shove. Seething at two humiliations in one day.

Mouthy bitches!

Livid all the way home, Darren kept thinking about how somebody had to pay for it, hands in his crotch, fantasising about the way he'd make them do it.

LUCY WAS in the common room, feet up, eating crisps and watching *Superman,* dreaming about changing places with Lois Lane when Donnelly sent an eight-year-old to say he wanted to see her. She didn't stir. 'Tell him OK,' she said, eyes glued to the TV. 'I'll be there in a bit.' She finished the crisps and shoved the empty packet down the side of the cushion. When the film ended she stretched herself and went to see the priest. The thought came that he'd probably changed his mind about her being there, was going to tell her they didn't have room for her after all.

So what?

Wouldn't make her any worse off than she was before.

She walked in without knocking and left the door open behind her. Donnelly stared irritably. 'You took your time. Next time I send for you, don't keep me waiting.'

'Come and fetch me yourself then,' she said smartly. 'How'm I supposed to know it's important if you send a kid? What's it about anyway? Want me to go?'

'There's a job available if you want it,' he said tightly. 'Domestic work in exchange for bed and board. Up to you, but better than the streets.'

'Here?'

'No. With people who support the refuge.'

More goody-goodies. Lucy scowled, trying to work out where the catch was. There was always a catch. His sort built them in.

'What if I don't like it?'

'Leave.'

'What? Just like that?'

'Your choice, Lucy. It doesn't matter to me if you accept or not!' He waved his pudgy hands in front of him dismissively.

'Can't hurt I suppose,' she said grudgingly. 'Not if I just give it a try. I'm not hanging round, though, if it sucks.' She fixed hostile eyes on him. 'Can do that, I suppose, can't I? Turn round and tell 'em to stuff it.'

'If it's what you feel like doing.'

'I'll think about it then.'

He stared at the desk, turning his pen end on end. 'I need to know by tomorrow.'

'That's when I'll tell you then. Tomorrow.' She put a sneer in the last word and saw annoyance. Good!

She told herself she'd clean up somebody else's dirt two weeks at the most, and that was it. A week here, two weeks there, and the rain would be stopped; she'd be off looking for Rollo then, 'cos he had to be somewhere.

She hugged the thought in her head like a warm friend. Him and her and the baby. Council couldn't not give them a flat then. Not when they were a family.

SKEETER AND DARREN were drinking in the Black Swan, Darren fancying himself in tight black Levis and stack-heeled boots, his melting-treacle eyes weighing up the available talent and not finding anything he'd want. He parted his fingers, combed them through his hair, and tuned back into what Skeeter was saying.

'...don't see why we had to have the sodding things!'

Darren's eyes stopped melting and hardened up. ''Cos it's what I said. That's why.'

'Yeah, well, what I think is it's twenty-four quid down the drain an' I could use that. Need new trainers for a start.'

'Shut it!'

'You what?'

'I said, shut it.'

Skeeter drained his third half of Tetley's and went for another. He came back, drank half, said, 'I don't see...' and then had the breath *oofed* out of him when Darren short-armed into his ribs. 'That bleedin' hurt!' he complained, rubbing, and got another punch to help him remember it had. He lapsed into silence, massaging the soreness.

A girl came in, jaunty-hipped, black tights and skimpy black skirt, hair brown and shoulder length, curling under at the ends. Darren perked up, measuring her, eyeing the door to see if she had a boyfriend in tow, then a dumpy little blonde sailed out of the ladies, pulling at her skirt, breasts bouncing. What'd she want to wear a frilly blouse like that for, silly cow! His lip curled as she high-heeled it to the bar and said something to the brunette. They both giggled, squinting at him and Skeeter, giving the come-on.

Darren's elbow hit the rubbing hand. 'The dumpy cow's yours,' he said in Skeeter's ear, and went over to break the ice.

TWO

THE RIVER WAS already high before the rain started, the hills and high ground still shedding pockets of melting ice from a long, hard winter, sodden earth fast turning into vast paddy-fields. Water rushed along the ditch on Parson's Lane, buffeting the body, tangling leaves and other debris in its hair. One shoe came loose and moved away, bouncing and bumping towards the storm drain.

SKEETER QUITE LIKED the blonde once he found she talked to him and didn't make him feel a freak. But then, he liked most women, and couldn't understand what Darren's problem was. Not that it showed up when he was into a chat-up, all spice and honey then, nothing to show all he wanted was a fast shag. Skeeter bought the blonde a rum and coke, and asked her if she'd seen *Pulp Fiction* while Darren moved in on her friend. He'd seen a ferret do the same trick with a rabbit. Mesmerise it with its little black eyes. When the brunette said her name was Sharon, Darren smirked and looked at the blonde. 'And I bet you're Tracy,' he said. She stared right through him. Then she turned her head to Skeeter and said her name was Joanne. Darren hadn't liked that, her paying more attention to Skeeter than him. Skeeter looked at the barman and lifted his finger for another half, making out like he hadn't noticed.

The more Skeeter looked at the brunette, the more she reminded him of his cousin—the married one who lived in Brighton. It threw him. Made him wonder if he should warn her in case his uncle had slipped up. According to his Mam, his Uncle Ted had put it about a bit. 'All that free love there was in the sixties,' she'd said. 'Seemed to think it was specially for him.'

Closing time they left in a foursome, the girls putting up little umbrellas and Darren with his arm round Sharon's shoulders, like he was onto something good. Knowing Darren, that was a dead cert. Didn't waste time asking, just went on and did it. It puzzled Skeeter they never complained. Like Darren had been right all along and that's what they wanted.

A good shag by an expert.

He fumbled for Joanne's hand.

'If you like…'

'What?'

'We could get a curry.'

'Be nice that,' she said, squinting a smile, and raised her voice. 'Hey, Shar! Fancy a curry?' Sharon broke step and turned her head.

Darren said, 'Or a pizza.'

'Fancy a curry myself,' said Joanne. Skeeter squeezed her hand.

'I don't know,' said Sharon. 'We'd have to split up.'

'I'd see you got home all right.' Darren said, looking down at her, slicking back his hair again, Mr Nice Guy and butter-wouldn't-melt. Skeeter started to say he fancied a pizza after all, then stopped when Darren gave him a look. 'Where'd you fancy we go then?' said Darren, looking down again. 'Romano's?'

'Be nice.'

Joanne said, 'Sure you'll be all right?'

'Yeh, I'll be fine. See you tomorrow—enjoy the curry.' She turned back to Darren. 'Don't give me any more to drink though or I'll never get home.' Joanne and Skeeter watched them go down the street.

'Think she'll be all right?' Joanne said. 'He looks a bit—well—you know—*fond.*'

'You want to get a pizza instead?' Skeeter said uneasily, liking the feel of her hand in his, and worried what Darren would say if they went to Romano's after all.

'Nah,' said Joanne, turning away and heading for the Raj Poot. 'She'll be all right. Got a no-fail turn-off if he gets too pushy.'

'What's that then? Black belt at karate?'

'Better than that,' said Joanne as Skeeter opened the curry house door. She shook drops from her umbrella and grinned at him. 'Brother's a policeman.'

SUNDAY MORNING Lucy was down on the floor cross-legged, playing with a couple of toddlers and sipping at a mug of tea. Donnelly came from his office and stood watching the interplay, unnoticed by Lucy until the back of her neck prickled and she looked up and saw him. She wrapped both hands round the mug and eyed him mistrustfully, shrugging when he said they needed to talk again.

'Yeah, all right,' she said, flat-faced. 'I get the picture. There's no job and you need the bed. So what? Doesn't matter anyway. Didn't ask for anything did I?'

He said, 'Bring your tea, Lucy,' and walked away.

She watched him cross the grubby carpet and took her time following, barging in when she got there, door banging against its stop. Donnelly looked irritated again, which was what Lucy had been aiming for, but the woman who was with him showed no reaction at all, just fixed her eyes on a point above Lucy's head and kept her face straight. Lucy looked from one to the other. Donnelly said, 'Close the door. And this time do it without theatrics.'

Sulkily, she obeyed.

The woman's eyes moved. Abruptly she asked, 'How far on are you?'

'You the one that wants her house cleaned?' Lucy said. 'What makes you think I won't run off with the silver?'

'For one thing, running isn't easy in late pregnancy, and for another there isn't any silver,' said the woman dryly. 'We're talking about a nursing home, not a private house. Your baby could be born there, if you stayed until term. Father Donnelly tells me you're facing this quite alone, Lucy, without family support.'

'Well, he's wrong then,' said Lucy. 'I've got a family what'd give support. I just don't want to know them is all.'

'Were you pregnant before you left home?'

Lucy stared back at the light brown eyes and could read nothing in them. Who'd she think she was? Mother Teresa?

'I don't need this,' she said resentfully. 'Questions. And I don't need to answer if I don't want. There's plenty of places to have babies. I don't have to have it in a field.'

'Lucy, you've got quite an attitude. To be frank I don't care if you come to me or not.'

'Makes two of us in the same mind then, doesn't it?' Lucy came back. 'Don't even know who you are.'

'Di Carpenter. Does the name make you wiser? Of course not! What makes you so touchy, Lucy? Are you in trouble with the authorities?'

'No!'

'How old are you?'

Lucy stared back at her stubbornly.

The woman turned in her chair. 'I think that's the problem,' she told Donnelly. 'She's under sixteen.'

'Then she's Social Service's problem, not mine,' he said, and picked up the telephone.

Lucy said quickly, 'I'm not under sixteen.'

He let go the receiver, picked up a pen and reached for a scratch pad. 'Date of birth?'

'Twelfth of February 1981, which makes me sixteen. All right? And I don't need you, or *her!*' She swung her head sideways and scowled again.

The woman got to her feet.

'I think I've heard enough for one day,' she said. 'Lucy, if you want to accept the work offer, tell Father Donnelly before your week is up. Up to you.' She fastened her trenchcoat, picked up her bag, and walked out.

Lucy stared after her, vexed, then saw the smile on Donnelly's face.

'Stuff it!' she said with rude emphasis, and tipped her three-parts-full mug of tea into his waste basket.

THE CEDARS was a sprawling three-storey residence, pebble-dashed and painted white in an acre of ground, built in the 1920s for an importer of fine cloth. In the 1950s the local council had turned it into a children's home, and in 1990, Carl Fielding bought it from them for less than its worth and converted it into a private clinic.

Nine months ago, when Paula Williamson first drove up from Somerset, she'd been apprehensive and defeatist. Making the journey at all on the say-so of an adoption worker had seemed nonsense, but it was a straw, and straws were about all she had left. When she got there, Fielding impressed her. Not just the way he took her proffered hand in both of his as if it really mattered to him why she was there, but the way he'd listened to her outpouring of misery and not made light of it. She was used to gynaecologists giving her pep talks on getting on with life and accepting her infertility, but not to being heard and understood. When he'd asked about the possibility of adoption she'd told him bitterly of the final insult. She was too old and Chas was too old. Thirty-seven and fifty-four. Of course if she could have had her own baby at that age everybody would flock with congratulations, not tell her she was over the hill. She sat silently after that, watching him doodle on a pad, waiting for the shake of head she knew would come, but instead he got up to call Chas in from the waiting room and told them how much it would cost if he were to make them a life raft from a straw.

DARREN was smarting again. Twenty quid he'd spent in Romano's and nothing to show but a hole in his wallet. *Tight bitch!* He'd pulled her up the alley just before her block of flats, laughing about it, nothing nasty, thinking about how up there in the dark she'd pay for her supper and a bit more. But she wouldn't go more than a few yards, not without a fight, and there'd been another couple walking past saying 'Goodnight, Sharon,' and getting a good look at him as they went. He'd still thought he was in with a good chance, way she'd let him inside her blouse, but when he went for more she'd nutted him and yelled about her brother being a policeman. Didn't believe it, but he'd had to back off so his nose didn't bleed all over his new shirt.

Knew where she lived though, which door and which window. Ground floor, third left. On Sunday night he was back there with Skeeter in tow, wet hair and drips down their necks. Lights were on in some of the flats but not Sharon's. He shook the can of spray paint and put it in Skeeter's hand. 'Go on then, write it. On the window like I said.'

Obediently Skeeter crossed the grass and stood on the concrete walkway. The stream of red came out like blood. He added two drippy squirts to dot the i's and took the can back to Darren. 'She'll know it's you,' said Skeeter.

'Can't prove it,' said Darren, and wondered what she'd do when she woke up Monday and found *Sharon is a fucking whore!* writ large for all to see.

THREE

MONDAY MORNING rain sheeted down like a glass curtain, spitting down chimneys and dripping in through broken roof tiles. On the motorway, windscreen wipers failed to keep up with the downpour and small cars disappeared in the spray from lorry wheels. Drains backed up and spread lakes across town roads; each passing set of wheels drenching pavements and pedestrians alike. The river brimmed and broke its banks, fields drowned and ditches flooded. The body lifted and lingered, like a traveller without destination.

Further along, where the road dipped, Parson's Lake became impassable. A Mini became stranded, its front end near submerged in water. The police hauled it out and set up traffic barriers, and the weather forecasters stayed glum.

DONNELLY more or less herded Lucy into his office Monday afternoon and told her she could either make up her mind about the work offer then and there, or forget the whole thing. The knee-jerk reply she wanted to give was on her lips when she saw the deluge teeming past the window, and thought better of it. She shifted her feet and swallowed the words, saying sullenly, 'When would I have to go?' instead.

His fingers stopped prancing on the blotter.

'Now.'

'Now? Why? I got another four days—she said so!'

'I need the bed.'

'Oh, right! Said I could stop a week.' She crossed her

arms and gave him a black look, thinking he'd a mouth like a monkey's bum.

'I said unless we needed the bed. We need it.' His eyes shifted from her belly to her face. 'Well?'

'Don't have much choice, do I? I'll go see what it's like, but I shan't stop, not if I don't fancy it.'

He got up from his chair and shoved his arms into a black parka. Lucy glanced at the window again and stayed silent. He felt in the jacket pockets for car keys and looked satisfied. Magnanimously he let her stick her head into the common room to say goodbye, but didn't allow time for anything else. When he took her outside she looked at the green Renault suspiciously, but got into the passenger seat without quibble and let him drive her away from St Ursula's. It was a simple act that Donnelly hoped would also drive her out of his life. Lucy's own thoughts weren't much different.

She stuck her feet out, and crossed her ankles, staring out the windscreen at the rain. In two places street drains were blocked and Donnelly didn't bother to slow down, driving through the deep puddles and raising wings of water. A brown mongrel, already wet, got soaked in the spray and shook itself wearily. Donnelly kept his mouth shut and didn't so much as glance in her direction. Silence suited Lucy fine, the last thing she wanted was getting talked at by a poxy priest.

Stupid prick!

She eased a hand inside the zip pocket of her jacket, fingered the four pounds sixty-nine left from begging, and decided if the worst came to the worst it was enough to feed her for two days. Thinking that gave her back a sense of security. If this place he was taking her to sucked, it didn't matter. She'd just cut out fast and go back on the streets.

Yeah!

Out on the main roads, away from town, traffic was light, more like Sunday than Monday except for the heavy lorries. Windscreen wipers made semicircles that washed away before the arc was completed. A cyclist gave up on the road and took to the pavement. Lucy stared at the sky, grey like somebody had painted it with a big brush, and told herself when the rain stopped she'd be gone anyway.

Four miles north of Malminster, and half a mile past the thick trees of Stye Woods, Donnelly turned into the driveway of The Cedars, and bundled Lucy in through the nursing home's back door.

Suspicious and defiant, the last thing she expected was to be met with a bright smile, be given coffee and chocolate biscuits, and then be left alone to relax in Di Carpenter's office.

MOLLY WAS THIRTY, had blonde hair, a penchant for large earrings, and a gravel voice from smoking too many cigarettes. It was a vice she was trying to give up. None of those things mattered to Donnelly; the turn-on for him was her forty-six-inch bust. He stopped at the first payphone and told her how long it would take him to get there.

Swallowing distaste, telling herself his money was the same as anyone else's, that, repulsive little toad or not, she'd still be fifty pounds the richer when he left, she got into the red satin basque, G-string and black leather thigh boots that Donnelly found entertaining.

Suppose she told him the price had gone up. Inflation. Could she squeeze another ten out of him? Compensation for a disgustingly moist skin.

Sixty?

Maybe. She put on a black satin wrap bought at Littlewoods, and tied the sash, ready when she opened the door to up the ante. He simply stared at her and pushed in without reply.

Molly let the door close and followed him upstairs, standing legs akimbo and arms crossed as he rummaged in the big cupboard.

'You know the rules,' she said. 'Money first.'

'You'll get it.'

Her hand went out, palm up. 'First!'

He came out of the cupboard empty handed and looked at her. 'Fifty.'

'Sixty.'

His face screwed up. He began to sob. Wailing like an infant. 'Nanny's being horrid to Lenny!'

'Sixty,' said Molly, shortly. 'Or you don't get spanked.'

FRIDAY NIGHT, Finnegan's Fair had pulled onto a field site just off the main road behind the shirt factory. Every year it pitched on the same site, and on the same week. Usually, the weather was better.

Finnegan had eyed the sodden ground and falling rain, and known he'd be out of pocket if it kept it up all week—in two minds whether to pull back out the next day and move on. Except Saturday morning it was down to a heavy drizzle and he'd no way of knowing it'd be pouring again by Saturday night.

All the fun of the fair for two dozen punters slipping and sliding in mud. Sunday wasn't much better. Darren went down there, late afternoon, nosying round, wasting time until he cornered Charlie Finnegan and asked about a job.

Finnegan's nose practically glowed in the dark, veins spreading out from it and purpling his cheeks as he stamped in the mud with heavy feet. 'Yeah,' he said. 'I'll give you a job. Get yourself a brush and sweep this lot up!'

When he walked away, laughing, Darren followed.

'I did two years with Staceys.'

'Should have stayed there.'

'Went bust.'

'That's a good recommendation?'

'Weren't my doing.'

'Tell me about it,' said Finnegan, as he climbed back in his van and shut the door.

Sunday night they laid boards down between the stalls, old pallisters, anything they could find, and still lost more money generating electricity than they made on rides. Darren showed his face again.

'What you want's somebody to drum up trade,' he told Finnegan.

'Somebody to stop the pissing rain you mean.'

'Free ride tickets, that's what you want.'

'You what?'

'Tickets. Hand 'em out in town—it'll pull punters in won't it? Give us a wad and I'll pass 'em round.'

'Sod off.'

'Suit yourself,' said Darren. 'See how you feel about it tomorrow.

Monday afternoon he was back, Skeeter in tow, hanging around until Finnegan came out, gloomy as the weather and, looking at a third no-profit day, willing to try anything. 'Here,' he said, shoving a Tesco bag at Darren's chest. 'Fetch in a good crowd or don't show your face here again.' Barrelling away towards the dodgems when Darren shouted after him.

'Payment?' Finnegan shouted back, without looking. 'Wanted a job, didn't you? You'll not get one any other way.'

THERE WASN'T TIME for more than a quick recce round the room before Di Carpenter was back, eyes roaming the office like a squirrel checking nuts. Lucy didn't need to be told why.

'Haven't nicked nothing,' she said pre-emptively. 'So you needn't look. And I haven't asked for nothing, either.'

She thumped her cup and saucer down and headed for the door.

'Oh, for Pete's sake! Checking the firm's property gets to be automatic. God! but you're touchy! Sit. Finish your coffee.'

Without looking at Lucy, she moved the cup and saucer to the end of the desk and dropped a folder on the place it had been. Wrongfooted, Lucy dithered.

'There's more coffee in the percolator if you want it,' Carpenter said as she sat herself behind the desk. 'And pour me one at the same time, like a good girl. Black—no sugar.'

Lucy did just that, frown still fixed on her face, and perversely over-filled the cup so dark liquid slopped and swam in the saucer, annoyed not so much by the task as by its telling.

She set the cup down ungently on the desk. Carpenter soaked up the spillage with paper tissues and didn't make an issue of it.

'Lucy, what I do here is hire, fire, and make sure the clients are happy. But I'm also a midwife. If *you* decide to give birth here, I'm the one who will deliver you. *Do you understand?*

''*Course* I understand! But it's nothing but an if, is it? Don't remember I ever said I was having it here.'

'You have to give birth somewhere, and you need to arrange it soon.'

'Tell me about it. Look. Coming here wasn't my idea.'

Carpenter shrugged. 'The door is right behind you, and it's open. Feel free to walk through it.'

'I will when I'm ready. Might as well find out what's on offer first, mightn't I? What the job?'

'Oh I see! This is an inspection?' Carpenter laughed, but without humour. 'Well, miss! Understand something. I don't plan to offer anything until we get a few facts straight.

First—if you stay here, you answer exactly the same questions as every other pregnant woman. Understood?'

'What sort of questions?'

'The kind you refused to answer at St Ursula's. Age, name, next of kin...'

'Name you know, age you know. Next of kin? Forget it! Far as I'm concerned, I don't have any.'

'...And because you're pregnant, any genetic diseases in your family or the father's,' Carpenter finished. Then asked. 'Do you *know* the father?'

Lucy's face blanked out. 'What you mean is, was I the school bicycle? Yeah, I'm right, aren't I? You're thinking, *silly cow went tarting and got caught!* Bet it makes you feel all pure and good does it? Thinking that?'

'Lucy, you can shag the town band if you like. How you got pregnant doesn't interest me or the clinic. Genetic faults and the father's ethnicity do though.'

'If you mean were he black—then he weren't!' Lucy said heatedly. 'Not that it'd matter if he was.'

'Sickle cell anaemia,' Carpenter said blandly.

'Well, since he weren't black he didn't have it. And there didn't seem much wrong with the rest of him.'

'You still have contact?'

Lucy's eyes dropped. She shrugged.

'There's the question of maintenance payments.'

'Yeah, well, I don't need help from him. I can manage on me own. Look, is there a job or isn't there? 'Cos if there isn't, there's no point hanging about.'

Carpenter said, 'Have you thought about adoption?'

Lucy crossed her hands over her belly and in loud anger snapped, 'Fuck adoption! Fuck you! Nobody takes my baby—*nobody!*'

Reddening, Carpenter said, 'Don't be stupid, girl, it's a routine question. In a national health service unit you'd not only be asked that, you'd have to cope with a string of social workers filing in and out every day as well.'

'So what? They'd try an' find me a place to live then, wouldn't they?' Lucy came back aggressively. 'Me *and* the baby. More'n *you* can do. I'm not as daft as you think.'

'Lucy, tell me, how long is it since you had an antenatal check?' The girl looked at her blankly. Carpenter said. 'You never had one, did you?'

'Why would I? Haven't been ill.'

'Have you seen a GP? Did you talk to one when you got pregnant?'

'Oh, yeah, I did that all right. Real sweetheart! Told me dad I was in the club, didn't he?' She dropped her head and started picking at a nail.

'What did your father do?'

'Doesn't matter, does it? What's it to you? I'm not going back home if that's what you think. Forget it!'

'Did I say you should? We're not getting anywhere, are we? Have you made your mind up?'

'Haven't said what the job is yet.'

'Light cleaning, some kitchen work. Taking out the tea trolley. In exchange you get bed and board plus twenty pounds for each complete week worked when you leave. Enough to rent a bedsit and give you a permanent address to claim benefits. Now—would you like to see the room you'd occupy?'

'Might as well, I suppose,' said Lucy grudgingly. 'As long as I don't have to promise I'm stopping or anything.'

'No promises. Later there might be, but not now. Drink up and we'll go.'

'It's drunk,' said Lucy, clattering her cup and saucer onto the desk again.

Take away the smart tongue, thought Carpenter as she eyed the girl, and all you had left was a stick insect with a big belly. She locked the door behind them, her smile no more than skin deep.

Stick insects weren't fit to look after babies.

TUESDAY AFTERNOON the swollen grey underbellies of cloud drifted east, trailing dirty elephants in their wake. By early evening the sky had lightened to the colour of sea-fret, with rain no more than a clingy drizzle. The change suited Darren fine. He told himself he couldn't lose. He stayed away from the fairground until close on nine, then wandered down to collect his prize. Finnegan eyed him unfavourably.

'Doubt you've made any difference. We'd have had more down tonight anyway with the rain gone.'

'How many ride tickets have come back?' said Darren.

'Haven't counted.'

'I'll hang round 'til closing time, then, won't be any hardship.' He wandered off, Skeeter slouching at his side, a dozen free tickets left but not using any until they were out of Finnegan's sight. 'He's right you know,' said Skeeter. 'Half of this lot are here 'cos it's given up raining.' Darren stopped in his tracks and stared into the washed-out blue eyes.

'Plan to tell him that?'

'Don't be daft.'

'What's it matter then?'

'Don't suppose it does.'

'Too bloody right,' said Darren, and gave Skeeter a shove up the Whirler's steps.

'I don't like this one, makes me throw up,' Skeeter complained.

'Sit by yourself then,' said Darren and chose another car.

FOUR

A SLOW FLOW of lying water began to ease grudgingly back into the river. Lazily the body stirred and moved with the flow, one hand brushing brambles, and leaving small shreds of skin.

WEDNESDAY MORNING Darren cleared out his room while the landlady was out shopping, and didn't bother leaving his two weeks' owed rent.

On his way to pick up Skeeter he called at the Army Stores and bought an inflatable mattress and two sleeping bags, throwing them in the back of the Transit with the rest of his stuff. Skeeter was out on the pavement, a duffle bag and a cardboard box at the side of him. 'Gerrin then,' said Darren. 'Make it look like you're willing.' Skeeter put his stuff with Darren's and climbed in the front.

'Not sure if I am,' he said. 'Willing. I mean, what's so good about a fairground?'

'Get away with a lot of things when you're on the move,' said Darren. 'Might be sodding rich when we come back.'

That'd be a laugh, thought Skeeter. Way it ran out his pocket like water. 'Petrol's a bit low,' he said.

'I'll get some after dark,' said Darren, swinging an uneven left. 'No sense paying for it.' Skeeter knew what that meant. Him going out with a pipe and can. Hands loose between his thighs, he sat and thought about his lot while Darren headed down the Scissett road to the shirt factory, and pulled onto the fairground. Parked between a Fordson truck and a rusting trailer, the Transit looked right at home.

LUCY'S ROOM was up in the eaves. The ceiling sloped over the bed and the window overlooked the car park, but it was hers, and she didn't have to share. Wednesday night she lay on the bed watching TV and felt pleased with herself. Not a bad bargain, bit of work in exchange for this. All she'd been asked to do so far was peel a few spuds and help tidy the rooms. *And* she'd got a dress to do it in. Naff-looking thing, but it gave her a chance to wash her jeans, and it was nice, being around other women that were waiting for babies. One had given her a box of chocolates. Said she had too many and didn't want to put weight on. Lucy had put them on the bottom of the towel trolley, and then taken them back to her room. Later on she'd remembered her manners and gone back to say thanks. The woman had been reading a book but she'd looked up when Lucy went in and smiled. The smile made Lucy ask, 'When's it supposed to come? Your baby.'

'Any day now. Why?'

'Are you scared?'

'No. Not a bit. We've been waiting a long time you see. Are you?'

'Nah,' Lucy said. 'Bet it's a piece of cake.' She dithered, just inside the room. 'Do you want a boy or a girl?'

'It will be a girl,' Paula Williamson said with a brief smile. 'I know that already. What about yours?'

'Dunno.' Lucy's hands smoothed over her dress. 'A boy'd be nice, but I s'pose a girl'd be easier. Doesn't matter really.'

'Why? Won't you be keeping it?'

''Course I shall!' Her forehead puckered, then cleared. 'Oh, I get it now. Asked you that too, did they, when you came in? If you wanted it?'

Paula started to shake her head, then thought better of it. 'Something like that,' she said, and turned back to her book. Lucy felt better. Maybe Mrs C was right, and it wasn't just her that got asked after all. Cheerful about that, she went back to work. Funny really, the way some people wanted to know what they were getting before it was born.

DARREN LIKED HIS BODY, had a love affair with it almost, working out twice a week and most days running a few miles too. The running did more than keep him fit. Joggers were like milkmen, never got noticed. People moving in, people moving out. Luggage getting loaded up for holidays, women locking up nice and careful, setting off for bus stops, shopping bag in hand. And Skeeter in the Transit, not too far away to do a quick break and enter. Useful things, cellular phones. The weight of his—stolen not bought—thwacked against his thigh as he ran.

A yellow Fiat Punto passed him on Maple Drive, engine slowing. Fifty yards along the blonde at the wheel made a right turn. Darren picked up a little speed, then dawdled at the drive entrance. Bending one knee and dropping down like his laces needed a retie, he swung his head right, watching the woman empty out the boot. Two supermarket bags bulging groceries, and a blue and silver dress carrier from La Ronde to tell him she had plenty to spend. She slammed down the tailgate and hefted the bags, long legs encased in beige leggings, a ginger-coloured jumper showing off her breasts. He watched the pale hair fall forward as she bent, wondered if she'd ring the bell or use her key. With a key, chances were she'd be home alone. He shifted feet, fiddled with the second lace. The blonde headed for the front door, setting the bags by her feet while she hunted for the key, unaware she was being watched by a man with rape on his mind.

TED BURNS had been a milkman fifteen years, and in all that time he'd never once been this late. He fumed at the annoyance of it, as irritated as his milkless customers. First, the float he'd set off in from the dairy had broken down on Oak Avenue. Halfway along and right at the bend. And he'd had to sit there waiting for close on an hour before they sent a replacement. Then he'd had all the crates to shift from one float to the other.

Fractiously he started off again, up one road and down another, the estate a warren of near-identical streets with names like Hawthorn Crescent, Elder Close, Beech Grove. Couldn't see the trees for the wood was Ted's personal joke, repeated often, but dependent for smiles on the day and the weather. Today he couldn't even raise much of a smile himself, his delivery problems multiplied by thrumming rain and a nagging tooth. He told himself if the rain stopped he might see the funny side. It might be a nice estate when the sun shone, streets frilled with trees that matched the names—only the sun wasn't in sight and every time he stopped his float some blamed overhanging branch or other showered the back of his neck. *Frigging weather!*

On Lime Crescent the road had been dug up. A wide, uneven trench with mounds of clay-based earth and bedraggled men. Water flowed freely in the trench bottom, brown and muddy, and three Yorkshire Water vans stood with rear doors open; one with a generator throbbing in the back and trailing cables. A compressor pounded and shrieked, the vibrations aggravating his tooth. He loaded his hand crate and trudged through the mud. The trench was wide, the pavement impassable. Gingerly he crossed over shaky planks and back again, ten crossings, ten houses, taking twice the normal time, and still another load to fetch from the dairy for the council estate. Unless the dairy took pity and sent another float.

KIM FITTON had become resigned to lying uncomfortably bound and frightened in her home on Maple Drive until her husband came home at six. She tried not to picture how his face would be when he found her, his revulsion and horror at the state of the bed and the acrid smell of it all. Rape was something that happened to other people, it wasn't meant to happen to her. Kim's mind replayed it in detail, her own internal horror video that wouldn't be turned off. Shame, anguish and the agonising fear her attacker would come back vied for supremacy. She couldn't stop shivering and nausea added to her wretchedness. Ever since the front door had banged, and the house declared its emptiness, she had wept, stopped, and wept again, the hair at both sides of her head salty soaked, wrists and ankles chafed raw from trying to free herself.

Deliberately she dragged her mind from her own state to the groceries littering the hall floor, imagining frozen food melting and soaking into the carpet, forcing herself to concentrate on trivialities like remembering the grocery bill and ticking off each item she'd bought. Anything at all that would disrupt the video being better than its constant viewing.

A cramp started in her left calf. She flexed the knee as much as she was able and pushed down hard with her heel. The cramp grew worse and made her sob. She straightened her toes, pointing her foot like a ballerina, sucking in a gasping breath of air as the pain eased.

It began to rain again, gusts of wind pushing it against the window. At eleven she heard the meter reader knock on the back door and screamed for help. The knock wasn't repeated. Tentatively, because she hadn't done it for a very long time, she tried to pray.

A SHEP SWOOPED LOW, a kamikaze bird almost taking his cap off, close enough for Ted to see the wetness of its feathers, iridescent as petrol on wet tarmac. It landed on the lawn ten feet away and beaked a solitary piece of bread. He massaged his jaw where he'd bitten down on the worrisome tooth and found it didn't help. Nothing for it but the dentist. His stomach squeezed in horror at the thought of such necessity.

Miraculously, for the space of three seconds as he got back on the float, the throbbing stopped. Then he eased out of the crescent at the crossroads and near enough got turned over by a dirty white Transit that swerved round him in a screeching curve. When he stopped on Rowan Close his heart was dancing boogie.

By the time he got to Maple Drive it was close to noon, and he'd collected a few edgy comments about the late delivery. Ted plodded on, doggedly, intent to get finished, thinking it was always the same; forget about the three hundred and sixty-four days he got there on time, and remember the one he was late.

At the Fitton house he put two bottles of half-fat in the milk holder by the back door and thought he heard a woman's voice, high pitched like his wife's in complaint. He didn't hang around to see if it continued. Three doors down he thought about the Fitton house again, and wondered how a bag of frozen peas had got stuck fast in the front door. He tried to tell himself it didn't matter. Not his business. Wasn't as if it was an old person living there. With an old person he'd have made sure they were all right. Went with the job. Milkmen and postmen. Unpaid social workers. What everybody expected.

He made two more deliveries and then walked back. The corner of green plastic still stuck out at the bottom of the doorjamb, and when he bent, he could feel two peas inside, soft under his fingers. Ted dithered. Now what did he do? Lean on the doorbell and then say, *''Scuse me, love, thought you'd like to know there's a packet of peas hanging out.'*

He eyed the parked Fiat and, expecting to get an earful, rang the bell.

Upstairs, Kim began to shout again, the sound diminishing as it left the bedroom, crossed the landing, and floated down the stairs, indistinct by the time it reached Ted, outside on the step. He pushed up the letterbox flap and looked into the hall. The groceries still lay on the floor, eggs broken and yolks spilling. Kim heard the rattle of flap and exchanged shouting for screaming. Ted went cold. *God Almighty. Sounded like a frigging murder.*

He tried to get in the front door and failed, tried the back and found it locked, and did the only thing he could think of, put his mouth up close to the letterbox and yelled that the cops were coming. Kim stopped screaming and wept quietly. Hearing the sudden silence Ted went colder still, and had to knock on two doors before Mrs Henderson at number thirty-two let him in to use her phone, mouth rounding in a little 'O' as she heard him make the call. Two minutes and the whole street'd know about it, he thought. Resigned to the idea of never getting the deliveries finished at all, he went back to wait outside the Fittons'.

FIVE

THE BODY MOVED unevenly with the flow of water, drifting towards the storm drain under Parson's Lane, then slipping past the vandalised grid into darkness. Other debris—broken branches, discarded cans and bottles, sandwich wrappers and used condoms, household rubbish and a dead cat—swept with it until further passage was blocked by the unbroken grid at Stye Beck.

Journey ended, face pressed tight against the bars, the corpse eyes stared sightlessly up at the freedom of the sky.

TED WAS a worried cage-bird on a perch. Moving from foot to foot without progress in any direction, nervously listening for noises because what the hell would he do if some nutter ran out before the police came? Weak at the knees when he heard a siren blast, he wiped sweaty palms down the sides of his wet jacket, relief running through him like a flood-tide.

Three minutes, that's all. Not bad. Showed they could move fast when they had to. Still thinking about that when two uniforms slammed out of a Panda and came running like they might grab him by mistake.

He worked on looking innocent, grimacing when he got a blast of cold air on his aching tooth and thinking it was just one sodding thing after another, nursing the tooth with his tongue.

A uniform stopped in front of him.

'Are you the one that rang it in?'

Nodding and nervous, Ted said, 'It was the peas. I mean, in a house like this who'd leave 'em stuck in the door?'

The eyes in front of him clouded. Thinks I'm a nutter, Ted thought. He moved. 'See? And a right tip inside. Here, have a look,' lifting the letter flap. 'Groceries all over the place.' The policeman bent, took a look and straightened. The second man returned from explorations round the back, and shook his head. Then he took a look through the letter-flap as well, and banged on the door.

'Won't get an answer,' said Ted. 'Tried it already.' Ungently he got moved away. Ornamental glass shattered. A shard ripped a triangular tear in blue serge. Upstairs Kim heard voices and pounding feet and couldn't stop herself vomiting, staring at the bedroom door wide-eyed and wretched in the mess. Ted, coming upstairs uninvited behind the two policemen, took it all in, the bed, the woman, the smell and the mess, before anybody realised he was there. He didn't need telling he wasn't welcome. What with hanging about in the wet, and near getting killed, seeing Mrs Fitton tied up like that was the final straw. He just made it to the bathroom, and was still sitting there, green on the toilet lid, when the uniform he'd talked to before came looking for him.

THERE WERE TIMES when Chief Inspector Morrissey regretted not having a woman police officer in CID. It was all very well turning to uniform and 'borrowing', but there were times when a permanent presence would be valuable, not least in the present rape case. He was also well aware that women officers resented having the majority of rapes and domestics tossed in their direction. Resentment didn't alter the fact that the majority of victims preferred to have another woman interview them instead of a male officer. At a time like that, any male might remind them too bitterly of their attacker. He'd put the same thoughts in front of Chief Superintendent Osgodby, getting him used to the idea, and at the same time had slipped in the notion that

Barrett might well be a better asset as an inspector than a sergeant.

Especially with Beckett still deskbound.

Nothing to do with his stomach now, but something the medical report termed euphemistically 'a psychological disability'.

Osgodby had taken it all in, sitting behind his desk sucking on his teeth irritatingly. He reminded Morrissey that to be in line with the latest thinking, Barrett would have to spend a year back in uniform if he were promoted. 'We haven't adopted that policy yet,' said the DCI. 'A bit of fancy footwork could still push a promotion through.'

'Make an exception, you mean.'

'I wouldn't say that, not exactly, exceptions are made after the law, not before it. Depends if you have an urge to let a good detective get away.'

'Establishment…'

'Beckett leaves us one down. He's dead weight.'

'Not in theory.'

'Theory isn't feet on street.'

Osgodby doodled. 'Leave it with me, John, I'll pass on your thoughts.' End of discussion, thought Morrissey. Stay as they were and don't rock the boat, but he still ran through likely women candidates on his way downstairs.

Rosie Quinn would have been more than gratified to know about Morrissey's concerns. It wasn't simply the fact that she came in for more than her fair share of rapes and domestics that made the problem; it was not being able to follow them through. Rosie got to comfort and cajole, while the men got to do the investigating, and she didn't need to be a feminist to see that as unfair. Calling it rules of the game made no difference. Equality of opportunity looked fine on paper but didn't translate into fact. Top and bottom of it, Rosie thought, men just didn't like admitting women were any good.

When she got back from the hospital with Kim Fitton's statement, she told Bill Grice, her sergeant, she'd like to stay with the case. No venture, no gain. His answer had been a swift negative. Then Morrissey stopped by to say thanks and got a brief, 'Part of the job, sir', in exchange. What else did he expect, she thought, head down again, filling in her worksheet. Thanks for letting her do CID's dirty work?

SKEETER had wanted to know all the details, and Darren had told him he'd have to wait, get the work done with first and then he might tell him about it. Later. Like, when they were on the move. Then all through the afternoon he'd kept letting little titbits out for teasers, watching saliva gather on Skeeter's bottom lip. Amused at how easy it was, pulling Skeeter's strings. Like that Russian bloke and his dog. Pavlova or something. Grinning when he thought of Skeeter down on all fours and drooling 'cos he'd heard a bell. Dogs, humans, all alike. Just knowing which buttons to push, that's all.

He caught Charlie Finnegan looking at him funny and hefted the big spanner thoughtfully, appreciating its weight. One day he'd learn to push Charlie's buttons too.

Skeeter got careless with a hammer and flattened his thumb, swearing and sucking at it.

'Go get a plaster, daft big daisy,' Darren said derisively. 'Need a sodding nanny.'

Dripping blood, Skeeter wandered off without answering, feet sinking into turfless mud. Finnegan watched him go, then went over to tell Darren that next time he wasn't there at the time he should be, he could take his reeking van and find another fair.

Darren carried on dismantling the Moon Ride, impassive until Finnegan ran out of words. Only when the flow stopped did he squat back on his heels and let the boss see his pale, hostile eyes, not shifting an inch until the other man spat on the ground and moved away.

By six-thirty there was nothing left on the field except churned mud and waterlogged detritus, the wagons and rides already on the M62 heading for Hull.

In the white Transit, Darren sat splay-legged while Skeeter drove, that day's rape forgotten in the greater pleasure of planning the next.

BARRETT HAD STOPPED wearing a waistcoat and couldn't get used to the idea of being without. At times of stress, thumbs and fingers still reached to pull down on non-existent corners.

Like then.

Morrissey saw the movement and schooled his face. Comparisons with comfort blankets were best forgotten until some more appropriate moment. He said gruffly, 'So the whole thing is a blank. That's what you're saying. Mrs Fitton didn't get a look at her attacker, no strangers were seen on the street, and apart from plenty of semen, we've got no clues.'

'Height possibly. She's five-five and says he wasn't more than three or four inches taller. And we think he's got dark hair. Shan't know that for certain though until we get forensic's take on pubic combings.'

'It's something.'

'Not enough.'

'Something,' said Morrissey firmly. 'Eliminates blondes and redheads for a start.'

'Yes. I suppose so.' Brightening a bit because if the DCI wasn't being negative, why should he? 'And there'll be no worry about genetic fingerprints when we pull him in. He's left enough to float a boat. I might get more when I talk to her myself.'

Thinking but not saying there'd be no might about it. It

all came down to experience, and there were questions he'd have asked that Rosie hadn't. Difference between uniform and CID, knowing what to ask.

Morrissey gleaned the conceit of thought from the Detective Sergeant's expression and said idly, 'When new regulations come in, any promotion for a CID officer will mean putting him back in uniform for a year. You've heard about that?' Barrett flushed. He'd heard about it all right, and didn't like either alternative.

Catch-22. He didn't want to stay a sergeant, and he didn't want to go back in uniform.

He said stiffly. 'I read the report, sir.'

'I hope everybody has,' said Morrissey. 'It'll save any standing on toes.'

'I wasn't...'

'I'm not suggesting you were, just making an observation, but when you do see Mrs Fitton, it might be as well to have a woman officer with you.' He started shifting papers on his desk, lifting and tidying, carved stone face giving nothing away.

'I thought I'd take Rosie,' Barrett said inventively. 'Better for Mrs Fitton to see a face she knows.'

'Good thinking.'

The DCI continued to tidy.

'Probably won't still be on shift.'

'Possibly not.'

Amazing, thought Barrett, how much Morrissey could get across without verbalisation. Downstairs, looking for the watch sergeant, he saw Rosie's bent head in the front office. Reddish hair, springy and clean. Better her than Woodsy he thought, suddenly cheerful again, and went to arrange it. Fifteen minutes later, in a hospital corridor that echoed voices eerily, he found out it was all wasted effort. Kim Fitton had enough sedation in her to keep her snoring until morning.

THE TRANSIT VAN was just that. A van and nothing else. No fittings, no refinements except for the inflatable mattress and a mix of cardboard boxes. The two sleeping bags were unrolled and Skeeter was in his, half asleep, Darren at the side of him lying on his back, a bent arm under his head. 'Want to hear what happened with the tart then?' he said. 'Only chance you'll get.'

Skeeter's eyes opened.

'Yeah, all right, I'm listening.'

'Bet you are,' said Darren. 'Haven't got the bottle to do it yourself.' In a flat monotone that changed in pitch as he talked he began to recite the obscenities he'd inflicted on Kim Fitton.

When he was through and the van filled with near silence, it stank of spilled semen, and the both of them were breathing hard.

THE SEDATIVE WORE OFF just before seven next morning, and for some reason the haziness that usually comes between sleeping and waking was absent. Kim woke to immediate memory of her rape, and for a brief second was immersed in the terror of being at home on the sullied bed, then the clean roughness of hospital sheets and smell of antiseptic broke through and told her she was safe. Close on the heels of that relief came knowledge that if she went home, safety would vanish.

When her husband came at eight and reached out to touch her, all she could do was flinch away from him and curl into a ball.

SIX

THE MINI-FLOOD on Parson's Lane drained away, and the road reopened to traffic. Stye Beck returned to its peaceful flow. Efflux from the storm drain slowed to a trickle, and the grey overcast changed as the month changed, and became clear blue. A motorist, braking hard to avoid a woman in pink, walking near the dip of the road, ran into the ditch. When he climbed out of his car to look for the woman, and to find a phone, she had vanished, and the nearest BT telephone was a mile away.

FRIDAY MORNING, sun slanted in through the window and stroked Lucy's face. She opened her eyes and looked at the sloping ceiling. When the sun comes out, she'd told herself, when it stops raining, I'll be gone. Remembering made her uneasy. She climbed out of bed and took off the pink cotton nightie. That wasn't hers either, just borrowed like the rest of the stuff in her closet and drawers. Made her wonder where it came from. Patients, according to Mrs C. Leaving things behind to be given to people who didn't have much.

It had bothered her at first, being thought of as a charity case. Then she'd thought, 'What's it matter? 'S'what I am,' and got on with her work.

The thing she'd noticed most was the money. All the women were well heeled. Probably why they were there in the first place. NHS not good enough. When she said that to Mrs C, she'd got a dirty look and a tight mouth in reply. Daft bringing it up in the first place. Wouldn't expect *her* to admit it.

Only, after a bit, Mrs C had said a lot came 'cos they

couldn't get pregnant, and Lucy knew all about that. Test tube babies and such. Couldn't be much fun to get old and not have any kids. Not if you wanted them.

Auntie Fee never had. Said so all the time, and ended up getting four. Didn't know whether to laugh or cry.

'Can't keep it bloody zipped, can I?' she'd said. 'Not way he carries on.'

Lucy could have told her a thing or two.

Next time she went into Paula Williamson's room she'd changed the water carafe and glass tumbler, and stayed a minute longer than she needed to talk about names. 'If it's a girl,' she said, 'mine, I thought about Melanie, like Melanie Griffiths. I'd want her to grow up like that, you know, doing something special.'

Paula had looked surprised. Then she'd smiled. 'My choice is Rachel Elizabeth,' she said. 'But the names don't belong to anyone we know. I wanted her to start life without anyone else's baggage.'

Lucy's face fell.

Paula added quickly, 'But Melanie is a nice name too, especially when you've chosen it for such a good reason.' Lucy nodded and took away the used carafe and glass, ten yards down the corridor before she decided Mrs Williamson hadn't been slighting her after all, and went back and told her so.

DARREN KNEW ABOUT HULL, or thought he did. Busy port and foreign ships. Bawdy pub talk he'd picked up about seamen and prossies, and the place being one big red-light district after dark. He knew it wasn't true of course, exaggeration pure and simple like with most things, but he liked the idea. Not that he'd any intention of paying for it. Free samples and a bit of force if he had to, prossies didn't make a fuss about that kind of thing. Twenty yards away Skeeter started manhandling a swing. Darren eyed him reflectively, wondering why he bothered dragging the silly squit around. Skeeter, struggling, feeling his end begin to slip and knowing Darren's eyes were on him, didn't wonder at all. Saw the whole thing clearly with himself the butt of jokes and cleaner up of shit. Brassed off at being landed with a job he didn't want, in a place he didn't like, the only problem circling his mind was why he couldn't get up enough bottle to go home.

BARRETT AND ROSIE had to cool their heels in the hospital corridor until the clinical psychologist was through with Kim. For some reason Barrett had expected a white-coated male to emerge, but instead it was a redhead in her forties whose looks gave him a quick buzz. He swallowed down surprise and asked about Kim, his eyes seeking and finding her name badge. P.J. Barrington. He wondered what the P.J. stood for but didn't ask. No sense risking a put-down with Rosie along. P.J. ignored Barrett and smiled at Rosie.

'You were here yesterday? You handled it very well.'

Rosie said uncomfortably, 'It didn't feel that way.'

'Take my word for it.' She switched her attention to Barrett. No smile for him, just a measuring, 'I hope you have the same amount of diplomacy.'

He hoped so too, but he wasn't going to tell her that. Bristling, he said stiffly, 'My remit is catching the man who did it, that's my prime concern, diplomacy comes second. If we don't get him, he'll do it again.' She inclined her head and walked away.

Kim was in bed, sitting up and staring at nothing, thoughts turned in. Barrett and Rosie were the last people she wanted to see. She closed her eyes and pretended they weren't there. Barrett felt uncomfortable, suddenly wished he'd let Rosie do it on her own. He pulled up a chair to the side of the bed, and sat on it, making himself smaller, less threatening, and began to ask his questions. Kim answered them all, voice even, and didn't once open her eyes until they were gone out of the door and she heard it close behind them. At four that afternoon she left the hospital with her parents, and went back to her childhood home in Durham where her father owned five butcher's shops and her mother sat on the local council.

The way she felt then, it didn't matter to her if she never saw Malminster, or her husband, again.

MORRISSEY'S HOME on the north side of Malminster was a bay-windowed 1930s semi with gardens on three sides, and at that time of year the garden would normally have been his joy and relaxation. Instead it was his bane. Semi-hardy shrubs he'd worked hard to cultivate had died in the hard, long-lasting winter, while the month of heavy rain that followed almost without break had turned the whole garden into a morass. Self-seeded green things turned mushy in the mud, while others—boxes of them—propagated in the greenhouse, grew spindly waiting for the sun. And now it had come he still felt pessimistic.

Four rainless days did not a summer make.

He wondered how much would ultimately struggle through, how many bulbs had rotted in the ground, and felt pity for market gardeners who depended on soil for their living. A mild gratitude stirred in him, that he'd put off becoming one of them for yet another year. He tended his greenhouse and tried to ignore the rest, potting on into fresh loam and hoping for miracles.

At seven he went back indoors and left his gardening shoes on the back step, ruffling his wife's hair as he passed and getting flicked with flour for his trouble. His fingers snaked to the pie dish and came out with a slice of apple that he put in his mouth with a grin. Familiar rituals cementing relationships. When he went upstairs, Mike was in his bedroom squatting in front of the stereo, flipping through a stack of tapes. When his father came in he set them down and got to his feet, his stance defensive.

'No need to stop,' said Morrissey mildly.

'It's all right,' Mike said. 'I wasn't doing anything in particular.' He sat on his bed and waited. Morrissey turned the wooden chair and straddled that, facing him. Mike looked tired, colourless under a pale tan. His father tried to dismiss it as imagination but it wouldn't go away.

'What's this about leaving school?'

'You've been talking to Mum.' A statement not a question. Morrissey dipped his head in acknowledgement.

'I don't see why not,' said Mike. 'Might as well leave now and get a job. Work my way up. No guarantee I'll do better getting A-levels is there?'

'Opens more doors.'

'Maybe.'

'A bit sudden, isn't it?'

'Dunno.' Mike dropped his eyes, leaned sideways and picked up a bunch of tapes, turning them over in his hands.

'Get a job where?'

A shrug. 'I don't know. Job Centre I suppose.'

'Mike...'

'So how old were you?'

'Different circumstances, mine was Hobson's choice. I'd have stayed on if I could.'

Mike showed a flicker of interest. 'Done the whole thing and gone to uni?'

'Probably.'

'And read what?'

Morrissey shook his head and saw no advantage in looking back. He rested both arms along the back of the chair and set his chin on them, hunched awkwardly because of his height. Mike waited for an answer, hands still, eyes on his father. Morrissey turned back his inner clock, saw himself Mike's age. No sense saying he'd have studied law, Mike would see through that for what it was. A plain lie.

'Classics,' he said gruffly.

Mike nodded. Silence stretched. His hands went back to turning over the tapes. His father sighed and tried again.

'I thought you'd decided on law?' Another shrug as Mike chose not to answer. Morrissey wondered what had happened to the custom of fathers laying down the law and sons obeying. Got thrown out in the sixties, that's what, just a spit too late for *him.* For the first time in years he wished his own father had done a little more in the line of consultation.

'Gone off the idea?'

'Not especially. It's the time involved. Two more years at school, three at uni, and a degree that gets me a job emptying dustbins.'

'What gives you that idea?'

'Remember Pete Truscott?'

'Winger?'

'He got a first in history. I saw him, emptying bins.'

'Did you talk to him?'

'Didn't think he'd want me to. There's been others in the papers, it isn't just him.'

'Compromise?' Morrissey bargained. 'Two more years at school and then please yourself.' Mike looked at him suspiciously. Down in the hall the telephone began to ring, and Morrissey heard Margaret answering, then her voice, calling him.

Whenever he tried to talk to Mike, work intervened.

He put the chair back in place and fought down an urge to hug his son and embarrass the both of them. Mike squatted by the stereo again and went back to sorting tapes. When Morrissey said, 'Think about it?' Mike nodded without turning his head. No hardship in doing that. His father might not know it, but that was all he ever seemed to do these days. Think.

WHEN THE FAIR CLOSED at eleven Darren wasn't there. Luckily for him Finnegan didn't know that. If he had known it Darren would have got the sack.

At the other end of town, near the passage called The Land of Green Ginger, Darren was eyeing the local street trade. The first time he made an approach he guessed wrong and offered twenty pounds to a brunette in a skimpy black dress waiting for her boyfriend to come out of the gents.

When he told her what he wanted her to do and she screamed, the boyfriend came out on the run, zipping his flies and looking murder.

Darren didn't wait to find out.

When he couldn't hear the epithets any longer he slowed down and got his breath back. A car trawled the kerb slowly. Twenty yards up it stopped under a streetlight.

A blonde in black basque, skimpy red skirt and ankle boots hipped over and leaned in the window. Terms agreed, she got in the passenger seat. Darren's lip curled. He turned around and went back the way he'd come.

Down the side of the station another brunette saw the white T-shirt and dark trousers and hoped he was off the German freighter, because the Germans always had plenty of money. When she found he wasn't she went with him anyway, trade being slow.

Down the side of the fish warehouse he took more than she'd bargained for, and when she limped home with aching ribs and a split lip, and said her night's takings were in Darren's back pocket, she got another good hiding from her pimp for being so stupid.

THE SOUND EDGED into the dream Lucy was having and woke her. Flat on her back, eyes open, she waited for it to come again, listening so hard she could hear the silence. Then a baby's wail echoed in and she slid out of bed and padded downstairs, pulling on the navy blue bathrobe whose sleeves were too long as she went.

She wanted it to be the Williamson baby, told herself if it was nobody would mind her being nosy enough to want to see, eager as she went down the corridor and stopped outside the door. Only, when she opened it the room was dark, and she could see a hump under the bedclothes and hear the even breathing that said Mrs Williamson was in there and asleep.

She withdrew quietly and stood in the corridor, head down, trying to remember exactly what she had heard. Didn't have to have been a baby. Could have been cats. Same sort of noise, sat there yowling and randy. Had to have been, hadn't it? Stupid cats.

Instead of going back to her room she went through the fire door at the other end of the corridor, down the back stairs to the ground floor delivery room and found that was empty too. There was no carpet in this part of the clinic, and her bare feet left dark imprints that faded before she had taken a full step. She shouldn't be in there, she knew that, Mrs C had told her never to go inside when she'd let her look through the open door the first day she was there. Germs, that's why. It didn't stop her wanting to look though, not when it was where hers'd be born if she had it at The Cedars and not a proper hospital.

It worried her a bit, the big round light, and the metal things on the bed. Nearly like an operating theatre. She dithered, worrying about her chances of getting caught if she went right in, but about to do that and risk it when she heard the lift coming down and turned tail, running for the central stairs, not waiting to see who was in it, in a hurry to get back to the attic and her own room, curling up under the pink and white duvet when she got there, ears pricked, listening for the cats.

SEVEN

FIELD MIST CURLED UP and thickened into hanging white ghosts that the sun ate up before midday, as it sat high and hot in a sky of intense cerulean blue. On Parson's Lane, traffic with wound-down windows shed snatches of music—reggae and rap—a byte of Mozart—all of it disturbing the grave-quiet place where gathering heat released the stench of decaying meat. A golden retriever out walking with its master sniffed the air and paddled into Stye Beck towards the smell's source, droop-eared and limp-tailed when called back before curiosity could be satisfied. A few minutes later, trotting along Parson's Lane where the road passed over the drain, the dog's hackles rose and it refused to go any further.

WHEN LUCY WENT into Paula Williamson's room again, midmorning, it was empty, bedclothes folded into a neat packet on the mattress. The book Paula had been reading the day before sat on the low table, waiting for attention, page marked with a red silk thong.

Puzzled, Lucy left fresh water and went out again, bumping the trolley over the hump at the top of the stairs and riding down in the lift to leave water in the four occupied rooms on the ground floor. She didn't talk to the women in those—mostly because they didn't talk to her.

Stuck up cows.

And anyway, they weren't having babies, they were having *treatment*—whatever that might be.

One was sitting on top of the bed eating chocolates, and

put the lid on real quick, not even offering. Squatting there with the box on her fat thighs—like Lucy had the lurgy.

Lucy stuck her nose in the air, and went out with her head up.

She'd taken the trolley back to the kitchen, washed the carafes and glasses, and had them cupboarded in neat rows when she heard the lift moving again, purring like a steel cat as it went to the first floor.

On her way back upstairs she heard a baby cry—and this time there was no mistaking it. Smiling, Lucy speeded up her feet, turning down the corridor to Paula Williamson's room and bursting in through the door. It didn't matter that Mrs C was in there with the sour-faced nurse who always looked at Lucy as if she were a piece of beef ready for the cleaver; what mattered was the perspex-sided crib at the foot of the bed.

Leaning over the crib's side, she grinned with pleasure. 'Aw, look at her,' she said, one hand dropping to her belly again. 'Just look at her, isn't she gorgeous? Can I pick her up? Can I? Just for a sec?'

Flushing with anger, Carpenter said, 'Out!' enforcing it with a quick shove. Lucy resisted the urge to shove back, but got her scowl on again.

'Only wanted to see,' she muttered.

'You've seen. Now get on with your work.'

Lucy turned, glowering.

Rotten cow!

Who'd she think she was, pushing and shoving.

'Out!'

Stiff-backed with resentment Lucy went.

Mid-afternoon, sitting in the kitchen, hands wrapped round a mug of tea, thinking how, with the weather bright and sunny, she might as well move on, she listened to Diane Carpenter lecture her about bursting into patients' rooms uninvited.

Drinking the tea in long sips, and debating the chances of nicking a couple of packets of the stuff before she left, Lucy wondered why it wasn't up to Mrs Williamson to say that, and not Mrs C. In half a mind to ask that when she caught the look in Mrs C's eyes and thought better of it.

'Wasn't bothered about cuddling it anyway,' she said, and left it at that.

WESLEY STREET ran at right angles to the park, east to west, two rows of small terrace houses eyeing each other up across a narrow road with speed humps at each end. The humps were a necessity; without them drivers took a fast and reckless short cut from one main road to another, and heaven help pedestrians in between.

Saturday night, the three youths who crossed over from the park were noisy. None of them were old enough to drink legally, but that hadn't stopped them getting hold of two six-packs. Cocky and sure of themselves in the half-light, they looked and behaved like they were set to cause trouble, lifting gates off hinges and peering through front windows. When they looked in through number fifteen's, Beryl Roberts rang the police. The call was logged at nine-thirty, but because Beryl made a habit of complaining, and the controller had heard it all before, from barking dogs and crying babies to strange coloured lights in the sky, it was given low priority.

Outside number twenty-six two of the youths hoisted the third shoulder high so he could pee in the pillarbox.

Fixing a broken sash in his front window, Geoffrey Harland saw the whole thing, picturing the letters soaked and evil-smelling at the bottom of the box, and one of them his, painstakingly composed to his daughter in New Zealand.

Rage took over from caution.

Hammer firm in his hand, he went out onto the pavement

and told them to get off his street. They pranced around, called him an old fart and worse, and then fanned, one to either side and one facing. Taunting.

'Come on then, piss-pants—what you waitin' for?'

'What's up, grandad—you got to pee in a bottle?'

Harland swung the hammer, felt his arm grabbed and twisted, and cried out with the pain of it. Deep under his ribcage a fist thudded home. Breath whistled out of him, emptying his lungs, and he dropped to his knees. His head felt light and out of control. Vaguely he was aware of them running down the street, of the dog that was with them sniffing him, nose wet and whiffling before it followed.

His hands felt warmly wet and red oozed out between his fingers. Dimly his mind accepted that the fist had held a knife.

From the far distance of a million miles Harland heard his wife's voice, and tried to anchor his consciousness to the sound of it, blackness fringing the edges of his field of vision.

When the ambulance arrived seven minutes later he was dead, his wife on her knees cradling him.

Face wet, eyes bewildered, she refused to release her hold, repeating over and over, 'I told him not to go…I told him not to go…'

When the first Panda car got there the paramedics were still trying to pry her loose.

'RACHEL ELIZABETH. She's lovely.' The baby felt light as she held her, hardly there at all with the fluffy blanket wrapped round. 'Might not call mine Melanie after all,' Lucy said. 'Thought I could get a book with names and things in it, pick something nice, something special—just for her.'

Paula smiled. 'You're determined to keep the baby. I can see that.'

‘’Course I am! Wouldn’t like to see anybody try to stop me either.’

‘Suppose it’s a boy?’

‘Dunno. Gary’s nice.’ She squinted at the other woman’s face, looking for approval, and found none. ‘Doesn’t have to be Gary, there’s others. Kurt—like Kurt Russell, or Kevin after Kevin Costner. They’d be all right.’

Paula eased herself against the pillows and held out her arms. Lucy handed back the infant with reluctance.

‘Don’t you like them either?’

‘Call him Luke. Luke and Lucy go well together.’

‘Luke... Luke.’ Lucy rolled the word around on her tongue and liked the sound of it. ‘’S’nice,’ she said. ‘Yeah—Lucy and Luke—Ta!’ Beaming, she picked up Paula’s tea tray and headed for the door, turning as she got there. ‘Can’t imagine anyone wanting to give their baby up, can you?’

Paula hugged the baby closer, eyes fixed on its face. ‘No,’ she said. ‘No, I don’t suppose I can.’

UNIFORM’S URGENT REQUEST for CID presence landed in front of DC Smythe, on solitary late shift in the big CID room. The DC took himself off in a hurry. Any chance to remedy past mistakes had to be good. By the time he checked with DCI Morrissey the police surgeon had pronounced Harland dead, and Scene of Crime were busy. Blue and white tape cordoned off the area and uniformed men were knocking on doors asking for witnesses. The only thing Smythe hadn’t yet managed to do—and he was regretful about that—was talk to Mrs Harland.

By the time he arrived in a flurry of wheels a near neighbour, who avidly watched *Murder She Wrote,* had fed the weeping woman two sleeping tablets and knocked her out completely.

‘Seemed the best thing in the circumstances,’ said the

neighbour comfortably. 'That upset she was, and no wonder, poor woman. I've seen a lot of these things on TV, and they always sedate the widow. Saves her having to be pestered by the police.' She stared him baldly in the eye as she said that.

Smythe eyed her unkindly. 'Mrs Harland's own pills, were they?'

'Mine. Nothing wrong with that, is there? I went home and fetched them. Share and share alike. She never had any need for sleeping pills, not until now.'

'Did you think to call her doctor?'

'No need, love, not when she's asleep.'

'What's his name and what were the pills?' he said roughly.

'Don't get like that with me,' she said. 'Shirty. I did her a good turn. And you won't get Dr Redman, it's only a locum what comes after six o'clock.'

'What were the pills?'

'What pills?' she said, and went into the Harland kitchen to brew a pot of tea. Fuming, wondering exactly what it was happened to women when they got older, Smythe went outside and radioed control to get Dr Redman out. 'Him personally. Not the locum.' More than satisfied fifteen minutes later when Redman arrived and gave the woman a dressing down.

He included that in his verbal report to Morrissey, and felt well pleased when the Chief Inspector told him he'd done everything that needed to be done, and then left it to Smythe to talk to Mrs Harland next day.

Not that the DC welcomed the task. It was the part of an investigation he hated, talking to the next of kin. White faces and red eyes made him wish he was a thousand miles away. He gentled his voice, but it made no difference, all he got was, 'Go away,' in a flat monotone.

He said, 'You want us to catch them?'

Her eyes lifted and measured him. 'The dog bit one of them a few months back.'

Smythe looked around, saw no pet hairs. 'Dog?'

Voice flat and hollow she said, 'Magistrate ordered it put down—there's justice.'

'I'm sorry.'

Her shoulders moved. Not quite a shrug. Not enough interest for that. 'Won't bring him back will it? Him or the dog. What'll happen if you find them? Will they be hung? Can you promise me that? No, 'course you can't—but they should be.'

'I'm not disagreeing,' Smythe said. 'I'm not saying they shouldn't be—just it can't happen.'

'That's what I thought you'd say,' she said, and closed her eyes.

All she said after that was another, 'Go away.'

He was back in the car, going steady over the speed humps, front gardens stiff with police in blue coveralls searching for the knife, mind half on that and half on the road when he realised she'd given him at least one name, and drove back to the station cock-a-hoop. Check with records and this one was solved already.

Pleased as punch at the thought it'd be marked up to him and look good on his sheet.

EIGHT

THERE HAD BEEN only the smallest drift of breeze during the night hours to carry the ripe, rancid smell in among the trees of Stye Wood. Small creatures, to whom such scents were ambrosia, had come to see, noses twitching. Most had turned back, unwilling to enter the waters of Stye Beck. A pair of foxes, less timid, had scratched at the iron grill throughout the night, barking in short, staccato bursts of frustration. At six-thirty a tractor driver taking a sow to boar noted the rotting sweetness and recognised its origins. When he got back to the farm he told his boss it stank like a dead sheep.

At nine, milking finished and breakfast over, the two of them went back to look…

MONDAY MORNING Smythe was cheerful, the Harland case wrapped up, and a pat on the back from Morrissey. If all police work were that simple the job'd be a doddle. Grinning to himself at Woodsy's sour face over in the corner. A while now since Smythe had been flavour of the month and he liked the feel of it. Three young toe-rags under lock and key and all of it down to a zealous magistrate having signed a dog destruction order.

'Anybody wants me, I'm going to talk to Harland's widow,' he said. 'Tell her the good news.'

'Yeah, well, tell her how collaring 'em was down to her dead dog, then, and not you.'

'Mawky sod!' said Smythe, and stalked out, hesitating halfway down the stairs when the telephone rang behind him, counting the repeats until Woods picked up. Six. Grinning, he took the last flight at a trot and went out the back door, starting up his car and moving off in one smooth action, turning right, out of the police yard and across the traffic before anyone could call him back, glad something was going to get Woods off his butt.

THERE WAS a Panda car parked just beyond the dip in Parson's Lane. Barrett and Woods pulled in behind it, a sweet rancidity already reaching into the car. Woods swallowed a couple of times and clamped his jaw. Barrett felt near wonderment that his own stomach sat unprotesting. It hadn't always been so. Past embarrassments flicked across his mind's viewing screen as he got out and looked down the banking towards Style Beck.

His eyes took in the other men's wellingtons, and the mud, and sent him to the car's boot. 'Only got the one pair,' he told Woods. 'Don't suppose you thought to bring any.'

'Didn't know I'd need 'em, did I?' said Woods, busy with his handkerchief.

'Get your feet wet then, won't you,' answered Barrett unsympathetically, yanking off his own shoes and shoving his feet into rubber.

Woods ignored him. What point stating the obvious?

At the side of Stye Beck, farmer and farmhand stood uneasily, slightly apart from two uniformed police, all four wearing the same expression, and none of them wanting to see what flopped out from behind the storm grid if it fell to them to take it down. 'Definitely human?' was all Barrett asked before he stepped into the slow-moving stream. Woods thanked God for his lack of boots and stayed where he was.

Water seeped through and around piled-up debris behind the metal barrier, pushing out small bits of detritus that flopped irregularly into the stream. Just above water level a hand poked out between the bars, small bones exposed, flesh ragged and friable. Barrett's stomach lurched with its old unpredictability. He eyed the hand warily and worked out options. No sense just pulling out the grid, letting everything in there tumble in a rush. Not until they knew what it was hiding. Human, yes, male or female he couldn't tell.

He clamped both hand and handkerchief across his face and bent closer. A mat of hair, mud-soaked and leaf-flecked crowded the bars. Came down from the other side of the road, that much was obvious. Question was how? Could be a hit and run, knocked into the ditch, then swept through the drain when it flooded. Could equally well be some poor sod fallen in half drunk and not got out.

The third possibility, that murder had been done, he tried deliberately to put from his mind, knowing that whatever the truth was, taking down the grid would send a mishmash of evidence out into Stye Beck and halfway to the river if they weren't careful. He turned around and waded back to the path.

'Better get it shifted, then,' said Woods, trying for nonchalant. Barrett eyed him uncharitably.

'Thought that out carefully have you?'

Woods hadn't. He shoved a mint in his mouth, a Polo, full of bits of lint from his pocket but better than nothing. 'Don't see there's an alternative,' he said. 'Could go in from the other side but it'd be a bit awkward, need a froggie, and with that smell he'd want a cylinder. Bit narrow for that. Too tight a squeeze.'

'That's a fact,' said Barrett. 'Two and a half foot diameter, I doubt it'd even be considered.'

'I'll get this lot started in on shifting it then,' said Woods, taking a step away, convinced he'd grabbed the initiative and one up on Barrett.

'You'll get yourself back to the car,' Barrett answered flatly. 'The grid stays where it is until we get the right cutting equipment. It'll have to come down bit by bit from the top. Tell Control we need SOCO and a forensic team down here to go with it.'

Woods's shoulders hunched. Time was he could really rattle the DS. Now it was water off a duck's back. Halfway back to the car he got an extra strong breath of the stench. His stomach heaved. At a stumbling run he just about made it to the hedge bottom before he threw up.

LUCY WAS UP in her room, supposedly taking a mandatory sleep. Like going back to day-nursery. Rows of little kids on foam mattresses, and a blanket over. Most of them sleeping, but boredom with a big B for those that didn't. She'd put the television on low and watched *Neighbours,* then got bored with what came after and turned it off. Now she was up at the window looking out over the car park and across the fields at the back. Over to the right she could see the trees of Stye Wood, heat shivering over the top of them like a ghost. Further away still the river ran, but she couldn't see that because of the lie of the land, only the way fields rose up sharply behind it. Midway was a road she didn't know the name of, that didn't get much traffic, except that now it was busy and she wished she could see more clearly what was going on.

Must be an accident of some sort. All the comings and goings seemed to be of white vans and cars—plus a bright red fire engine that had gone now.

Elbows propped on the sill, she watched the perfunctory flash of a blue light as a white van moved away.

Yeah, accident. Had to be. Wishing for a pair of binoculars when the loose board creaked in the corridor and sent her scurrying for the bed. Curled up, eyes closed, pretending sleep, she told herself whatever it was, it'd be bound to be on *Calendar News.*

When the door opened and let someone into the room

she lay quietly and breathed rhythmically, until it closed again as they went out.

When the board creaked down the passage she sat up.

Mrs C. Had to be. Was only her wore *Apogée.*

'It's French, Lucy, and very expensive.'

Like Lucy was too thick to know it for herself.

Back at the window, kneeling on a chair, chin resting on crossed arms, she returned her attention to the distant road.

COPELAND WAS BACK at his desk, the shut-down look on his face showing which way the court case had gone. Smythe eyed him, pulled his own chair out, and flopped onto it. Nothing ever did go the way you expected.

'Chucked it out?'

Copeland looked up from his writing.

'Hundred hours community service.'

Smythe nodded, started hunting out a pen that hadn't either dried out or gone scratchy and thought it was like him with Harland's widow. He hadn't expected her to look happy, not so soon after it happened, but he'd expected something. Satisfaction, thankfulness, just a look crossing her face, but instead—nothing. Might as well not have told her. He'd stood in the hall, eager as a kid wanting a pat, and she'd stared back at him like a zombie.

'Won't bring either of them back will it? Him or the dog,' she'd said, and practically pushed him out.

'What's on then?' He motioned at Woods's empty desk.

Copeland kept on writing.

'Dunno, only just got back. Probably a plum—usually is where he's concerned.'

Yeah, thought Smythe, disgruntled, dead right it was, and if he'd turned himself round when he heard the phone ring instead of wasting half the morning it could have been his.

NINE

PARSON'S LANE was closed to traffic again, diversion signs at both ends while men with grim faces who would rather be anywhere but there took the grid apart. Not given the choice of absence they worked for the most part in silence, breathing air through face masks that made them look like aliens but filtered out most of the stench. For that they were grateful, wishing only that what their eyes must see could be sanitised too.

Detritus was removed by the handful, examined and largely discarded. Some of it went into bags. Mid-afternoon the last section of grid came down. The body rolled and sighed. A fat rat ran out between the legs of the men and escaped up the green bank towards the trees. When the body was lifted out, two fingers and a foot were missing. Word went round that what had been found was once a woman.

'FUNNY SHE HASN'T BEEN missed,' said Barrett. 'Or at least, it is if she's local. We've had no one go missing since the Brindley business.' He sat at his desk, chair half swivelled, looking at Morrissey, the same thought in both men's minds. Morrissey dismissed it first.

'Can't see there being a connection. Too far out of town for a start, and if she'd been in there since February there'd have been less of her.' Barrett, who had been there when the remains went into a body bag, pushed that thread of thought away. Bad enough to know the post-mortem was still to come, and a ringside seat for him guaranteed. He cleared his throat.

'Not many houses down there, no more than a couple of dozen right the way along the lane, so they won't take much getting round. Then there's the two farms. If she's from down there somebody must have missed her. Unless she lived alone.'

'Wouldn't be unusual.'

'Make it that much harder, though. Especially if she'd kept herself to herself.'

But it had to be done, hard or not hard. Didn't matter how simple the explanation might turn out to be, a woman was dead, and they needed to know how and why, thought Barrett, who'd long since stopped expecting anything to be easy. He looked at the wall clock, and saw both hands were on four.

Not much point expecting council housing officers to fall over themselves that close to home time.

Better to do it tomorrow anyway, when they'd got all the house-to-house reports back from Parson's Lane. Might even get lucky for once and not need to bother if somebody had a neighbour they thought had gone on holiday and turned out to have been in the drain instead.

It wouldn't stop him having to be at the post-mortem though, nothing could stop that.

He remembered how Warmsby's face had closed up when the grid came down and he'd waded through the effluent stream to look at what was there, mouth stretched thin, eyes hooded and no jokes. First time Barrett could remember the Home Office man looking at a body without some kind of witticism. He remarked on that to Morrissey, being stoic because like Warmsby himself, at tomorrow's post-mortem he'd have to see it all again.

'Let Woods attend,' said the Chief Inspector. 'Time he was bloodied.'

'He'd spend most of his time horizontal.'

'Time he learned policing isn't all missing cats,' Morrissey said unsympathetically. 'I seem to remember it being part of what he gets paid for. Survived it yourself, didn't you?'

Barrett didn't remember having been given much choice, he'd been told to get in there and keep his stomach down, and that had been that—with Morrissey wolf-grinning when he hadn't managed it. Thought of putting Woods in the same situation brought perverse pleasure.

'It's something to think about, sir,' he said. 'I suppose I could find myself a bit stretched if I did it myself.' Exchanging a look with Morrissey that said he'd make certain of it.

THE LARGER PART of Malminster's Asian community lived in the terraced houses behind the industrial estate off the Middlebrook Road, but not all the house were Asian-owned. A half-dozen pensioners who had brought up families and spent most of their lives in the terraced rows had stayed put.

The terraces themselves ran at right angles to the circular access road that fed traffic into and out of the big warehouses, and at their other end, where until a year ago a parcel of derelict land had formed a hazardous playground, stood end-on to six new rows of town houses that were part of the town council's redevelopment scheme.

Life was peaceful, except for one sore thumb.

Willie Beam had moved into one of the few landlord-owned terraced houses six months ago, making himself look respectable when he negotiated with the agents, and paying a sizable deposit up front to show he was solvent. He omitted to mention one thing. The way he made his money.

Willie's dream had always been the same. To get rich. Didn't matter how so long as it didn't entail work, and he'd picked up the notion that satisfying consumer demand ahead of anyone else was the road to take. And right then he was on a roller.

Far as he knew he had the only crack house in town and demand growing by the minute.

Willie was happy with his lot. The more rocks he made, the bigger the queue to buy, and his operation was strictly cash.

'Put it in my palm,' he'd say, holding out a lean paw. 'Let me hear it sing. That's the only music I hear.'

He made no exceptions. Not even for Eddie Gunn, who ran a string of girls and fancied he could keep them in line better and get more work out of them if he fed them crack. Start them on freebies, then make them pay. No more holding back on takings then. What they didn't hand over like good little toms, they'd spend on crack. Like Willie, all Eddie wanted was money.

He'd have been in pig's heaven if Willie Beam hadn't been awkward. 'Cash up front, and come in person,' is what he told Eddie. 'How'm I supposed to know who you got working for you? Some *man* comes knocking on my door saying, "I come from Eddie," how you expect me to know he's telling the truth? Could be some *man* I don't want to know. Like Mr Police*man.*'

Eddie didn't like that, fancying himself as Mr Big, but he didn't put on the swagger for Willie that he brought out in front of the girls, just stubbed out his thin cigar on Willie's shiny low table. 'Right then, Willie lad,' he said, 'if that's the way you want it. A week to think about it, after that I shut you down.'

'Yeah,' said Willie, eyeing the new heatburn. 'You do that. And the price just went up.' He hustled Eddie out onto the path and watched one of Eddie's lackeys leap to open the car door like a proper chauffeur. Audi, he thought, watching it drive away. Eat it up for dinner when I get me Porsche.

THE FAIR was getting ready to move again, this time over the Humber Bridge and down to Brigg. Darren, having found Hull to his liking, was regretful. He'd been helping out on the dodgems, riding car backs and collecting late fares—and riding for other reasons on the ones that held pretty girls, his tight jeans, lean good looks and slicked back hair encouraging them to pay for another ride.

He'd had more than that out of two of them. Sweet sixteens, and him making well sure they'd been more than kissed when they went home. Grinning when he remembered having them. Up on the hill in the tight knot of trees above the fairground. One had come back the next night for more, the other had gone away crying. He'd boasted about it to Skeeter, but Skeeter hadn't said anything, just turned over in his sleeping bag and acted like he wasn't interested. Darren had swung his fist over in a wide arc and given him a thump on the ear to get his attention.

'Don't act like you're not bothered,' he said, nasty. 'Just 'cos you can't never get it up.'

Skeeter had swallowed the pain and added it to a long tally card, and gone back to thinking about Joanne. He'd been doing that a lot. Been nice, that night, going for a curry. He wondered if she'd forgotten him. Then he started wondering who she was with and what she was doing, wishing he'd told Darren to get stuffed and stopped on in Malminster where he wanted to be, a part of him dead for years wanting to scrub his slate clean and start again. Couldn't though. Not now. Bloody stupid, way he trailed Darren like a kicked dog, and no bite left.

A DESCRIPTION of the dead woman went out on local radio, along with a police plea for information. The same plea went out on *Calendar News,* together with video footage of the dismantled grid and yawning darkness of the drain's mouth. As always, a studio number for enquiries was given along with the local police number, but with the exception of one caller wanting to know if finding the body meant the smell had gone, and he could now start taking a short cut down the lane again, the telephone lines stayed silent.

Lucy saw the fluttering blue and white police tape, and cluster of vehicles, on her television at ten-thirty. At first she didn't realise why the scene looked familiar, then memory clicked in and combined it with the long-distance view through her window.

When she saw the drain she shuddered, imagination sharing the body's cramped space, reliving the panic of being trapped. Suppose she'd been alive in there, not dead like they thought. *Suppose she'd tried to get out, pushed and pushed and pushed, and cried she'd be good! Suppose she'd done that.*

Shivering as she thought about it.

Like being in the coal bunker, it'd be, only worse.

She hugged the pillow for comfort—glad that in the bunker it had been only spiders, not rats, her eyes glued to the screen, wondering who the poor, silly cow had been.

TEN

SOON AFTER nine p.m., as dusk wrapped itself between earth and sky, the forensic team called a halt. The amount of debris remaining within the storm drain would keep them busily sifting for at least another twenty-four hours, and if that search failed, it would be widened. One finger bone had already been found, but the missing foot had not. The green canvas screens were left in place overnight, and the diversion signs taken down.

PC Halloran, left behind in his Panda to keep watch and bored with all the inactivity, listened to the radio and had problems staying awake. At one-thirty, a fresh set of car headlights crested the rise near the entrance to Randall's Farm and shone bright in the PC's face. He slitted his eyes and waited for it to pass, but instead the car braked heavily, lights veering erratically across the centre line as it slewed. The back end came towards him, gliding like an overweight skater, sideswiping him and the police car into the nearside ditch. Halloran felt his collar bone snap and swore. Stuck inside the car, unable to open either door, the PC radioed for help.

When a second Panda got there, the car driver was still pacing the road, looking for a woman with bright red hair and a pink tracksuit, who he swore had run out in front of him.

TWO SUPPLIES MEN were up in CID early Tuesday morning, moving furniture out of DI Beckett's office and carrying it downstairs. Barrett, crossing the corridor looking for Woods, watched the desk disappear with mixed feelings.

Refurbishment was a buzz word and almost every office in the place had already been given the treatment. One of the exceptions up to now had been Beckett's long narrow space with its too-small window. To Barrett's mind, if they'd finally got around to it, it could mean only one of two things: either the DI was moving back into CID, or they'd found a replacement. He didn't like either option.

Woods had his feet up on the desk, mug of coffee to the right, bacon butty brought up from the canteen in his hands, half eaten. He eyed the DS warily, half guessing what was to come. 'Didn't have time for brekky.'

'Isn't too greasy for your stomach, then?' asked Barrett, eyes on the butty. 'No cholesterol worries?'

'Not much point,' said Woods. 'If that doesn't get me, something else will.' He took another bite, filling his mouth. Barrett watched the rhythmic jaw movement.

'Best get something solid inside,' he said, with unkind pleasure. 'Put a bit of weight in your stomach before you go out. Post-mortem's at ten so I don't advise being late, not when the DCI'll want every last detail.'

'Why me?' said Woods, butty suddenly unpalatable.

'Why not?' said Barrett, trying to keep a straight face. 'Need somebody there with a responsible attitude. Good observer. Not uncomfortable with either of those virtues are you?' Smythe, busy at his desk, but appreciating Barrett's drollery for once, looked up and grinned.

Woods saw the trap but couldn't avoid it. Chewing and glowering, he shook his head. All in all the DS was getting to be a pain in the arse, and high time somebody took him down a peg. Still thinking about that two hours later as he parted company with his butty in the mortuary sink.

MORRISSEY READ the house-to-house reports with a feeling of dissatisfaction. Warmsby's initial opinion, grudgingly given, that the body had been in the drainage system no more than six weeks, added to the problem. The dead woman's clothing had already been bagged and sent to Forensics; the garments cut off with delicate care, so as to avoid even more disintegration of the tissues they enclosed.

Lightweight sports shoes with a Marks & Spencer label. Fine for walking, but useless for running or jogging. Sweat bottoms and collared top, both pink, and from Dash. Nothing else worn but bra and briefs, on what had to have been at best a bitterly cold day. He moved around from his desk to the wall map and ran his finger the length of Parson's Lane.

Barrett knew what the DCI was thinking. The woman had to have been coming from, or going to, somewhere close at hand to have gone out in such light clothing. But the house-to-house reports said differently. If anyone was missing, no one was admitting it. No wife, daughter, friend or distant cousin of any resident of Parson's Lane need be considered—if they took the householder's word on it. He went to Morrissey's side.

'There's two field paths, but I can't see her having come down either one,' he said, picking the first out with a firm finger. 'This runs up from Randall's Farm across to the river. Can't see why she'd be coming from that direction, no houses or anything, and not the weather for a picnic. The other path…' Twisting his head to get a different angle. 'There. Good long one that. Gets a lot of summer traffic, ramblers and such. Runs straight across farmland, give or take a few stiles, cuts the corner off a copse just here, and comes out on the main road. Three-mile hike. Might have come that way, but if she had, she'd have needed to be going somewhere.'

'And you don't find that likely?'

'Depends if everybody we've questioned told the truth,' said Barrett. 'She wouldn't have walked from there, to here, unless she'd had somewhere to go. And I can't see her setting off on a three-mile hike anyway, in that weather, and in those clothes.'

'If she walked at all,' said Morrissey, moving to the window and lowering his buttocks onto the narrow sill. 'But we've nothing to say she did, have we?' He loosened his tie, the waft of breeze through the open window warm against his face. 'So far it's just an assumption. Nothing more.'

Barrett shifted, unwilling to commit himself. He didn't need to be reminded she could have got there by car, and he didn't like to think how wide that would mean casting a net either.

'There's always a car,' he admitted grudgingly.

'It's a possibility,' said Morrissey. 'You've worked that out for yourself.' He eyed Barrett. 'What don't you like about the idea?'

'It widens the net too much. But I can't discount it, not when it's the best reason we've got for her being in light clothing. What I'm hoping is for something concrete to come out of the post-mortem. Give us a firmer place to start from.' He put his hands in his pockets and started playing with loose change. Morrissey noted the movement. Not much better in his mind than pulling at a waistcoat. 'I mean, all right,' said Barrett. 'She could have been driven there. She could have had a tiff and got out to walk. It happens. Dark night, muddy verge, easy enough to fall. Except—why didn't whoever was with her go back to look? Report her missing when she didn't go home?'

Morrissey, arms folded, eyes watchful, said, 'Don't need help from me on that one either. Not when the answer's written all over your face.'

Barrett studiously watched a fly walking across the calendar. Too right he didn't need any help on it, not when there were only two alternatives. One, she hadn't got there by car, and two, she had.

And if she had, the way things looked, the driver had most likely killed her.

THE POST-MORTEM had almost ended when Barrett entered the white-tiled room, with its stainless steel sinks and over-bright lights, stepping in quietly, green paper gown draped over him like a nun's habit, face mask dipped precautiously in strong-smelling Dettol. Woods's eyes were fixed on the wall in front of him, across the other side of the steel table, reluctant to admit that the thing below their level of vision was human. His skin above the mask had taken on the parchment hue of nausea and was filmed with sweat, and when Barrett came in his eyes rolled rather than moved in the DS's direction.

Barrett eyed the table's burden, noting Warmsby's lack of banter, and felt the old familiar tightening in his gut. He stepped in closer and tried to close his mind to the rank smell. Warmsby lifted his head, nodded, and went back to separating a gelatinous mess, saying sourly, 'Always knew you were a masochist.'

'Not that,' said Barrett. 'Looking to get a firm fix on cause of death is all. I don't suppose...?'

'You'd be right not to,' Warmsby said. 'Nine times out of ten. Have you seen the state?' Barrett had, but like Woods was trying to avoid looking. The pathologist finished what he was doing and dropped the discoloured sample into a specimen jar. 'Kidney,' he said matter of factly. Woods swayed a little and turned tail. Warmsby folded the macerated skin and ribcage back into place. 'I think your colleague there has had enough,' he said. 'That's his third exit.'

'He'll do better next time,' Barrett answered unsympathetically. 'Been there myself.'

Warmsby's eyes examined him. 'Initiations are painful

events. Most of us survive. I suppose you plan on standing around until I hazard a guess?'

'We've nothing else to go on.'

'I'm marking it as probable asphyxiation.'

'Accidental, then?'

'Possibly, but unlikely. Mud and grass particles in the nasal passages, more in the trachea. No water to speak of in the lungs so she didn't drown in the ditch. I'd say her face had been pressed into a muddy surface and held there until she suffocated. And in case you hadn't noticed when they took her out—she was pregnant. Close to full term.'

'What?'

'Behind you,' said Warmsby. 'On the trolley.'

Barrett turned. A macerated foetus hung, suspended in fluid, filling a tall specimen jar. Bile rose and burned the back of his throat. He swallowed it down. Dragged his eyes away and fixed them on his feet.

Not one murder but two.

He battled with the idea, tried to escape from it.

'Make it hard to get out of a ditch if she fell in,' he said, still doggedly looking for alternatives to the unthinkable. 'Awkward, being that size. Unbalanced.'

'You asked an opinion,' said Warmsby. 'You've got it. What you do with it is your business.' He rinsed off his hands, discarded the gloves, and with flat emphasis and a frosty glare, added, 'I don't recall ever having said you'd like it.'

ELEVEN

HALLORAN HAD HIS ARM in a sling, high up across his chest, collarbone immobilised but still shooting pain if he forgot and moved his upper body without thinking, as he did just then, irked and irritated at being asked the same question three times. He'd already said there'd been no woman, what did the Sarge want for God's sake! Bright moonlight like that, he'd have seen anything bigger than a mouse. He said it over again, carefully, so there'd be no misunderstanding. No woman. Looking at him, Sergeant Acer decided enough was enough and let it drop. To his mind, if there'd been a woman on the road she'd have had to run like a bloody rabbit to get out of sight that fast.

Halloran said, 'If he hadn't been drinking he must have been on something else.'

'Nowt that showed up,' said Acer, levering himself off the low settee. 'Must have seen a ghost.'

A NIGHT'S SLEEP hadn't made much difference to Woods, his stomach still felt hot and uncomfortable and the rest of him unfit for anything much but looking miserable. Barrett took note and split the house-to-house reports between himself and Smythe, the DC starting at the south end of Parson's Lane, himself at the north, managing with his usual lack of tact to alienate Smythe twice in quick succession by reminding him not to cut corners.

Smythe, having heard graphic details of the decomposing foetus from Woods, hadn't intended to cut anything, never mind corners, and stared at the DS resentfully, wondering how long one simple mistake would be hung like an albatross round his neck.

More than a year already and it still clung like a bad smell.

He followed Barrett's black Escort up the Middlebrook Road and left at the roundabout still simmering. Three miles on, he swung his elderly 300 series BMW into a sharp right-hand turn, giving Barrett's unseeing back two fingers as he did it.

It'd all be a waste of time anyway, he told himself as he pulled up outside the first house. These repeat house-to-house questionings always were. Ask the same questions, you got the same answers.

That premise stayed true until he got to Hargreaves Farm, a mile from Randall's and on the other side of the lane, and nearly collided with a tractor driven by a farm labourer who seemed to have been overlooked the first time round.

'Was down in the five acre, when they come round before,' he yelled at Smythe, voice near drowned by tractor noise. 'Shifting sheep. Daft buggers. Them got no sense. Don't s'pose farmer's missus thought to mention it to 'em, like. Invisible man, that's me. I comes and goes and nobody knows.' He grinned broadly and turned off the engine. 'I seen you down the Cock and Crown with that Zoe. Not for a good long while, though.' He eyed Smythe speculatively. 'Wouldn't be you what put her in the club, would it? Must be six months gone now—size of her.'

Smythe's mind did fast sums.

When it came up with a negative his relief showed. The farm labourer's grin grew. 'Had you sweating there a bit, didn't I?'

'Not at all,' said Smythe. 'Just trying to remember the name.' The lie hung between them like a brick and the other man's grin widened.

'Bernie Parks,' he said. 'Case you want it for your book. Bit of a goer, our Zoe is.'

Smythe said, 'Forget Zoe. It's the woman we found in the drain that interests me.'

'No accounting for taste,' said Bernie cheerfully.

Smythe said sourly, 'Any idea who she was and how she got there?'

'No. Got no ideas at all. Dunno what she looked like even. Only thing I've heard is she stank like hell, and I'm right glad it weren't me what found her. Can't be nobody from the farm, though. I can tell you that much. 'Cept for farmer and his missus there's nobody up there. Last visitor they had was back last summer when missus's brother come over from Australia, and he's gone again now.' He eyed Barrett speculatively. 'What'd she look like then? That one in the drain.'

Woods's horror story drifted to mind. Smythe blocked it out and repeated the official description instead. Bernie took it in and didn't need to think.

'Red-haired and pregnant round here I wouldn't have missed. Not anybody local to these parts she wasn't, I can tell you that. She'd have been noticed, 'specially with me going up and down the lane the way I do. I'd have seen her for sure.'

'In broad daylight, maybe,' said Smythe. 'Not after dark, though. It's easy to miss somebody walking at night.'

Bernie shrugged, reached for his starter, then thought better of it and leaned back out. 'Might still have seen her, if she'd been a regular. Got a girlfriend lives down the other end of the lane. Up past Randall's. When I'm not working here, I go down her place. I'd have seen a redhead for sure if there'd been one about. An' if I hadn't seen her—she would have. Eyes like a hawk my woman has when she's in the van.' He eyed Smythe. 'And it's an F-reg Toyota in case you're wondering. Use it when we go out to a club or something.'

'How often's that?'

'Couple of times a week.'

'Did you notice anything six weeks back? A parked car on the lane after dark?'

'Wouldn't be unusual, that, there's cars parked up outside the field gates most nights. Courting couples mostly—or marrieds having a bit on the side.'

'What about somebody parked by the ditch?'

'Too risky. Put a wheel over that, and they'd have a right time getting out. That'll have to be it, squire. Time I was getting on.' He pulled back inside his cab and put ear-muffs on.

Smythe opened the car door and got a leg inside. The tractor engine started then died. Bernie shouted down. 'Was a van there about a month back now I come to think of it. Close on two in the morning it'd be. Dark coloured. Don't know who it belonged to. Ask Susan. If it had a name on she'll like as well have seen it. Same as I said, she's got eyes all over the place when it's me what's driving.'

'And she lives where?'

'Number seventy-five. Down the other end,' said Bernie, and started the engine again. Smythe got back in his car, hurriedly. Bernie bellowed, 'She won't be home, not 'til half-six. Works in Woollies,' and pulled out onto the lane, scraping past Smythe's car with half an inch leeway, and grinning as he went.

'WHAT'S HAPPENING with the Harland stabbing?' said Morrissey. 'Why no charges yet?' Smythe, just back in with Barrett, felt his jaw twitch.

'We're still making enquiries, sir. The knife hasn't turned up yet and one lad's mother swears he was home.'

'You realise we can only hold them another twenty-four hours. If they're not charged before that they walk.'

'Yes, sir.' Smythe pulling himself up stiffly and wishing he'd told Barrett he had other fish to fry. 'I'd best find out if there's anything new come in.'

'There hasn't,' said Morrissey. 'And uniform are getting a bit peeved at doing all the work. If you had to go out this morning the Harland enquiry should have been delegated to Copeland—or Woods if Copeland wasn't available. Haven't forgotten the rules, have you?'

'No, sir.'

'Well make sure you don't, I don't want a slip-up on this one. Go on then, get busy. We want charges, not eggy faces.'

Smythe turned on his heel and went out smarting.

Morrissey's basilisk eyes turned to Barrett. 'He needs closer supervision on this, we don't want another oversight. If the file's up to date they've only been interviewed three times in forty-eight hours.'

Barrett's hands moved up to the missing waistcoat and came away uncomforted. 'We could do with DI Beckett back,' he said. Then blurted resentfully, 'I can't be in two places at once. There's a rape and a dead woman besides Harland. And I thought that one was well wrapped up.'

'Well it isn't,' growled Morrissey. 'One of the three youths changed his story, and now his mother swears he was home with her.' He sighed. 'You'd better spend the rest of the day making sure it doesn't go by default. Fill me in on the other two cases first, and then get on with it. Crying for an extra pair of hands won't help.'

'I could put Copeland to help with Harland, that'd leave me free for...'

'Twenty-four hours out of your life won't make that much difference,' said Morrissey. 'Not unless you get hit by a bus. I want this tidied up by someone I can trust.'

A sop of sorts that made Barrett feel half gratified, half got-at.

'There's nothing at all happening on the rape except for forensic stuff,' he admitted. 'Kim Fitton's still up in Durham. If I want to talk to her again I'll have to go up there. Must be laughing his head off, whoever it is did it, getting in and out without being seen. One of the neighbours saw Mrs Fitton turn her car into the drive, but she says she was on her way to the kitchen and didn't see anything else.'

'Think she's telling the truth or keeping out of trouble?'

Barrett moved his head non-committally. 'Can't see any reason why she'd lie.'

'He had to have been on the street before the car got there,' said Morrissey. 'No other way he could have taken her by surprise as she opened her front door. He can't have been more than yards away from the house when she got home.'

'I've talked to the neighbour three times now,' said Barrett, 'and she's not changing her story. I'll go back again when the youths have been charged.'

'Let Copeland try his hand with her. Women seem to go for the lost look.'

'Anything's worth a try, I suppose,' said Barrett, stolidly. 'I'll send him off now then, shall I?'

'When you've briefed me on this morning's expedition. Anything new on that?'

'Nothing from my end of the lane. I haven't had a chance to get Smythe's report.' His voice took on a resentful note. 'I was about to do that when you came in, sir. I'll debrief him before I get to work on the other.'

'Let me know if he's been lucky,' said Morrissey. 'What about the woman herself? Any thoughts on identity?'

'We need to put out another press release,' Barrett said, firm on that, sure of his ground, telling Morrissey instead of asking. 'We want the media to know it's a murder investigation now, so they give it a better spotlight. Let's tell them what we know on age, height, hair colour... Pregnancy.' His eyes met Morrissey's and saw his own dark anger reflected in them. 'From what Warmsby said, she was close to term. Must be a doctor, midwife, hospital clerk somewhere that remembers her. And then there's the rings—we could put out a photograph of those and hope they jog a memory somewhere.'

'That it?'

'Unless Smythe's picked something up.' He dithered, then said, 'The rings worry me. They don't fit in with the rest of her stuff. I mean her clothes carried middle-class labels, but the rings were cheap silver. They don't fit together.'

'Oxfam shopper?' suggested Morrissey. 'A lot of people are.'

'It's possible.'

'But you don't think it's likely.'

'I've got nothing concrete to say it isn't.'

'A hunch.'

'Something like that,' Barrett said uneasily.

Except he'd never believed in hunches, not even when they proved right. Just a bit of logic that he couldn't pin down, that's all it was.

Morrissey grinned. 'Give it another twenty years, you'll be used to having them by then.'

'Yes, sir.' Not believing a word of it.

'I'll take your ideas upstairs, Neil, but keep me briefed on what's happening.'

Didn't he always? Barrett thought, disgruntled as he headed for the door, halfway to it when Morrissey said, 'And send Smythe back up, I might as well debrief him myself and save you the time.'

'Sir,' said Barrett stiffly, and closed the door behind him with an ungentle hand.

EDDIE'S 'STAFF' amounted to Sam Bates who drove for him, Tony who did his collecting, and an elderly woman who came in to do his cleaning, but he liked to make out he was better equipped, and to that end called on one of the local youth gangs if he wanted a bit of harassment done. The day after his conversation with Willie Beam, Eddie sent Sam round with two hundred pounds in tenners and instructions not to come back without the crack he wanted.

An hour later Sam returned with a thick lip and the two hundred still intact, sent off like a whipped dog because Willie had had two friends with him who outweighed Sam by a couple of hundred pounds.

Eddie was less than pleased.

Half an hour later he was back at Willie's place himself and laying down his own rules. Willie took as much notice as he had the day before. 'You want it, you come and get it for yourself,' he said, flat-faced. 'No middlemen. Don't worry me none if you go some place else, I can sell as much as I've got.'

Eddie exchanged his money for goods. 'Six days,' he said. 'Yesterday it was seven. Better do some thinking.'

'I done all the thinking I need to do,' said Willie, and showed him the door.

THE ONLY THING Barrett told Smythe was that Morrissey wanted him back upstairs. When Smythe started in asking why, Barrett snapped, 'Now! Move it!' and walked away. As he climbed up the rubber-topped stairs to the DCI's office, Smythe told himself it had to be the Harland case again.

Something else he'd forgotten to do.

Wracking his brain for what that might be, and then slicking his hair back before he knocked on the Chief Inspector's door.

To his worried ears the 'Come in' was intimidating.

Uncharacteristically Smythe's palms began to sweat. He wiped them on the back of his pants and told himself it was the hot weather, but they were greasy again by the time he turned the door handle.

Morrissey said mildly, 'If you've done something as serious as the look on your face, you'd better tell me about it and get it over with.'

'DS Barrett said you wanted to see me, sir.'

'He didn't say why?'

'No, sir.'

'But it gave you a guilty conscience.'

'Not exactly, sir.'

'Explain not exactly.'

'I thought it might be something to do with the Harland case again. Hingeing on what you'd said earlier, sir.'

Morrissey nodded. 'Except for this morning's oversight you did well with that case. Relax.' Smythe did so, visibly, and the Chief Inspector hid a smile. Nice to know he still kept them on their toes. 'What I called you in for was your report on this morning's little exercise. Detective Sergeant Barrett drew a blank—did you?'

'Not exactly, sir. I found a farm worker who hadn't been interviewed first time round. Claims there's usually a few steamy-windowed cars parked up on Parson's Lane, late at night. He drives up and down there a lot, collects his girlfriend from number seventy-five and then brings her into town for a drink, or the pictures. When he takes her home the cars are there—but on the other side of the lane, not the ditch side.'

'Doesn't help us much, not unless he saw the woman.'

'No, but he said there'd been one night when he'd brought his girlfriend home late—two or three in the morning, and there was a van on the same side as the ditch. Says he didn't notice much about it but his girlfriend might because she never misses a thing.'

'And you've done that?'

'Not yet, sir, she works in Woolworth's. I thought I could call round tonight, after she gets home.'

'In here, first thing tomorrow if there is anything.'

'Yes, sir!' Suddenly bushy tailed again, waiting for whatever else was asked, but Morrissey simply dismissed him and went back to his paperwork.

Going back downstairs to find Barrett, Smythe grinned to himself. Talk about luck. If he'd done the north end and Barrett the south it'd be the DS getting friendly looks, not him. Soon as he got his second-part sergeant's, a career jump might be likely after all.

LUCY WAS TIDYING UP the staff room as she did every evening, collecting used coffee cups and squirrelling away half-empty biscuit packs to nibble on later.

On one chair, a copy of the evening paper had been dropped untidily, and when she picked it up her eyes went straight to the three-inch, double-column write-up on the front page with its broad header: *Murder Investigation: Police Say Woman's Death Was No Accident.*

Sitting in the chair, feet up on a coffee table, she read the report avidly, one hand dropping to her belly when she saw the woman had been pregnant.

The silver rings weren't mentioned until almost the end, and when she read their description Lucy's hands went chilly-damp.

Slowly she read it through again, then dropped the paper on the floor, sitting elbows on knees, resting her head on crossed hands and trying hard not to cry.

TWELVE

HAYES TROD the shrub-lined path to the mortuary every night, shining his torch on the high windows and quivering in the small of his back at every crack of a twig. Low-powered bulbs in the internal corridor gave out a dim glow along its length. The first few times he'd gone in there, it had scared him shitless, then he'd realised the dead only walk in nightmares and horror movies, and grown braver. That night—when he'd locked the door behind himself because he didn't want anyone else wandering in and giving him a fright—he turned around and saw a woman in pink.

'Here,' he said, covering fright with bluster. 'What the hell do you think you're doing in here this time of night? And how'd you get in anyway?' The woman didn't answer, simply turned and went into the darkness of the room behind her. When Hayes got there and flipped on the lights, the place was empty of anything except refrigerated drawers.

LUCY'S MISTRUST of the police kept her dithering half the morning, but at eleven o'clock when she'd collected in the coffee cups and given out fresh water, she put on her leather jacket and let herself out of the back door. The thought that when she got to the main road there might not be a bus along for quite a while didn't worry her any. She'd just keep walking and thumb a lift, it had always worked in the past, and she didn't see why it wouldn't work now.

Then she wondered if that's what Mandy had been doing, thumbing a lift, when she ended up dead, and dropped her arm. A mile further down she raised it again, thumb up, already tired by the heat. A Volvo stopped, a few yards in front of her, and the driver looked back, then put his foot down and sped off when he saw she was pregnant. Lucy stuck her tongue out.

She crossed the south end of Parson's Lane and walked up the rise, taking off her leather jacket, and showing patches of perspiration under her armpits. Fifty yards on another car stopped and she eyed it warily, taking in the taxi sign on its roof. Some hopes he had, she didn't have money for a bloomin' taxi!

When she drew level the door opened and a lilting Asian voice said, 'Malminster?'

''S'all right,' said Lucy, without stopping. 'Can't afford a ride.' The car moved slowly, keeping pace.

'The car is empty. You want a ride or not?'

Lucy stopped that time, bending to see the driver. Old, she thought. At least fifty. Wouldn't want to grope her. Not at that age.

'For free?' she said.

'If you don't tell my boss.'

'Who's your boss?' she said, getting in the back.

'Me,' he said. 'I'm the boss. So you don't tell me I give away my money. All right?' His teeth were yellowed when he smiled, and a faint smell of betel juice dallied in the air.

'All right,' said Lucy, smiling back. ''S'nice of you. Do something for you sometime.'

He pulled away from the kerb and speeded up. 'You look after your baby. You do that for me. All right?'

'All right,' Lucy said again, thinking she'd like to see anybody stop her, and leaned back, comfy against the nylon fur that covered the back seat.

EDDIE HAD BEEN smarting over Willie and he didn't like that. When he did business he did it his way, and he was looking for the means to give Willie a fright. Then he heard a bit of passing gossip that gave him chance to stir things up, tittle-tattle from civilian staff at the police station.

It seemed that while CID had been busy with rape and death, uniform had been trying to finger a break-and-enter artist who had got away with a lot of stuff. What irked uniform the most was that none of the stuff had turned up on sale locally.

Sixteen video recorders, as many televisions and a range of other electrical goods had been spirited out of houses and disappeared. Logic said they'd been sold out of the area, but there was still a nursed hope that they were stashed away somewhere waiting to be found when the right information came in.

Eddie got the gossip from a part-time yob who hung out at the Cat and Garter, and it gave him what he thought was a great idea.

With Eddie's instructions written on a piece of paper so he couldn't get it wrong, the yob got sent to a phone box with a tip-off for the police that would cause Willie some anxiety. He did what he was told then went back to Eddie wreathed in smiles because he knew they'd bought what he fed them hook, line and sinker. When he handed back the bit of paper he got a tenner for his trouble.

The tenner went straight down to the bookmaker's and got wagered on the three-thirty at Redcar. It lost.

To Eddie's mind he'd done a good morning's work. Willie Beam in for a bit of worry, the police looking stupid, and a pirate radio that'd given Eddie's girls some bad publicity about to go off the air.

And all for a tenner.

LUCY'S MISTRUST of the police was profound, and she'd dallied outside the police station, getting as far as the steps and walking away again, for a good twenty minutes after the taxi dropped her off. When she finally went in through the doors it was close to one o'clock, and there was a thought in the back of her mind that Mrs C would be wondering where she was. Let her. Wasn't as if she was a prisoner or anything. Up to Lucy if she wanted to go somewhere—or walk out altogether come to that.

She went up to the counter hesitantly, with the hairs on her neck prickling, and ready to turn tail at the least excuse.

Luckily for both of them Rosie Quinn was doing desk duty. Taking in Lucy's bulge and nervousness, Rosie added a smile to her voice.

The friendliness wasn't something Lucy had expected. Without stopping to think she blurted, 'I know who it is. If I tell you, can I go then?'

Rosie eyed her. 'Know who who is?'

Hands knuckled as far into her jacket pockets as she could get, Lucy said, 'Her from Parson's Lane, the one that's dead. If I tell you who it is, can I go?'

Rosie said, 'I'll have to write it down. How about we go somewhere private and have a cuppa? Would that be all right? I could do with a cup of tea.' Trying to keep her voice level and friendly as she watched Lucy's flight response first strengthen, then die.

'S'pose so. If it's just a cuppa.'

'Just a cuppa,' lied Rosie. 'Hang on there while I come round.' Lucy stood where she was, but up on the balls of her feet, ready to run if she had to, eyeing Rosie warily when she stuck her head out the inner door. 'Come on then, let's find somewhere quiet.'

Lucy said stubbornly. 'Why can't we stay here?'

'Because I'd get the sack if we did,' said Rosie. 'Got to do it by procedure or not at all.'

Procedure? Lucy knew all about procedure. Used to come up on *The Bill* every week before she left home. Funny how she'd liked watching it. She frowned. Now if it was that June Ackroyd offering her a cuppa, she could trust her.

She tilted her head a little and examined Rosie's face. Got a bit of a look of June except she was younger. Making that the deciding factor she shrugged resignedly and let herself be led away.

EXCEPT FOR HEAT that made him prickly hot, Morrissey was feeling happier again. The third youth's alibi had disappeared when Barrett pointed out to the boy's mother that conspiring to pervert the course of justice also carried a jail sentence. Her face had swung from disbelief to fear. Finding out there were witnesses who'd already sworn her son was with the other two when Harland was stabbed, had helped make up her mind.

By this time tomorrow they'd have been up before the magistrates and sent on remand. Three more yobs off the streets.

He ran a finger inside his collar, loosened the top button and let his tie hang slack. The thermometer had moved up into the eighties. Ridiculous in so short a time. He thrust head and shoulders out of the open window looking for a current of breeze and found none, only a dry oppressive heat that bounced and shimmered off the oven-on-wheels he had to drive home in—unless something dragged him out of the office before then, in which case he'd cook even sooner.

Freak heatwaves were a pain.

About to pull back in and turn on the fan when a half-dozen police in shirt sleeves came out the side door. Four piled into a police van, the other two into a patrol car. He watched them make a right turn out of the yard, towards the Middlebrook Road, then withdrew his head and went downstairs in search of enlightenment. Part of the protocol between uniform and CID was a requirement that they communicate with each other when something was going down, the idea being that if each knew what the other was up to, there'd be less chance of spoiled operations. The sight of six uniformed police taking off in the early afternoon worried him. Not the time of day for pub fights—even if anybody had the energy left to start one.

On the second landing he met Phil Whalley coming up, the inspector's top button neatly fastened but his shirt ringed with sweat. 'Let me guess,' said Whalley. 'Same errand I'll bet. You coming down to find out what's happening, and me coming up to tell you. Saw 'em take off I suppose?'

'Bad timing,' said Morrissey. 'Five minutes either way, I'd have missed it.'

'No big secret, it's the break-ins we've been having, and you know about them. We've had a tip-off where the stuff is. Can't afford not to take a look.'

Morrissey watched Whalley's busy handkerchief mop, eyeing the amount of extra weight he'd started carrying around, hands straying to his own waistband in a spurious shirt-tucking movement. Forty-five wasn't a good age to turn apple-shaped, so what was behind the rapid girth change?

Simple overeating or something more profound?

Whalley's business. Not his. Not unless broached. What was his business though, was the amount of doubt expressed in the Inspector's 'Can't afford not to take a look.' He said mildly, 'How about the address? Is that a good indicator? Someone we know about?'

'It's an indicator all right,' allowed Whalley, glum as well as hot. 'And I'd rather it had been your lot sticking their neck out. It's one of the terraces behind the industrial estate.'

Which put it right in the middle of Malminster's Asian community, thought Morrissey, remembering how fast tempers could fray on a hot day and hoping everybody stayed calm. The probability of Pakistani involvement in the break-ins was less likely than that the call had been a hoax. A wind-up. Some right-wing yob out to make trouble, even. If it had been Morrissey's shout he'd have gone in quietly to take a look, one male and one female officer in plain clothes and an unmarked car. Same again watching the rear, just in case. Not uniforms, however well behaved. Nothing that could be construed as an insult.

'Let's hope it goes right,' he said gruffly.

'Aah... Thought you'd see the problem. Can't afford not to send anybody though, and I told 'em to keep it soft and quiet, no fuss. Didn't want to include one of yours in it, did you?'

'Uniform put in the legwork, uniform get the credit,' said Morrissey, blandly tongue in cheek, and hoped self-control held with both sides so it worked out that way.

THIRTEEN

PETERS, the mortuary attendant, was accustomed to the cold, but the past few days he seemed to have felt it more intensely, especially in the storage room. He told his wife about it, when he got home. She put his sausage and chips on the table, got the HP sauce out of the cupboard, and sat watching him eat. When he started mopping his plate with a piece of bread she said matter-of-factly, 'Probably one of them's not ready to go yet.'

'One what?' he asked uneasily, knowing very well what she was going on about.

'Spirit. What did you think I meant?' she said, pouring his tea. 'When did it start?'

'Dunno. Monday, or round about.' He remembered then, what it was they'd put in the drawer when the post-mortem was done, and drank his tea off in a hurry, near scalding his lips. 'I'm going back to work,' he said, scraping the chair back, and put his jacket on before he had to remember anything else.

WHEN WILLIE HEARD the two engines stop, and doors bang, he took a look out of his window, saw the patrol car, the van parked behind it, and shirt-sleeved police climbing out of both, and thought he'd been rumbled. 'Shi-it!' he howled, and grabbed his money stash ready to dive out the back door. Then he saw the law wasn't coming his way and relaxed a bit.

In the terrace across the road Mustaph Ali, known as Muz, heard all the noise too, and took a look out the attic window. Behind him in his hand-built studio a rap record spun gently on its deck. It had taken him five years to save money enough to buy the radio equipment in the attic, and it was his joy and fulfilment with which he spent every spare minute. Muz had taken it on himself to provide Malminster with its first pirate radio and he was proud of it.

When he saw the police rushing to his own front door, and heard the pounding fists, his immediate thought was they were going to break it down. Panicking, he locked himself in the attic, stopped the music and, perched on the edge of his chair, shouted in loud excitement, 'Police raid, police raid! Any moment it is they are breaking into the studio. If you hear me now, come to help. This is important. Come to help or you will lose your radio.'

Since he didn't think to specify the kind of help he needed, some of those near enough to give immediate response turned out of the rows of terraces and new houses built on the wasteland, and made a small crowd outside Muz's home, waiting around to see what all the excitement was about.

Downstairs, Muz's sister had opened the front door and had the police push past her, coming in with heavy feet and urgent voices, waving a search warrant and talking about stolen goods.

Upstairs with his headphones on, Muz heard the general noise but missed Sergeant Grice's announcement about the warrant, so when feet pounded up toward the attic he jumped to the conclusion they were coming to break up his beloved equipment. Breaking out in a hot sweat he repeated his first distress call. Outside on the landing PC Dickson heard Muz's voice and tried the door knob. When the door wouldn't budge he shouted for Muz to open it. Muz refused. PC Dickson stepped back, positioned his foot, and kicked it in. The sound of splintering wood went out over the still-open transmitter.

Muz got up off the castored chair and sent it spinning.

It interrupted Dickson's forward rush with neat precision and toppled him into just the right position to knock himself out on a table. A trickle of blood ran down into the corner of his left eye. Muz didn't hang around. Halfway downstairs he met PC Sutton coming up to see what all the noise was about. The scuffle between them was brief. Muz fell awkwardly down the last six steps to the first-floor landing and broke his arm. Pain made him scream. That went out over the radio too, as did Sutton's loud curse.

Smythe, driving back through Malminster after another abortive visit to Maple Drive, heard the whole of it over the car radio and wondered what the hell was going on.

ROSIE SAID, 'It was the only way she'd do it, sir, on our own with a cup of tea. If it'd got any more official than that, she'd have walked.'

Morrissey said, 'You used your initiative and got the information we needed. We know where to find her if we want to talk to her again. You did well.' Rosie flushed.

'Thank you, sir.'

Barrett said, 'It's a pity the girl didn't know where the woman had been living before she went on the streets.' Then he caught Rosie's look and amended rapidly. 'Before she became homeless.'

'Lucy said she had a Yorkshire accent, which narrows it down a bit,' Rosie said. 'In fact...' She stopped, her look uncertain.

'Go on.'

'Well—I'm not sure, but I think she might know and just doesn't want to tell us.'

'Have to talk to her again then,' said Barrett. 'That's why it's best to have someone sit in. There's less gets missed.'

'I didn't miss it,' said Rosie. 'But I did decide not to push and miss something else. You don't know how nervous she was. And pregnant.'

'Couldn't be the same man that put Mandy in the club, could it?' said Barrett. 'Not both of them.' Looking at Morrissey, then retracting the idea almost before the last word had crossed the space between them. 'No, of course not. Daft idea.'

'Worth asking,' said Morrissey. 'Though I doubt you're likely to get a straight answer, even if it is.'

'Funny though,' Barrett said half to himself. 'Both her and the other one pregnant. Why kill a pregnant woman. Blackmail?'

'Left it a bit late to try that if you're talking an extortion attempt on the father,' said Morrissey dryly. 'Sort of thing to try at the beginning, not the end.'

Rosie shifted her feet and got herself noticed again.

'I'd thought it might have been her husband who did it, or a live-in lover,' she said, 'but it can't have been, can it, not if she's been living on the streets. I mean, how would he have known where to find her?'

There, she'd said it, let it be known she'd at least given it some thought. It might not be the most brilliant idea ever expressed in Morrissey's office, but at least it showed she kept her mind on the job. With two pairs of eyes on her she willed herself not to go pink, and waited for the amusement.

MUZ'S PAIN was acute and he milked it for all he was worth, until Sergeant Grice got him back on his feet and down the next flight of stairs into the living room, where Muz's sister rounded on her shaking brother and told him impatiently she'd known all along it was a mistake to let him put his stuff in the attic.

Belatedly, Sutton remembered why he'd been going upstairs in the first place and went back to look for Dickson, who was still face-down on the floor.

With the desk chair over on its side, and a blood-marked

table edge, it didn't take Sutton long to guess what had happened—or to recognise that they'd been sent in on a wild goose chase when he saw the radio equipment.

When the ambulance came, Dickson went out on a stretcher with half the neighbourhood watching. Muz followed, walking, arm neatly strapped, free hand raised in a fist because he remembered having seen it done on TV and thought it looked good.

Just before they shut the ambulance doors he shouted to his sister to turn the mike off. Sutton and Grice exchanged looks. Grice followed the sister into the house and up to the attic. When the red light over the consul went out, he said, 'That mean everything it picked up got broadcast?' She gave him a one-sided smile and nodded. Great! Grice thought. Do him a lot of good that would. Cock-up of his life and everybody listening. He told her they'd repair the broken door.

She shrugged. 'What about this lot, then? Taking it with you?'

'Won't fit in the van, will it?' he said with heavy sarcasm and walked out. When he got back to the street the number of onlookers had increased and there was some edgy muttering going on. Nothing left, he thought, except damage limitation. 'Right,' he said, to the uneasy police faces. 'Back on board. We've done what we came for.' When he moved forward a gap failed to appear. 'Clear a way,' he said brusquely. 'Come on now. Nobody wants trouble, so let's not play silly beggars.' He used his shoulder and pushed forward. Somebody else pushed back. Grice and the others shoved back harder and pushed a way through. A youth pounded on the side of the van. Two more joined in. A squad car arrived. As the van moved away a stone smashed into the offside rear light. The stone thrower got manhandled into the squad car and the small crowd became more vocal. Insults were shouted. A youth who ran at the side of the car got handed off and fell, taking a woman down with him. More stones were thrown.

By the time Grice got his men back to the station, word had gone up the chain of command that there'd been a major foul-up. Chief Superintendent Osgodby let it be known to all that the inevitable police inquiry would be far more efficient than that afternoon's operation had been.

LUCY COULD EASILY have walked away from the police station and gone back to her old haunts. Instead, she'd let Rosie organise a lift back to the nursing home in a police car, insisting it dropped her off out of sight. She left the leather jacket in her room and went to forage for food in the kitchen, making herself a chicken and lettuce sandwich under the watchful eye of the cook. While she was eating it Diana Carpenter came in and demanded to know where she'd been.

'For a walk,' said Lucy, her mouth inelegantly full. 'Not a law against it is there?'

'Next time tell me before you go,' said Carpenter, and walked out.

At six-thirty, when Lucy was in her room watching *Calendar News,* Carpenter came in. 'Shh,' said Lucy when she started to talk. 'I want to see this bit.' Carpenter pressed her lips together and folded her arms, thinking it was time Lucy learned a few things. She turned her eyes to look at the screen. The newscaster was female and tawny-skinned, strongly good-looking rather than pretty, and Lucy watched her avidly.

If she ever got a chance, wouldn't of course, not her, but if she did, that's what she'd like, sitting there, nice clothes, nice hair, all Yorkshire watching her and hanging on every word. Her lips moved in mock imitation until the words penetrated and she stopped with her mouth half open.

'...Found in a storm drain has been identified as that of

Mandy Sheard. No further personal details are known, but a police spokesman said Ms Sheard was believed to have been homeless and living rough in the Malminster area for the past six months. An artist's impression is coming up on your screen now.'

Lucy's eyes took in the computer-enhanced photofit she had helped to compose. Out there, staring back at her on the small screen, the face looked somehow more like Mandy than had the black and white graphic she'd been shown at the police station.

The likeness disturbed her.

Without looking at Carpenter she said softly, 'I knew her, you know. We was mates for a bit. That's where I went this dinner time. Police station. I helped them draw that, make the picture.'

Carpenter eyed her reflectively. 'The police contacted you? When did they do that?'

'Didn't, far as I know,' Lucy said. 'It was me went down there and said I knew her. Then they had me help 'em do that.' She lay back full length on the bed, looking up at the slope of ceiling and thinking about the dead baby. 'Pity Mandy didn't get to come to a place like this,' she said sadly. 'Still be alive if she had wouldn't she?'

FOURTEEN

PETERS WAS ODD-JOBBING in the post-mortem room, wishing the hospital pathologist would go back to his own department and finish off his paperwork there. Always happened if he wanted to get home early, anybody'd think he'd telegraphed it. Ears wide he listened for the office door opening, and when it came geared himself for the expected 'Night, Les'. Instead of which, Gibson disappeared into the cold-room.

A chill drifted out and swirled round Les. He moved away from the sink and busied himself elsewhere.

A couple of minutes later Gibson came, rubbing his hands and asking if anything was wrong with the temperature control. Les said no, and made a show of checking settings, knowing all the time he did it they were right, because he'd already done it a dozen times.

'Same as it always is,' he said.

'Must be time I went home then,' said Gibson, and clapped Les on the shoulder as he said goodnight. Les watched the doors swing shut and balanced like a sprinter, ready to follow him out the minute he heard the outside door close too.

BY SEVEN THAT NIGHT, with the stone-throwing youth still in custody, there were around sixty youths gathered outside the police station, some hiding their faces behind check scarves, all of them noisy and restless. Three times they'd been told to disperse, three times they'd shouted demands for the stone-throwing Arshad Majid to be released. Passing cars slowed and gawping onlookers collected on the other side of the road. Some of the youths were young, laughing nervously with excitement.

Half a dozen police in day-to-day uniform stood nervously outside the police station's front door, shifting from foot to foot as they waited for the youths to make a move. It looked like a weird ballet. The youths edging forward, then back again as courage failed.

A TV crew arrived; cameraman, reporter and a couple of technicians spilling out of a van. The crowd began to role-play more vociferously, every man a hero.

Osgodby came down from his office in the full glory of his uniform and tried to ride the crest of voices, but his own was drowned out by the mob. Shoulders stiff, he went back inside.

Ishmal Habib came, driving his car carefully and getting out with a worried face, this kind of confrontation something the Asian community leader had never expected to happen. When he faced the crowd and called for the young men to go home the answer that came back was a rolling cry for violence. None of the youths moved away. Grim faced, he went up the stone steps and into the building. Behind him the crowd edged forward, filling the pavement and jostling at the bottom step. Osgodby gave the order to break out riot gear and took Habib upstairs to his office.

Having only recently been elected to the town council, the community leader felt a weight of responsibility for his new position. It was like straddling two horses and waiting for the painful moment when one would veer away.

Sitting in Osgodby's office when the pleasantries were over, sparse grey hair, well-fed appearance and rimless glasses marking him as a thriving businessman, he looked glumly at his tea cup and stirred sugar into the liquid, wondering where it would all end.

'It's the young men,' he told Osgodby. 'They no longer listen to what we tell them. They go to white schools where they hear your own children talk about violence, but never about right and wrong, and they think this is how they should behave. Now you see the result of it all outside on the street. You have already told me you were misinformed, that the mistake was yours. What is the cost of a rear light? I myself will pay for the damage to your van. Why can you not forget Arshad's hot-headedness and release him, so we can all go home peacefully? Our community is the most law-abiding in Malminster, you yourself know that.'

'I can't do it because if I did it would look like police weakness,' said Osgodby, who in his secret heart would have liked nothing better. 'It's a matter of law and order. We have to take a stand.'

'Taking a stand is not always good,' Habib said sadly. 'The young ones feel alienated. And angry. They speak the English language, and with local accents like the white boys—but they don't get the same jobs and they are angry about that too. Don't you understand?'

'I understand all right,' said Osgodby. 'But it isn't my job to sort out society's problems. I've enough on my plate trying to keep the peace.'

Habib drank his tea politely and got up to go, hoping Osgodby hadn't made a mistake in his decision, but fearing the worst, and when he stepped out onto the street the fear was confirmed.

For a few seconds the noise died, and into the silence Habib injected the news that Arshad would not be released that night. A buzz began. Habib told the crowd to go home and got angry insults in reply.

Walking back to his car he was shoved and jostled and the TV crew caught it all.

By ten o'clock Asian youths had driven in from other towns, wanting to join in the action. A bus load had come down the M62 from Manchester, and more from Dewsbury and Bradford. All of them assembled in the roads behind the industrial estate where people in the terrace houses watched disbelievingly. The older men went out and told them to go home, but it was a waste of time.

In a noisy, sweeping mass the mob wound its way down the Middlebrook Road leaving a trail of damage as it went. Car windscreens were smashed and bricks thrown through shop windows. At Murphy's Electrics some opportunists turned their attention from rioting to looting and went off with a good haul while the rest of the mass of young men crowded the road. Traffic heading into Malminster from the motorway roundabout made haste to turn around and go back. Halfway down the hill, just before Fischer Comp., a wall of police in riot gear blocked further progress. Youths broke away into the side streets and began to overturn parked cars. Two were set alight.

Stolidly the police began to push back up the road, long shields making a moving wall. Bricks, stones, side-mirrors ripped from cars, anything handy that could be thrown, was thrown. On the fringes someone lit a petrol bomb and lobbed it over police heads. It hit a helmet and exploded. The man wearing it staggered out of the flames and collapsed. The police mood changed from one of containment to dour anger. They dropped back, then charged, batons swinging indiscriminately. Rioters fell and police tripped over them. More petrol bombs were thrown. One went through the plate-glass window of a car showroom and exploded among the cars. Fire engines and ambulances trying to get through came under a shower of missiles.

At three a.m., as if on a signal, the mob began to melt, cars headed back down the motorways and shadows drifted into back streets.

By four a.m., the only evidence of the mob's existence lay in the enthusiastic reportage of television and radio news teams, and the trail of destruction and overflowing police cells left behind in its passing.

BEING CONFINED with Darren in the back of the Transit had given Skeeter a close-up he would rather have done without. Resentment and rebellion were growing side by side, impaired only by a slowness of thought connection. Last night Darren had drunk a full half of whisky on top of four cans of lager, and got restless. When Skeeter undressed and turned his back to crawl into his sleeping bag, Darren had grabbed him by the balls and asked if he fancied a prick up his arse. Skeeter had hardened, shrunk, and then been immobilised as Darren tightened his grip.

A second hand came, up on his left hip, and Darren with it, kneeling on the sleeping bag behind him, voice thick.

Skeeter had heard that sort of thickness before, up on the hill when Darren took the girl from the dodgems, the one that went home crying. Quick and rough, he'd been, ramming in like a hammer, wolf-face turned up at the moon. Skeeter had seen it, watching in the pale dim-dark, and in the back of the Transit memory had run electric. The hand shifted from his hip.

A zipper slicked.

Skeeter's heightened senses scented Darren's crotch, panic overcame pain, and he'd kicked back, wild and hard. Darren had fallen backwards, trying to take Skeeter's balls with him. Then Darren's weight had rattled against the Transit doors and he'd let go.

When the pain had let him move, Skeeter had got back into his jeans. Only then did he go to look at Darren, who hadn't moved since his head hit metal.

If he'd been dead Skeeter wouldn't have cared.

But he hadn't been, he'd been snoring gusts of whisky-heavy breath, and Skeeter had yanked up the open zipper with one quick pull—careless with it—then he'd shifted Darren to the other side of the van and spent the rest of the night uncomfortable in a swing-boat.

THE SKY had cracked with dawn when Morrissey drove home through streets already busy with traders boarding broken windows, and council workmen earning overtime. A smell of burning hung in the air, and a lone fire tender still stood outside the burnt-out Rover showroom. Morrissey fixed his mind on the thought of three hours sleep and blanked out the mess, negotiating a roundabout empty of traffic and letting the car coast idly down Forest Drive to his home.

Save for a lone thrush in the lilac the house was silent. He left jacket and shoes in the hall, heading zombie-eyed for the settee, where he spread the travel rug from his car. Naked except for boxer shorts, he slept instantly and deeply until Margaret woke him at eight with a cup of tea, and the smell of breakfast drifting in from the kitchen.

'I suppose you *have* to go in this morning?' she said, half angry, half affectionate. 'I heard you come in.'

He came up on one elbow, swung his legs down, began to apologise until she stopped him. 'The thrush woke me,' she said. 'That and the empty bed. The bathroom's unoccupied, I've made sure of that, and don't even think about walking out of the house without eating.'

He came upright and kissed her, nostrils filling with her familiar scent. 'Don't know how you put up with me,' he said gruffly. 'Just toast. I'll eat it on the run.'

'You'll sit down at the table,' she said firmly. 'They can do without you until you've eaten.' The telephone rang. 'Until you've eaten,' she repeated, and went to answer it. Morrissey followed her into the hall, and watched her lift the receiver. She waved an imperious hand at him and said loudly, 'No, you can't, not right now, he's in the bath.' Morrissey took a step towards her and she scowled death at him. 'Yes, I'll tell him that, he'll be glad to know it wasn't urgent,' she said sweetly. 'It might even give him time to swallow down some food.' She listened again and her lips twitched. 'That's all right, Neil, I'll send you a butty—I expect you're hungry too.' She put the receiver down and looked at her husband.

'Yes,' he said hurriedly, and took the stairs two at a time. Meeting Mike on the half-landing, he exchanged a comradely grin, both of them glad of the reminder that on one level at least they could still communicate.

BARRETT WAS EARLY, at his desk by eight and sifting through reports, something niggling at the back of his mind that he couldn't bring into focus. Then he read through Lucy's statement and the words *St Ursula's* opened a window he hadn't seen before. Kicking himself—because where else should he have started the enquiry but at the women's refuge—he went downstairs to the computer room and waited to be told how many other women had been deposited at St Ursula's, courtesy of Malminster police.

WHEN MORRISSEY got to his desk Barrett was on the point of leaving. 'Not so fast,' said the Chief Inspector, and dropped the bacon butty Margaret had made on Barrett's desk. The DS eyed it suspiciously, but opened the greaseproof bag anyway and caught the scent of its contents—cold now but still causing a spurt of gastric juice.

'I was on my way out,' he said, looking at Morrissey. 'Don't ask why I didn't think of it before, but we missed the women's shelter.' Morrissey shed his jacket and waited for more. 'The girl Rosie interviewed yesterday,' said Barrett doggedly. 'According to her, she was picked up by one of the patrol cars and taken there. I got to thinking if it had happened once it could have happened before.'

'And you found Mandy Sheard?'

'I found a woman calling herself Mary had been taken there in March. Might not be connected but the pregnancy would fit, so it's worth looking at. Logical when you think about it—could be them that kitted her out.'

'You don't think they'd have noticed if she'd gone missing?'

'She might not have been there long enough for that. Could be she stayed around to get fed and some clothes on her back, then went walkabout again. Won't know until I ask.' He looked longingly at the butty. 'Better get off.'

'Ten minutes won't kill,' said Morrissey. 'Take your canteen break before you go.' Grinning to himself when Barrett didn't need telling twice.

FIFTEEN

WOMEN SINGLY he could deal with, more than one and he felt outnumbered, and Peters had got talked into something he was regretting. For one thing, if Gibson caught him doing it, it'd take a bit of explaining. He thought about ringing home and telling his wife it was off, but then he didn't have the courage for that either—not after the stick she'd given him last night for being ungrateful.

Mumbo-jumbo. That's all it'd be. A lot of mumbo-jumbo. And all for nothing.

DONNELLY GOT the phone call just before eight, Carpenter's voice cold, like a shot of ice-water in his ear. 'Lucy Walton went to the police yesterday, seems she knew Mandy Sheard. You remember Mandy?'

'I remember her. Why does it matter? She walked out didn't she?'

'Her ingratitude seems to have got her killed. Lucy identified her as the woman found in a ditch and told the police that. I imagine they'll be coming to talk to you. You won't mention The Cedars when they do though—not if you want to keep the arrangement going.'

'Why would it matter?'

'Bad publicity. The woman, Mandy, walked out on us—you know that. It isn't our responsibility that she accepted a lift from a stranger.'

'Is that what happened?'

'What other explanation is there?' Carpenter snapped. 'She left—that's all I know.' The slam of receiver at her end stung his ear. He put his own instrument down thoughtfully, and wondered how much such silence would be worth.

SMYTHE HAD KNOCKED on the door of Morrissey's office twice already, and the DCI hadn't been there—only Barrett, the first time, looking at him suspiciously when he said he had to see Morrissey, and wanting to know what about. 'He said he wanted to see me first thing,' Smythe countered. 'So I'm here.'

'Well, he's not,' said Barrett. 'He was up half the night with all the rioting, so he's probably still asleep.'

Smythe doubted that but didn't stop to argue, what he had to say was for Morrissey's ears, and more points for his merit badge. Now he knocked again and this time the DCI was in there and looking expectant.

'Come back with something positive?'

'She remembered seeing the van,' Smythe said, sounding pleased. 'According to her it was an Escort, dark coloured, but she couldn't tell if it was dark blue or black, and this boyfriend of hers, Bernie Parks, was in a hurry to get home. Said if he hadn't been she'd have told him to stop and back up.'

'Why would she have done that?'

'Said the driver was half bent over, leaning down into the ditch and she'd have liked to know what he was up to, but Bernie wouldn't stop, told her not to be so nosy and carried on back to her place. Upset her a bit to think it might have been Mandy Sheard. I think it'll probably upset Bernie too, when she gets hold of him. From the way she talked he's in for an earache.'

'Goes with the territory,' said Morrissey in a rare fit of masculine solidarity. 'Did this van have a name on it?'

'It had, but she couldn't read it, so that's not much help, but what she did have was a diary she writes in every day.' He pulled out his notebook. 'April twenty-eighth. They'd been to Casanova's, left about one o'clock, ate a curry in the van Bernie drives, and then went home. She thinks it'd be about half-past two in the morning when they passed the van. It's not much, but at least we can start looking for dark-coloured Escort vans, and we've got a probable time and date.'

'It's good information,' said Morrissey. 'Write up the report and bring it to me. Quick as you like.'

'Sir,' said Smythe, who loathed keyboards with passionate animosity, and didn't know why a civilian couldn't do it instead.

MALMINSTER had a different air about it. The shoppers were out as usual, going about their business, but on side streets and grassy areas police waited, on foot, on horseback and in vans for any repetition of the previous night's violence. Townspeople eyed them with looks akin to disbelief. Such things might happen in other places but not in Malminster.

Outside the police station a sullen group of youths still hung around, twenty or thirty of them, occasionally shouting for Arshad Majid's release. The police kept watch through the windows, but declined to offer the provocation of putting men outside, and the youths stayed on the pavements and away from the steps.

When Barrett drove out of the yard on his way to see Donnelly, a few jeers went up and he ignored them, turning right and then up through back streets to St Ursula's. When he got there Donnelly kept him waiting for close on five minutes, leaving him to cool his heels chairless in the corridor before opening his office door with a flourish and the minimum of apology.

'Detective Sergeant. What can I do for you? We usually only see the police when you have another stray for us, but since you're CID this must be a different errand. How may I help?'

Barrett noted the blandness, and forced neutrality over instant dislike.

'I'm looking for information about a woman who may have stayed with you—not less than five weeks ago, and not more than twelve. I take it you have records of women passing through?'

'We do indeed, without records we would have no funding. What was the woman's name?'

'Mandy Sheard.'

Donnelly let his eyes form O's of surprise. 'Detective Sergeant—isn't she the woman—the unfortunate soul—who was found dead recently?'

As if he didn't know, thought Barrett.

'I'm glad I don't have to explain it,' said the DS. 'We need to trace her movements in the weeks before her death, so if you wouldn't mind looking through your register, or whatever documentation you keep...?'

'But of course,' said Donnelly, spreading pudgy hands. 'Anything I can do that might help. Come in and sit while I get out the files. I have to tell you, though, the name isn't one I remember, and I usually have a good memory for such things.' He moved away around his desk, swaying on ten-to-two feet like he was clenching a tenpenny piece between his buttocks. Barrett watched, bemused by the gait.

'She may not have given that name. I need to see files for everybody in that same period.'

Donnelly stopped, and turned.

'Everybody? There's such a thing as confidentiality you know.'

'Not in a murder investigation there isn't,' said Barrett.

'You're sure it is that? There can't be any mistake?'

Barrett didn't answer, simply tightened his lips and stared back stolidly. Donnelly's eyes hooded. 'The women come to the refuge from fear. They expect me to keep their lives safe from other eyes.'

'I can get a warrant and take every file you've got if I have to,' said Barrett. 'But I don't think there'll be a need to do that, will there? Can I use your desk, or is there another office?'

This time it was Donnelly's rosebud of a mouth that thinned, compressing itself enough to annihilate his lips as he reached out a manilla folder, set it on the desk blotter, and turned back deliberately to lock the cabinet. 'I'll have someone bring coffee. How long do you imagine it will take?'

Barrett flicked through the folder.

'About an hour—shouldn't be any longer. Don't want to hold you up more than necessary.

He sat himself in Donnelly's chair and with the folder open began to turn the record sheets, eyes down, as if the other man wasn't there. Grinning to himself when the priest left and the door closed with a decidedly irate snap.

IT WAS ALMOST TEN when Darren came out from the Transit, eyes bloodshot and leary, blinking in the sun and looking for Skeeter, then recognising the need to pee and to wash himself before he did anything else.

Skeeter, wary and resentful as he greased axles on the Moonride, watched him go. Half an hour later Darren came back and squatted down, watching Skeeter's busy hands.

'Laid a right one on last night,' he said. 'Dunno where I went, or how the hell I got back, but I got a bleeding headache—an' a lump. Some bleeder must've hit me. You wasn't there was you? Wasn't you brought me back?'

'Didn't go out,' Skeeter said. 'Dunno where you went.' Carrying on greasing because he didn't know if Darren was lying or not. Wouldn't be the first time. 'Maybe you tried it on with some woman and came off worst,' he offered helpfully.

'Never,' said Darren, and then stopped, memory of having got out of the van for a pee and near-screeching when he opened his zipper coming to his mind. Could have been a woman, wasn't him got himself in that state. Bloody cow! 'Which way you working?' he said. 'Up or down?'

'Up,' said Skeeter shortly.

'Give us the grease-gun then, an' fetch yourself another. Nothing wrong with your head.'

Had to be, thought Skeeter as he handed the gun over. Wouldn't be where he was now if he was right in the head, would he? Thinking about how it was two days to payday and maybe this time, when he got his, he'd go back where he belonged.

A COUPLE OF TIMES Lucy had caught Di Carpenter looking at her measuringly, and felt uncomfortable about it. What was she supposed to do? Not say anything about Mandy being Mandy? Wasn't as if her taking some time off was criminal. Didn't even have to stay here at all if she didn't want—testing the idea of going back on the street now good weather was here and feeling an unexpected reluctance.

When she pushed the coffee trolley into the waiting room to see if anybody in there wanted a cup, she found just one woman, fortyish, with lines of discontent and eyes without warmth, expensively elegant in a powder blue two-piece, its top dragging softly over her pregnancy. As always Lucy eyed the lump with interest, working out how far on the other woman was in comparison to herself. This one looked as if they'd be neck and neck.

'Want a coffee?' she said. 'It's not instant or anything.'

'Coffee would be nice. Plain black,' the woman eyed Lucy reflectively. 'When's the baby due?'

'Next month—when's yours?'

'Next month.'

'Funny if we both had them together,' said Lucy.

'Yes,' said the woman. 'Wouldn't it?' and went back to the magazine, giving no more than a nod when Lucy put black coffee on the low table.

Lucy shrugged philosophically, and left her to it. Wasn't that unusual to meet toffee-nosed women in this place.

SIXTEEN

THEY'D DONE two P-Ms that morning on hospital patients, and the chill feel had wrapped itself around the room again. Twice Gibson had checked the thermostat and shaken his head, squinting at Peters as if it were somehow his fault, and now the place was cleaned up again and Gibson gone out of the office and back to Pathology.

And Peters's mother-in-law was walking around.

He followed her miserably, hoping she wouldn't sit herself down and go into one of those trances of hers. Be just what he needed—her talking in that funny voice, and her eyes closed, when Gibson walked in.

'Oooh yes,' she said. 'You got somebody in here all right, and she's wanting something.' She tipped her head a little on one side like an anxious bird. 'You what, love? Didn't quite hear you that time, tell me again?'

'I said…' began Peters.

'Not you,' said his mother-in-law. 'Shush! Can't you tell I'm talking to somebody? Go on, love, never mind him, never did have any manners. Come a bit closer and let's have a look at you.'

Peters moved away. Invisible was bad enough. Seeing, he didn't want. He got out a pile of packeted gowns and put them on the trolley by the door, his back to what was going on.

'I can see her,' his mother-in-law said. 'If you're interested. Pink tracksuit, nice one, red hair and a bonnie face, and she's holding her stomach like it hurts.' Her voice changed a little. 'Is that what took you, love? Something matter with your insides?' Peter's hand stayed itself in mid-air. He knew what had come in in a pink tracksuit and red hair, and he hadn't told his mother-in-law about it either. 'Whatever it is she wants, it's in this cupboard,' she said firmly. 'And it's locked.'

'There's just specimens, that's all.'

'Well, she thinks one of 'em's hers. You going to open it?' She tilted her head again. 'All right, love, all right, don't get impatient.'

Peters came, his keys in shaky fingers. Only one thing she could want in that cupboard and he knew what that was, too. When he pulled open the door his mother-in-law burst into tears.

'Her baby,' she wept. 'You took away her baby, that's what she's here for. Give it back.'

Wordlessly, Peters lifted the jar and took it into the refrigerated room. 'I could get sacked for doing this,' he said bitterly. 'Knew I shouldn't have let myself be talked into it.' He opened Mandy Sheard's drawer and a sigh of cold air settled there. 'Now what?' he said.

'Put the jar in with her and let's see what happens.' Like a bloody horror film, thought Peters as he did what he was told, and closed the drawer.

'Satisfied?' he said ungratefully, and went back into the P-M room to lock the specimen cupboard and wash his hands, hearing his mother-in-law's voice still rabbiting on in the cold-room.

Daft, that's all it was. Daft.

But he had to admit—the cold had gone.

BARRET HAD TAKEN a lot less than an hour to get through the file folder. And he'd come out empty-handed. Donnelly's face had stayed blank when Barrett told him that, but his eyes had looked satisfied. And smug. It was the smug part that Barrett didn't like, and he'd walked away from the front door with a feeling of having been had. It was a feeling he didn't enjoy and could find no logic for.

The metal of his car was hot, the air inside greeting him with dry, volcanic heat that made him back away and open all the doors. A faint rustle of breeze, not much cooler than the air, stirred papers on the passenger seat. After a couple of minutes he closed everything except the driver's door, hung his jacket on the courtesy hook, and got behind the wheel, which scorched his hands and made him curse. Footsteps out on the street echoed, and traffic sounds were overlaid with the kind of silence that comes before thunderstorms break. That was all they needed.

The notion came that it was like waiting for the devil to stretch himself—or someone to drop a match in a powder keg so Malminster would ignite.

He turned out of the car park towards the motorway roundabout, both front windows fully down. In Death Valley, California, it got so hot you could fry eggs on rocks and hear them sizzle, a useless piece of information he had carried in his head for years, but which he now remembered with a kind of gratitude for it not having got hot enough for that trick here. He pictured eggs frying on Malminster streets, and ran a finger round his collar where spurting sweat left it wet.

When he walked into The Cedars, the receptionist in her L-shaped island looked him over and switched off the automatic smile. Barrett, already conscious of his wilted and crumpled look, stared back at her resentfully. The electric fan above her head sent a cool airstream towards him and he stepped into it with gratitude, fighting back the urge to raise his arms and cool off his armpits too.

He fished out his warrant card, too irritable to waste time with niceties. 'Detective sergeant Barrett, Malminster CID. I'd like to talk with Lucy Walton. I understand she works here?'

'You need to see Mrs Carpenter,' she said.

'I need to see Lucy Walton.'

The woman punched intercom buttons and didn't answer. He sighed. It was too hot to argue. Let her get the woman she wanted, and if that one gave him any trouble, he'd argue then. He eyed the name badge pinned on the white blouse. Lenore Sutton. Uncharitably he rhymed Sutton with mutton, and stayed exactly where he was when she told him to go and sit down, making the most of the cooling downdraft, and watching the tiny light that said Mrs Carpenter's reaction to him being there was to use an outside line. Probably no link between the two, but the itch to listen in was almost physical.

Whatever nature the outgoing call might have had, the time lapse between the light going out and Carpenter's door opening worked out in seconds, not minutes. Barrett watched her come, his own face as empty as hers. Neither of them made any attempt to shake hands, and when she spoke it was straight to the point.

'You want to see Lucy Walton? Can I ask why?'

'Not something I'm at liberty to tell you,' Barrett said blandly. 'I won't keep her long.' Carpenter eyed him and turned to Lenore.

'Find Lucy for me and bring her downstairs. I'll keep an eye on the desk while you're gone, but be quick as you can.' Lenore's face settled into a deeper scowl, but she didn't argue. 'It's the weather,' said Carpenter, watching the other woman walk away. 'It gets to all of us.'

'It's hot,' Barrett admitted. 'Better under the fan.'

'It's also her time of life.'

'Not something I'd know much about,' said Barrett. 'How long has Lucy been here?'

Carpenter shrugged. 'Ten days or so, I can't be accurate without checking. Do you want me to do that?'

'I might at a later date, but not now, ten days is close enough. She works here?'

'She isn't a member of staff.'

'What then?'

'She came to us from St Ursula's, when they no longer had room for her. She does very light work in exchange for room and board.'

'A charity case.'

'I wouldn't say that. We have links with St Ursula's through donation, and when Father Donnelly advised us he could keep Lucy no longer it seemed natural to offer help. I don't expect her to stay—living on the street becomes a habit.'

'Lucy isn't the first woman you've helped in this way?'

'We've had, I think two, although not from St Ursula's. Both of them left after a few weeks. I don't know where they are now.'

'When was the last?'

'Oh, I don't know. Towards the end of last year.'

'Not this year. Not a woman with red hair, February—March?'

'No. Someone like that would be hard to forget. This is the woman Lucy knew I suppose? She told me she had helped with the photofit.'

'She helped with more than that,' said Barrett cryptically, and watched question marks spring up in Carpenter's eyes. 'Not that I'm at liberty to discuss it,' he said firmly.

'I expect Lucy will tell me, in her own good time,' Carpenter said. 'If she stays around that is. She's already talked about moving on now the weather is good.'

'If she does that, I'll want to know,' Barrett said. 'And I'll want to know it as soon as you do. The dead woman was pregnant too.'

'A lot of women are pregnant,' said Carpenter. 'Every

woman who walks through our door is either pregnant or wants to be. Does that put them all at risk?'

'It might. Given the right circumstances.'

'What are the right circumstances?'

'You'll know that when we've made an arrest,' said Barrett shortly. 'If Lucy Walton goes out, and isn't back at her expected time, I want to know. Understood?'

Colour crept under Carpenter's skin. 'Lucy isn't under contract, she's free to come and go as she pleases. I won't necessarily know what time she's coming back. Do you suggest I keep her under lock and key?'

'No. I suggest you have a quiet and friendly talk and point out the dangers.'

'I will—if you tell me what the dangers are.'

They glared at each other. Barrett snapped irritably, 'Mandy Sheard was pregnant and homeless. Lucy Walton's in the same state and—according to you—talking about sleeping rough. There's a link in that they knew each other, and until we know better that makes an unacceptable risk.'

Lenore appeared on the stairs, Lucy behind her.

'I'll talk to her,' said Carpenter. 'But I doubt she'll take notice. The girl has a mind of her own.' Her eyes followed Lucy's movements as she crossed the floor. 'You'll find that out for yourself—she'll tell you what she wants to and no more.'

Lucy caught onto the last sentence and grinned to herself. Stopping just short of Barrett, hands stuffed into her dress pockets, she told him, 'Like I said to that Rosie yesterday, I'm not talking to anybody but her, so if she's not here there's not much good asking me nothing.'

Carpenter eyed him sardonically.

'Since you're obviously not going to be long you can use my office. See to it will you, Lenore. I'll be in the staff room if you want me.' She strolled away, amusement in the curl of her mouth.

When Lenore had closed the door and left them alone, Lucy relaxed a little. 'All right.' she said. 'What do you want? I don't know nothing except what I told Rosie.'

'But you'd like us to find out who killed Mandy.'

'What do you think? We were mates.'

'It'd help to know who the baby's father is,' Barrett said. 'So we can talk to him.'

'How'd you expect me to know that?' said Lucy. 'I wasn't there, was I?'

'Mandy never talked about it?'

'Didn't say that,' said Lucy. 'Why'd you think it's him?'

Barrett sighed, trying to forget trickles of sweat. 'We think it was probably someone she knew.'

''Cos it usually is, you mean? Not always like that though, is it? Could just be a nutcase, there's a lot of them about.'

'We have to start somewhere,' said Barrett doggedly.

'Well it wasn't him.'

'We won't know that until we talk to him.'

'You know 'cos I just said so.'

'It isn't enough. Tell me who it is, Lucy, and let's get it out of the way.'

'Won't help any.'

'We'll find out eventually, it's just going to take longer,' Barrett said, 'and meantime somebody else could get killed.'

'Well if you're thinking that,' said Lucy logically, 'it couldn't have been the baby's dad that did it anyway, could it? Wouldn't have no reason to kill anybody else.'

Barrett's ears picked up.

'So you do know who he is?'

'Never said so,' said Lucy, and scowled at him. 'Don't see it matters anyway, if it weren't him.'

'Name,' said Barrett.

Lucy's lips clamped.

'Name?'

She stuck her hands even deeper into her pockets, so that the pull of material flattened her breasts, and made her look like a child.

'Dunno—'cept his first name was Gary. But he didn't do it.'

'How would you know that?' said Barrett with a sigh.

''Cos he come off his motorbike at Christmas and he's dead,' said Lucy. 'So you'll just have to think of something else, won't you?'

SEVENTEEN

THINGS WERE BACK to normal on Parson's Lane, the police tape gone, and the beck cleared of debris. New grids had gone up at both ends of the storm drain; thick, heavy-duty metal, stronger than the first, and the deep ditch bottom had been cleared out for the first time in twenty years in a fruitless search for clues. For the first few days after the police left, sightseers came and climbed down the bank to stare at the drain or ponder the ditch, each inventing a scenario for the killing that fitted their own mindset.

When the adults went away and left the place in peace, the children came back, paddling in the newly cleaned beck and playing catch among the trees, the sun high and hot in the sky and the water warm around their ankles.

The day after the chill went from the hospital mortuary the beck lost its warmth, and a different kind of silence hung over the area around the drain. Sensing it, the children spent less time there, playing instead in the wood, or in the pasture on the other side of the road—and for the first time since the body was moved the retriever refused to walk over the storm drain again.

MUZ WAS BACK ON AIR, arm in plaster, and after a visit from Ishmal Habib, worried about what he had started. That his misplaced cry for help could have provoked a riot was hard for him to understand—all he'd wanted to provoke was a stack of verbal protests to the closing down of his radio. He had explained the situation to Habib with many gestures of his uninjured arm, but Habib hadn't been impressed. The responsibility for the damage and injuries were Muz's alone, said the community leader, and he'd better make amends by getting everything quietened down. Muz brooded on that, as worried at the idea of losing face with his peers as he was about having caused the problem in the first place. But Habib's insistence would be placated by nothing else, and the threat from Muz's sister to forbid use of her attic took away his last vestige of choice.

Now, every fifteen minutes he sent out a plea for peace and reason, but tried to word it in such a way as not to seem an apostate. Mostly his listeners heard the music, but not the words between, and in the heat of Malminster's streets with the temperature at thirty degrees Celsius, groups of youths kept their positions, taunting the watching police to come and move them on, and egged on in their provocation by waiting news reporters eager for a story. At midday two bus loads of British Front supporters arrived and started a little provocation of their own. A barrage of stones and bottles were exchanged and a passing bus had three windows broken and five passengers injured by flying glass. Police reinforcements were brought in from neighbouring towns, and a running battle with the British Front supporters ensued as the police tried to herd them back onboard the buses.

One supporter and two policemen ended up in casualty, six supporters stayed behind in police cells, and while all that was going on Barrett tried to explain to Morrissey that finding out who the baby's father was had been no help at all.

'WHAT D'YOU MEAN, you're going to quit?' said Darren, aggressive in his stance, thrusting his face into Skeeter's so their noses near touched. Skeeter backed up.

'I mean what I said, I'm going home. 'S'what I want.'

'Don't matter what you bleedin' want,' Darren came back. 'It's me what decides.'

'Yeah. Well…' Skeeter's eyes shifted. He was going and that's all there was to it, he forced memory of last night to the front of his mind and stood his ground. 'You sodding decide for you,' he said. 'I've had enough,' and without meeting Darren's eyes he began to walk away, the back of his neck bunched up the way it had been since he was ten, in permanent anticipation of Darren's violence. Three more steps before it came—Darren hard yanking on his collar, a string of invective curling the air and Skeeter near-falling over backwards. 'Gerrorf!' he yelled, arms flailing, one making a lucky connection with Darren's nose and stinging enough to loosen his hold.

Skeeter skewed his neck a couple of times, snapping out the kinks, and straightened his collar. 'Told you to sodding lay off,' he said.

Mean-eyed, Darren stopped comforting his nose to curve a savage short jab under Skeeter's ribs. Skeeter doubled over. Methodically, as the other hit the ground, Darren put the boot in.

DIANA CARPENTER had wanted to know what Barrett's business had been, but Lucy had hedged. What she'd told him had nothing to do with anybody except Mandy, so Mrs C could like it or lump it. 'Might have to go make another statement,' she said off-handedly. 'Don't know for sure—but he said I might, so I suppose I'll have to stop on here a bit longer won't I, 'til I find out?' Staring at Carpenter's smileless face with one equally sour, hands as usual deep in her pockets.

Carpenter was the first to look away, waving her hand dismissively. 'Go up and make sure room ten is tidy and the bed made. There's a new client coming in this afternoon.'

'She like Mrs Williamson then, nearly due?'

'Just do it, will you?' said Carpenter. 'Now!'

Lucy turned around and walked out, hearing the telephone ping as she closed the door. Probably reporting back to the boss, Lucy thought, telling him she'd been talking to the police again, with any luck they'd throw her out on her ear and save her the bother of deciding for herself.

KIM FITTON had benefited from the counselling she'd found at the Rape Crisis Centre; enough so her fear had turned in greater part to anger. Not wholly though, and the idea of being alone in her own home in Malminster still gave her the chills. Which was why her father gave her the Rottweiler that had refused to leave her side since she'd arrived in Durham. 'Might as well,' he said gruffly. 'Not much use to me anyway since he's decided he's yours.' The dog sat tongue lolling, fond eyes signalling agreement. 'If he's too much bother you can always send him home. Feel safer will you? Having him there?'

'Much,' said Kim, and let her mind lick at the image of opening her front door with the dog at her side, amazed that picturing it didn't make her feel physically sick. 'I'll let Ken know,' she said. 'Get him used to the idea.' Smiling to herself as she said it, because she knew a dog would be the last thing he'd want.

Didn't like dogs, didn't like children.

And she liked both.

Discontentment joined resentment.

When she got back home late Friday afternoon Ken Fitton had redecorated the main bedroom and replaced the old bed with a new one from Ikea. The Rottweiler settled itself near the bed's foot and wouldn't let Ken anywhere near.

For the first time in almost three weeks Kim began to feel safe again.

DIANA CARPENTER'S flat at The Cedars had its own entrance, obscure behind the black-painted iron fire escape that came down the side of the building, twisted back once on itself at a half-landing and ended with its bottom step facing the wide turning circle at the front. The door to the private flat was immediately below the twist, and Carl Fielding had his own key.

When he walked into the living room, Carpenter was in the shower, and less than pleased to have to cut it short. She towelled her hair and watched him pour whisky. Without looking at her he lifted an empty glass and said, 'Want one?'

'Not right now,' she said flatly. 'I'm running a little short. I thought you had a dinner tonight.'

'So I have. I told Maria I had to check on a patient.' He turned. 'Aren't you flattered?'

'No.'

He shrugged, drank half the measure of whisky and poured more.

'I told you I was short,' she said irritably.

He lifted the bottle and eyed the level. 'You drink too much.' She snatched the bottle and carried it with the wet towel into the bathroom.

'What do you want?'

'Lucy Walton—that's her name isn't it? You weren't all that clear this afternoon. What is it she's done exactly?'

Carpenter came back into the room, finger-drying her hair. 'You won't make anything on this one.' She picked up the evening paper and folded it. 'Donnelly's waif and stray helped the police to put this together. Has he had his money yet?'

He took the newspaper in his hand and stared at the composite. 'I spoke with him this morning. He didn't mention this.'

'You didn't see it on local television?'

He threw the paper down irritably. 'I don't watch local news, it doesn't interest me.'

'This time it would have. What do we do—send her back?'

'No.'

'She's barely sixteen.'

He ignored her. 'I've been thinking about relocation and expansion. Somewhere warmer, more pleasant, fewer restrictions.' He saluted her with the glass and downed the second shot.

'What does Maria think?'

'Not something I intend to discuss with her.'

'Remiss of you.'

'Why? I wasn't thinking of taking Maria with me.'

She fluffed vigorously at her hair again, watching him through half-closed lids, a man without grace, face long-boned, eyes wide-set, *and hung like a donkey.* That last made her drop her eyes and turn away, but he'd seen already and curled his mouth. When he pulled loose the belt on her towelling robe all she did was smile…

DURING THE AFTERNOON the temperature had hit eighty-six, and there was no noticeable cooling when evening came. Muz's exhortations for calm fell on deaf ears. Tempers and an urge for violence ran parallel to the Fahrenheit scale. By nine p.m. sundry cars, vans, minibuses and a couple of hired coaches had delivered youths and young men spoiling for a fight into the outskirts of Malminster. Soon after nine-thirty the first trouble erupted when a service bus was forced to stop, its passengers and driver evicted, and the bus itself turned into a beacon of fire.

Police reinforcements poured in, sweating in heavy riot gear, and running battles emptied the streets of all but the foolhardy. And the cinema crowd.

Mike had been to see *Twister* with Adrian Blake and Robby Skirrow, both from his school year, and none of them expecting trouble. Malminster never had trouble. Not before midnight anyway. Conveniently burying what had happened the night before in the belief that it wouldn't recur, and then finding skirmishing already begun on the street outside the cinema. Behind them the rest of the audience backed up, retreating through swing doors into the foyer. Mike and his friends retreated with them. A brick crashed through plate glass at the side of the doors. Adrian said, 'Shit!' and tried to shove back inside faster, Robby and Mike doing much the same, but having been first out they were at the tail end of retreat. Adrian made it, and Mike was following when another brick came flying and took him an inch above and behind his right ear, pitching him forward into the backs of people in front, blood spurting and splashing over Robby's face and shirt and pouring out of Mike's head.

As the barrier of people in front moved away he crumbled like a discarded puppet, twitched a couple of times and lay still.

It was twenty minutes before an ambulance could get through to take him to hospital, Adrian and Robby in the back with him, and another twenty while the ambulance detoured to avoid the riot-torn streets. Not until they were in casualty, watching the trolley with Mike on it being wheeled away fast, did either of them think that maybe his parents should be told—and only then because a nurse not much more than two years older than they were, asked.

EIGHTEEN

BERNIE PARKS was driving without thinking much about it, one hand fondly kneading Susan's knee, the other on the wheel, one o'clock in the morning and driving home along Parson's Lane. By rights it was their night for Malminster and the disco, a curry on the way home, but when he heard about the rioting he'd turned around and taken her to the Cap & Plume instead, paying more than both the disco and curry would have cost him but thinking philosophically that upmarket surroundings and a better chance to show off her new dress would please her, so what the heck? His mind on that when she suddenly yelped at him to stop and near had him in the ditch.

'Bloody Norah!' He clamped both hands on the wheel for a change and looked at her. 'What the heck did you do that for? Near had us in the ditch.'

'Back up,' she said, looking through the back window.

'What for? I didn't see nothing.'

'Never do see nothing. I want to go back and see what that woman's after.'

'What woman?'

'Her in pink.' Hair came up on his neck when she said that but he backed obediently. ''S'funny,' she said. 'Where's she gone?'

'Field path,' he said shortly, and put his foot down to get away from the place. Best not tell her that chap that hit the police car had seen the same thing.

MORRISSEY couldn't sit down, impossible even to think about it, pacing from window to door and back again, staring out restlessly, the moon like a pale eye measuring him, dispassionate as its maker, caring nothing about flying bricks and compressed fractures, careless of subdural haematomas in the greater scheme of things, and Morrissey's raging futile in the face of such indifference.

Katie and Margaret didn't share his restlessness, both of them were more numb than anything, frozen in a nightmare that a surgeon in green theatre-strip would have to end and dreading his coming. Margaret cursing herself for not having stood firm in insisting Mike should stay home that night whether Robby and Adrian were going to the cinema or not.

Better to have stood Mike's anger at her for denying him manhood than face the sight of him on a theatre trolley. Anger would have passed—but this...shaking her head, holding agony tight so Katie shouldn't see, not knowing that Katie, hunched on her chair and silent inside herself, didn't dare to think at all.

Polystyrene cups mounted in number on the table. At three, Margaret gave her hands something to do and cleared them all. Five minutes later Morrissey went to the machine in the corridor and got three more, the coffee blandly unlike its name but drinkable.

At four-fifteen the surgeon came, tired-eyed, rubbing at the bridge of his nose, looking at their faces and doing what he had to do in telling them the surgery had gone well, fracture lifted, haematoma drained, pausing for them to take that in and seeing relief cover their faces like a mantle before, on a deeper breath, he told them about underlying damage to the brain tissue.

BARRET WOKE to the stridency of the telephone and lifted it knowing it had to be trouble connected with the rioting. Groaning when he looked at the clock and found it barely six when he hadn't crawled into bed until after two. And then he heard Morrissey's voice and the hollowness and woke up in a hurry, heaviness settling in the pit of his stomach as he remembered the smell and feel of intensive care. He was at the hospital before half-past and behind his desk less than an hour later, with Morrissey's caseload delegated onto his shoulders and weighing heavily—especially the idea of putting the Chief Superintendent in the picture.

But when Osgodby heard what Barrett had to say, he left his office immediately and went to the hospital, as upset and angry as the rest of the station. Ten minutes later Barrett too drove out of the yard, heading for The Cedars and what he expected to be difficult meetings with both Diana Carpenter and Lucy. For someone who had once rigidly followed procedure and eschewed hunches he was, he told himself, learning to use such things to his own advantage.

For some reason the idea of getting heavy with Diana Carpenter filled him with satisfaction—as did the receptionist's look of straight-lipped annoyance when he walked in through the door.

'You again!'

'Lucy Walton.'

'I'll let Mrs Carpenter know—why don't you...' She started to motion towards the waiting area, then caught Barrett's look of stolid immovability and gave up on the idea.

This time Carpenter came out of her office a little faster, demanding to be told why he wanted Lucy. 'The child will wish she'd never talked to you at all if you keep this up,' she said irritably. 'What is it this time?'

'Confidential—as is most police business.' Staring her down and wondering how popular she was with her staff, he remembered an S&M bust they'd made not long back and grinned to himself. Easy to picture her among that lot with her whips and thigh boots—his eyes sliding downwards despite an attempt to keep them on her face, the image making the grin show itself against his will.

Carpenter whitened instead of reddening, and said sharply, 'Get her!' at the dragon and went back into her office, slamming the door closed behind her.

He turned his face up to the fan again, appreciatively, and got ready to wait, but this time the dragon didn't move away from her desk, instead she snapped 'Send Lucy Walton out, to reception' down the internal phone and put the receiver in its rest without waiting for reply. Obviously she'd learned a lot from the boss.

When Lucy came she had a pink check triangle round her hair and a matching pinny over her dress. The pinny was lifted in mid-air as she dried her hands on it. 'Won't take long, will it?' she said. 'Got a stack of carrots to do.'

'It might,' Barrett told her. 'I want you to come down to the station with me.'

She backed up a step. 'What for?'

He shook his head. 'You're not in trouble, it's to do with Mandy.'

'Oh.' The tension went. 'Another picture or something.'

'Something like that.'

'I'll just go tell cookie she's on her own then,' Lucy said cheerfully. 'Hate peeling carrots, right mucks up me fingers.' Barrett watched her disappear back the way she'd come, hearing the click of Carpenter's door again as the dragon scurried out from the desk and across the corridor to tell her the bad news.

EDDIE'S MOOD wasn't good. Things weren't supposed to have turned out the way they had. What he'd set out to do was cause a piece of aggro for Willie, and now look what he'd got. Near killed his own bleeding trade. Nobody looking for girls with a sodding riot going on round their ears.

With inborn perversity he added it to Willie's tab; something else he had to pay for if he didn't get his finger out. He snarled at Sam to bring the car round and went to pay an early visit. If he was going to spoil Willie's day he'd do it early enough to make it memorable. Smiling like a weasel with a rabbit in sight.

Willie was down in his basement, doing some cooking, and it took a couple of hard knocks to get him to come up and answer the door. He looked at Eddie, then at Sam standing behind him, and grinned. 'Changed your mind then and decided to come yourself have you, Big Man? How much you want?' Sam put a hand on his chest and shoved him inside, crowding him through the door, Willie going back off balance and grabbing at the front-room lintel so he didn't fall. Eddie followed them, stepping in casually, satisfied he'd got Willie on the run and a walkover from now on.

He looked round the front room.

'Wouldn't like to live like this, Willie. Like to have a bit of class round me when I go home. Some good pictures up on the walls, a few nice pieces of Capo del Monte—you know what I mean. Class.'

'Yeah,' said Willie. 'Class. Right. So what you want? You make the place untidy.'

'Worried were you, when the heavies came? Thought they were coming here? Must have been a relief when they didn't. I can see you, standing there, ready to run. Wouldn't have made it Willie, they'd have covered the back as well as the front if they'd had a tip-off.'

'If they'd had a tip-off,' said Willie. 'But who'd do that?'

'I might,' said Eddie. 'Call the upset across the road a warning. All right? Next time they'll be coming here.'

'Please yourself,' said Willie. 'Best find somewhere else to do your shopping while you're at it, though. Can't get it here if the shop's shut, can you?'

Sam stared at him, hands twitching.

'That's not how you talk to the boss.'

'Might not be the way you talk to him, Sunshine, but I

don't have to clean his arse. It's a seller's market—and it's me that's selling.' He looked at Eddie. 'Was you what gave the tip-off then? Bet I know a copper or two what'd be glad to know about that.'

Eddie's eyes hooded, took on more than dislike. 'There's more than one way to shut you down. Dead men don't deal.'

'Who's going to do it then?' said Willie with a bit more bravado than he felt. 'Rambo here? Gone right out of fashion, that has. Seems a simple enough deal to me—you want crack, I want to sell it, but I don't deal through middles. Them's the rules.'

Eddie's eyes drifted from Sam to the Bang & Olufsen stereo, expensive and sleek in the corner. Sam's eyes drifted there too and his feet followed, the stereo's wires ripped away from the wall socket before Willie got his mouth open. 'Here,' said Sam, 'catch,' and with seeming ease arced the stacked components in Willie's direction.

Willie's hands went out involuntarily, then his brain took over and got him out of the way. Plastic cracked and shed fragments, metal fractured into sounds.

'Clumsy,' said Eddie, who had watched too many movies for his own good. 'Should've caught it. Made a right mess of it now, haven't you?' He grinned, teeth sharp, pointed and tobacco stained. 'Sam'll be round tonight. Don't send him back empty-handed or next time it'll be you what's in pieces.' He kicked a shard of matt black casing that had landed near his foot. 'Hope you was insured,' he said and walked out, Sam following like a shadow.

OSGODBY had never seen a man age so much in one night. Morrissey's tall, broad-shouldered frame appeared contracted to a lesser shape, and an inner and haunted weariness denied the outward implacability of his face. Osgodby put an awkward hand on the Chief Inspector's shoulder.

'Any change?'

Morrissey shook his head, the pain he felt physical in its intensity. 'There won't be anything for a good long while yet. I'm trying to persuade Margaret and Katie to go home and get some rest.'

'They won't go?'

'Another voice may do the trick,' Morrissey tried to smile but the act produced only a grimace. 'So might the offer of a ride.'

Osgodby nodded. 'You've got both,' he said. 'You know that.' He stared past the bank of monitors into the six-bed ward. 'How long?'

Morrissey gestured at the equipment as if it were an enemy he might kill without reason. 'If these things don't go off they start to lower sedation tomorrow. After that we wait to find out the damage.'

'Get something in the canteen, John,' the Chief Superintendent said, making it sound like an order. 'I'll take your place here. Go on—don't argue—it'll give me chance to soften them up.'

If such a thing were possible, he thought, watching Morrissey stride away, the knowledge that Margaret was as stubborn as her husband fixed firm in his mind.

NINETEEN

BERNIE'S GIRLFRIEND went into Malminster police station during her lunch-break, winding herself up to do that because she could end up looking a right fool. Rosie was on the front desk again, and Susan didn't know whether to be glad or sorry it was a woman there, and not a man. Men expected women to act three sheets to the wind, so it didn't matter about adding another one to the list, but women were different, and Susan didn't like to look a fool in front of her own sex. Still—wasn't any other way to find out what she wanted to know. Rosie gave her a friendly smile and asked what she could do to help, managing to look like she meant it too.

'It's that woman on Parson's Lane,' said Susan. 'You know—the one somebody called Smythe came to see me about.'

Rosie perked her ears. 'You want to talk to him?'

'No,' said Susan, a bit too fast. 'I mean it isn't like I've remembered anything, it's just like…' Her voice trailed off.

'Like?' prompted Rosie.

'Like that pink tracksuit she had on. Was it dark pink—sort of strawberryish?'

'You knew her, then?'

'No!' Vehement this time.

'But you know the pink was dark pink?'

'It was then, wasn't it?' said Susan heavily, and started to turn away.

Rosie said, 'You can't just go like that you know, not after what you've said. If you can identify the shade of pink she wore, you must know who she is. I can't let you just walk out of here if you have information that will help in a murder enquiry.'

'I haven't,' said Susan, and wished she hadn't come, dithering whether to risk looking a fool or not and deciding she had no choice. 'It was last night, you see,' she confessed reluctantly. 'When me and Bernie was driving home. I think I saw her ghost...'

DARREN AND SKEETER were on the road again, but this time without the fair. Skeeter, sore and resentful, was driving while Darren nursed a swollen jaw and exuded something worse. Going back to Malminster with his tail between his legs hadn't been part of his plans, but teaching Skeeter a lesson, Friday morning, hadn't gone the way he intended. Finnegan had come out of his caravan roaring like a bull, and with one mighty sideswipe taken Darren off his feet and near broken his jaw.

And then he'd told him to get off the site.

Not Skeeter though—just Darren, and that had made things worse. Darren wasn't used to coming out second. He'd argued, said it was just personal, nothing for Finnegan to get upset about, but none of it had made any difference, when the fairground boss said, go, he meant go, and he'd whistled up a couple of his heavies to make sure Darren got the message.

Twice he came back onto the ground to reclaim the Transit and both times got thrown off again, sharpish. The third time Finnegan had set his German Shepherd on guard outside the van, and Darren didn't even try. Dogs he didn't like, and the feeling was mutual.

Just before six a.m. Saturday he tried again, and found the dog gone and Skeeter asleep in the back of the van. Darren shook him roughly and told him to get his clothes on, they were going, and Skeeter was still too sore to argue.

'Going where?' he said as he pulled his zipper up.

'Back to sodding Malminster, that's where,' said Darren blackly. 'An' all your bleedin' fault!'

Skeeter got out for a pee without correcting him.

Half an hour later they were in a Greasy Spoon twenty miles away, the only thing that marked their having been on the fairground at all a gap in the circle of vans.

'I'm not going back skint,' said Darren darkly. 'Dunno what got into you, wanting to go home. Not as if there was anything worth going back for.' He eyed Skeeter, who was solidly shovelling fried egg. 'Well?' he challenged. 'Is there?'

'Is there what?' said Skeeter who knew very well but chose to pretend otherwise.

'Get a move on,' said Darren. 'I want to get to Rigby.'

Skeeter stopped with his mouth half open, a mess of chewed food plainly visible, and eyed Darren warily. Then he swallowed and said, 'What for?'

''Cos like I told you, I'm not going home skint, that's what for.'

Skeeter pushed his plate away, appetite gone. 'What you planning now?' he said dispiritedly. ''Cos I've just about had enough.'

Darren reached lazily into his back pocket and came out with the knife he'd threatened Kim Fitton with, weighing it in his hand, eyes on Skeeter, and Skeeter's eyes stuck on the flick-blade like they were magnetised. 'Had enough what, Skeet,' Darren said, voice flat as the blade. 'Breathing?'

BARRETT HAD HOPED that interviewing Lucy in the police station might improve her memory—but it didn't. Stubbornly she'd insisted that Mandy had told her nothing else about the baby's father, and he'd ended up paying for her to eat in the canteen and nothing new to show for it, telling himself there was nothing for it now but to hope the police computer could run through December's RTA's and come up with the right name. He'd also intended sending Lucy back to The Cedars in a Panda, but ended up taking her himself instead.

She had the same effect on him as a stray dog, and he couldn't rid himself of a niggling feel of responsibility. Most of the way back she sat as far away from him as she could get, staring out the side window like she'd never seen so much scenery before. Then she relented and said, 'You should have told me you was just going to ask all that again.'

'What difference would it have made?'

'Dunno—but I'd have known what you were up to wouldn't I? Makes a difference.'

'You have a real knack for getting backs up.'

She grinned suddenly. 'I do, don't I?'

Barrett squinted at her, felt his mouth twitch, and schooled it to stay stern. 'Yes,' he said. 'You do.'

'D'you think you'll find out who did it? I mean, how would you? Find out, I mean?'

'I think we'll find out,' said Barrett, sounding a lot surer than he felt. 'We're persistent. Things get added together until one day we begin to see a picture of what might have happened. And then we find out who fits in the picture.'

'Bet it's not as easy as that though,' said Lucy. 'Not going to get someone put their hand up for it, are you?'

'It's unlikely,' admitted Barrett.

'Them rings,' said Lucy. 'What you going to do with them?'

'They'll be given to her family.'

'What happened to the other one?'

'Other one what?'

'Ring.'

'You've lost me,' said Barrett. 'What other ring?'

'Mandy had three. Them two what was in the paper, and another one. The other one was nicer. Haven't you got it?'

Barrett slowed the car a little. 'Describe it,' he said carefully.

'It was like the others—silver, but it had this blue stone, not shiny or anything. Mandy said it was for her birthday, and everybody has a stone. Mine's topaz,' she said. 'Funny that, 'cos I like yellow.'

'And Mandy's was blue?'

'Yeah, turquoise. We had a look in that rock shop on Market Street and they had a lot of it there. Mandy said she was going to get a proper job again one day, and buy some earrings too, 'cos she liked it. Wish she had,' she finished sadly. 'If she'd had a proper job she wouldn't be dead, would she?'

'Can you describe the ring?' Barrett said, still driving slow.

'Told you. Silver, and a blue stone.'

'A round one?'

'No—longish. Sort of…' she looked around the car, saw nothing that would help, and did a sort of twirl with her index finger. Barrett sighed and stopped the car.

'Think you could draw it for me?'

'Easy.'

He gave her his notebook, opened at a clean page, and a pen. Lucy scrunched her forehead up and began to draw. 'Sort of diamond-shape,' she said. 'Like that. And then this stone in the middle was longish and thin. Looked nice, like it was old. Mandy said she got it second-hand some place.' She gave him back the pad and pen. 'Have you got it then? 'Cos she wouldn't have given it to anybody—not that. Liked it too much.'

'No,' said Barrett. 'We didn't find a ring like that. Just the two you saw. You're absolutely sure she would still have had it? She might have sold it to get money for food.'

'Not that she wouldn't,' Lucy said firmly. 'It was her lucky charm, that's what Mandy said. Always thought if she lost that her luck would run out.' She sat quiet for a minute, then said, 'And it did, didn't it?' looking at him with eyes grown big. 'I bet that's what happened. Somebody pinched it, and when she tried to get it back they killed her. Could have happened like that, couldn't it?'

'It could have,' Barrett agreed, unwilling to tell her the more likely explanation was that the ring was on the finger they hadn't found yet.

BARRETT WAS STILL in the canteen when word came that Ken Fitton was waiting to see him, and he swallowed down the rest of his bacon butty in a hurry and went to find out why—wishing after the first few minutes that he'd taken his time.

Fitton tried to make out he was being courteous in letting the police know his wife was home, but what he really wanted was to be told they had a suspect, so he could send the dog packing. Barrett took him into an interview room and tried to dredge up some flagging tact, but Fitton wasn't in the mood.

'She's wanting to move now—do you know that?' He said the words like an accusation, as if it was somehow Barrett's fault that it had all happened. 'Frightened to be in the house she says. So her father's given her a Rottweiler that won't let anyone near her. Including me! It hasn't made any difference to her wanting to move though, she still wants that.'

'I can understand why your wife feels that way, sir. Given the same circumstances…'

'You married?'

'No.'

'Then you're not qualified to give an opinion.' Fitton shifted on his feet, restless, wanting someone to take his anger out on, because how the hell was he supposed to feel about moving house when all he had was negative equity, and every cent he earned spent before it reached the bank? He said stiffly, 'How long do you reckon it'll take to sell a house where a rape's taken place, and the rapist is still on the loose? Think we'll get a queue of buyers?'

A queue of sightseers more like, thought Barrett. Bouncing on the beds and wondering if that's where it happened. Not that selling would solve anything, anyway, memory not being a piece of junk you could leave behind. Fitton knew that too, it was written all over his face. Barrett said, 'Now she's back I'd like to talk to your wife again.'

'No,' said Fitton.

'It isn't a matter of choice.'

Fitton glowered, frustrated at not being able to hit out, not having anyone specific to aim his anger at, and fast reaching the point where any target was better than none, even a policeman. Barrett shifted his balance, watching the other man's hands twitch and bunch. Fitton stuck his head forward. 'Why don't you get off your damned arse and find him?'

'Talking to your wife is a part of doing that.'

Fitton picked up one of the wooden chairs, weighing it in his hands, then he dropped it back on the floor, turned on his heel and walked out. Disgruntled and heavy-footed Barrett went out after him and headed back to his desk, stopped on the stairs by Smythe before he got there, the DC less brash than usual but still pushy to know what was going on.

'Anything new, Sarge?'

'No,' said Barrett shortly, and kept on walking. 'Except his wife's back. When he found out we'd have to talk to her again he wasn't best pleased.'

'I could do that,' Smythe said, keeping up with him. 'I

mean with the DCI away...' He trailed off, reading negativity in Barrett's face.

'Doubt she'll have remembered anything we don't know already,' Barrett said flatly.

Smythe started to shrug and give up on it, then changed his mind. 'Still needs to be asked, though.'

'Think it's necessary, or just voyeurism on your part?'

'I think we haven't been getting anywhere with it and any chance is better than none. I'd like to do it—take a WPC with me so Mrs Fitton has no worries.'

'Just because Harland was open and shut...'

'Not that,' said Smythe. 'I think if we don't get him he'll rape again, probably has already.'

Barrett went into the office, shuffled papers on his desk, made a neat stack, slotted them in a folder. He thought the same thing, and so did everybody else with half a brain; problem was he hadn't credited Smythe with enough interest in the job to think about it. The plain fact was that all the rapist had left behind was semen, useful for DNA fingerprinting but not unless they came up with a suspect to match it with. He waved at a chair in front of his desk. 'Convince me,' he said, 'that you won't mess up on it if I let you do that.'

TWENTY

THE RETRIEVER found a fox's scent trail and followed it deeper into Stye Woods, turning a deaf ear to its owner's demand for obedience, and speeding up as the man's thrashing feet came through the trees after it. Half a mile beyond the beck the dog began whiffling in circles until it found a narrow way through a thorn thicket and disappeared inside. When its owner came up, panting and in a rage, the dog was invisible except for the sound of its digging. Beating at the bushes with his stick did no good at all, except to earn him scratches that made his curses even louder. Glowering, he waited for the dog to be done.

Luckily for the retriever the earth was empty, the dog fox and its mate moved on by the noise of machinery and the smell of men busy at the storm drain and searching in the woods. One scavenged prize had been left behind. When the dog fox had entered the open end of the storm drain it had been in search of rats, and several had been killed and added to his meagre larder before he found carrion. The foot had already been gnawed and partly severed by rats, now the fox completed the mutilation and took the bounty back to his earth. Sated by the vermin and two unwary squirrels, the foot was put away for leaner times. Next day the men came.

Now, the retriever dug out the fox's larder and took the prize back to its owner, dropping the trophy on the ground at his feet and then sitting with lolling tongue waiting to be praised. A shred of desquamous tissue hung from the dog's muzzle and its tongue swung around to lick and swallow. The owner saw and, feeling his stomach clench, grabbed the dog by the collar, hauling it away before it might be tempted to do worse.

ROSIE HAD JUST FINISHED telling Barrett about Susan thinking she'd seen a ghost, when the message came through that a dog had dug up the remains of a foot that could well be Mandy's. 'It's to be hoped it is,' said Barrett. 'If there's another body out there I don't want to hear about it. Get the foot to Forensic and ask for a quick result.' He put the phone down and turned back to Rosie. 'I don't believe in ghosts,' he said. 'I do believe in people who make things up to get a bit of attention though. Think it might be a bit of that?'

'If you want me to be truthful, no, I don't. She didn't strike me as wanting attention at all—just the opposite.'

'Then either somebody's playing around or it's coincidence,' Barrett insisted firmly. 'Pink isn't all that uncommon a colour for women to wear.'

'I just thought you'd want to know,' said Rosie, wishing she hadn't bothered, and turned to go.

'Kim Fitton is back in Malminster,' Barrett said, 'and that means we need to talk to her again, see if she comes up with anything new. DS Smythe will be looking for you a bit later to go with him. Better for Mrs Fitton if you're along, she'll remember you.'

'I do what I'm told,' said Rosie, feeling even more that her role in life was to act as makeweight. 'Like everybody else.' And turned smartly on her heel before he could think of anything else he might use to reinforce knowledge of her place in the scheme of things.

MORRISSEY HAD SAT alone by his son's bed for close on three hours, big frame crammed into a chair never intended for anyone his height. Putting his head back would have been nice, but even sliding forward, legs stretched out with only the base of his spine making contact with the seat of the chair, he still got a crick in his neck. In all that time Mike had made no movement, no sound, with only the constant blink of a monitor screen confirming he was anything but dead, and the thoughts that had occupied Morrissey's mind as he listened to the muted beeps were of butted heads and lost time.

He was also too much of a realist to make rash promises to either himself or to Mike, that such things would change. Young stags forever butted their heads against the old, and the old were too stubborn to move aside or change their stance.

He began to count the slow drops of glucose-saline pushing though plastic tubing into the back of Mike's hand, supplemented every fifteen minutes by the whirring buzz of the driver, adding sedative to the mix. Mike's hand, like the rest of him, was in change. Half child, half man.

Something seen every day and never noticed until now, when the vulnerability of it bowed Morrissey's shoulders. He shifted again, the ward's over-warmth and plastic upholstery combining to create discomfort. His mind conjured up the relief of a cool shower, teasing him with unfulfilled anticipation like the grapes of Tantalus.

Mike's head jerked. A small fraction of movement that peaked a line on the monitor, and Morrissey's heart rate peaked with it. He reached for Mike's free hand, gripping it in an agony of misery and guilt, trying to pour strength through the contact of skin on skin while the sceptic in him denied the possibility that such might happen.

His grip was still as firm when Margaret and Katie came back at three o'clock, and with hugs and soft words made him go home to eat the casserole still warm in the oven before he fell into an exhausted and haunted sleep.

SKEETER'S APPETITE didn't return. He watched Darren clean his finger nails with the point of the knife and felt all the terrors of childhood wash over him again. But now there was something new added to them, and to the way he saw Darren. Part of the fear had given way to hate. But only a small part. Nowhere near enough to make him openly challenge the other—not yet. But it was the not yet that he hugged inside himself as they set off again, heading south into Lincolnshire instead of north towards the Humber Bridge and home.

Just outside Healstone they pulled into a lay-by while Darren rooted through his stuff and came out with the monkey mask. 'You too,' he told Skeeter. 'In the back and get it found.' Skeeter didn't argue.

Healstone was busy, a Saturday market lining both sides of the high street making it hazardous for both traffic and pedestrians. Skeeter drove along it obediently, then found his way back to their starting point along minor roads, parking in a slot outside the service door of an empty shop.

The sub-post office Darren sent him into was off the high street, on a narrow road that was part of the one-way traffic system. Small, flanked on one side by a baker, and the other by a florist and hairdresser, the post office held nothing but a counter at one end with a small room behind, the body of the shop lined with greeting cards. The surprise for Skeeter was in its business. He made a show of looking at cards and kept an eye on the counter queue. After ten minutes he bought an eighteen-pence stamp and went back to the van.

'Well?' said Darren.

'Just the one woman there. Like you said.'

'And busy?'

'Looked it.'

'Cash going in or out?'

'Fifty-fifty's what I saw.' His voice non-committal, that being as far as renewed rebellion would let him be, yet.

'Hard to tell, like, me not being as bright as you.' He let his mouth stay slack as Darren stared at him, and felt saliva gather in its corners.

'Stupid pissing arsehole!' Darren snapped, emphasising it with a short jab that caught a bruise still tender from the day before. Skeeter's mouth opened a little wider and let out his pain.

Darren's top lip curled as he dropped down out of the van and headed for the post office. Left behind, Skeeter rubbed the soft flesh over his kidney and looked at the keys, hung limp in the ignition.

He could take off. Nothing to stop him. Dump Darren's stuff and drive—except if he did that, it'd have to be away from Malminster. No more going home. Not if he wanted to stay alive.

He put his feet on the dash and leaned back, waiting. After half an hour Darren came, a four-pack of lager in one hand and a satisfied look on his face.

'Should be a walkover,' he said as he broke open a couple of cans and held one out to Skeeter. Skeeter took it and didn't reply. 'Going soft on it then are we?' Darren sneered. 'Scared of getting caught and having us bottoms slapped?'

'Haven't told me what you're up to, yet, have you?' said Skeeter, not that he needed to hear. Even a subnormal didn't have to be told what Darren wanted with a sub-post office.

'I reckon we'll come out with a couple of thou. Easy.' Pulling on the can, watching Skeeter's face, eyes half-hooded.

'Yeah?'

'Get a pressy for your ma on the way home if you like. We can stop somewhere, shop or something.'

Skeeter drank his can straight off, crushed the thin aluminium in his hand and tossed it out the window. ''S'wait and see, shall we?' he said.

'Want another?'

'Nah.'

'Right then,' said Darren, swallowing down his own beer and tossing the empty after Skeeter's. 'Let's go get on with it then.'

SMYTHE WAS UP CLOSE to the Fitton's front door when it opened, ready to flash his smile and warrant card, and then to walk right in. Instead he moved back so fast he slid down the step and made an ungainly windmill as he fought for balance. Rosie, who'd been a pace behind, swallowed a grin. The Rottweiler eyed Smythe like a juicy lamb chop and leaked saliva. 'Nice dog,' Rosie said.

'I like him,' said Kim. 'It was you I talked with in the hospital wasn't it?'

'That's right. There are some things we need to discuss if we can come in.' She turned around to Smythe, who'd got his composure back and was holding up his identification. 'This is DC Smythe, and he's the one who'll be asking the questions.'

'Isn't it always?' said Kim, tightly. 'The men I mean. Who ask questions. Too bloody many.' She stepped back from the door, her fingers looped through the dog's collar. 'Come in, I'll put Julius in the kitchen.'

'Julius?' said Smythe.

'Too many Caesars,' said Kim cryptically as she moved away. 'Sitting room on the left.'

Rosie moved in that direction and left Smythe to close the front door. Ikea furniture, with plain, Scandinavian lines, two angular uplighters. Everything looked immaculate. Not a book, magazine or ornament an inch from where it belonged. Two Chesterfields upholstered in cerise and white stripes faced each other across a low table, a pale cream rug between them. Easy, thought Rosie, to recognise a house without children. She wondered if the dog were allowed in here.

Kim came back and sat on the Chesterfield nearest to her, waving politely at the other. 'Do sit. I've put the kettle on if you'd like tea.'

'I would,' said Rosie before Smythe could open his mouth. 'I always feel better talking over a cup of tea.' Kim smiled at her, and Smythe took his cue.

'It'd be nice,' he said, sitting himself opposite, his hand going to straighten his hair. Rosie saw the movement and marvelled. What with Smythe and his hair, and Barrett pulling imaginary waistcoats, it was enough to make anybody think CID were self-obsessed.

That made her swallow a smile too as she sat with Smythe, the gap between them wide. 'I suppose the dog makes you feel more secure,' she said. 'It would me.'

'He's my father's really,' Kim admitted. 'But he seems to have taken to me. When Dad said I could bring him home I jumped at it. Ken isn't too pleased, he doesn't like dogs.'

'A lot of people don't. A good deterrent, though.'

'For a lot of things,' said Kim obliquely. 'I'll check the kettle.' She was up and gone while Smythe was still trying to work out meanings.

'What was all that about?' he said.

'All what?'

'The dog.'

'Nothing to do with police work,' said Rosie. 'You wouldn't understand.'

'Well when she comes back let's get what we've come to do, done. All right?'

'Of course,' said Rosie. 'I'm only here to make weight.' About eight stones' worth, thought Smythe, trying not to let his appreciative eye show. When Kim came back again he cleared his throat, ready to get started, but she didn't give him a chance.

Handing out the mugs, she looked directly at Rosie, and said, 'I suppose you've come to find out if I remember anything else?'

'Yes,' said Rosie. 'I suppose we have.'

'There's only one thing,' said Kim, 'so I might as well say it now and then it's over with. I remembered his after-shave. Distinct. Not distinct unusual, but distinct too much of it. You know what I mean?'

'You can put a name to it?' said Smythe, putting his mug on the table and getting out his notebook.

'No,' said Kim. 'I'm not that knowledgeable, but you can.' He stopped his pen in mid-stroke and looked at her.

'I can?'

'Yes,' said Kim. 'You're wearing it.'

TWENTY-ONE

EVER SINCE she found out that the body on Parson's Lane had been that of Mandy, Lucy had found herself drawn back to the attic window, recreating in her mind the flashing lights and police vehicles that had first attracted her eyes. Only now she added something different to the scene. Because she knew it was Mandy, the face of her friend was ever in the forefront of her mind.

From the attic, traffic moving along the lane looked like Matchbox models, bodywork catching the sun's rays and reflecting the gleam back at her across the fields.

The ring had lodged in her mind and wouldn't be shifted. Stubbornly the thought persisted that whoever had the ring now, had killed Mandy.

But Barrett didn't think so.

More fool him!

A blur of bright pink caught at the corner of her eye and she twisted her head to see better, but when she looked full at the place where it had been there was nothing but pasture and the dark, bordering hedge, behind.

SKEETER WAS doing the driving again, coaxing as much speed as he could out of the engine without blowing a gasket, anxious to put as many miles as possible between the Transit and Healstone before anyone went looking for the woman who ran the sub-post office. When his eyes weren't fixed on the road they ranged sideways onto Darren. Part of the way he fantasised about having an ejector seat on the passenger side. Shoot the bastard out in front of an eighteen-wheeler and watch the splash. He pictured that in his mind, bright red like paint. A big flattened hedgehog.

'You didn't have to go that far,' he said as they passed the Snaith exit on the way west. 'Could have just taken the money, like what you said.'

'Wasn't my fault,' said Darren. 'Got me excited didn't she? Should have done what she was told. Anyway...' he turned his face and grinned. 'She enjoyed it.'

Like hell, thought Skeeter, remembering.

'Didn't have to have watched, did you?' Darren said remindfully. 'Could have looked the other way.'

'Not bloody deaf though, am I?' Skeeter muttered.

'What?'

'Nothing.'

Darren reached back for his duffle bag and set it between his knees. Showily he counted out five hundred pounds in fives and tens, folded them in two and shoved them down the waistband of Skeeter's jeans. 'Your share.'

'Oh, yeah? And what's yours?'

'Don't matter what mine is. Gettin' too cocky, Skeet, better watch it don't get cut off.' Skeeter felt a slight rise behind his zipper and held onto the wheel tightly, remembering the knife.

WHEN ISHMAL HABIB heard about Morrissey's son he was beside himself. First he went to the hospital and apologised for the behaviour of the youths in his community, staring at Mike through the observation window with a sick recognition of having viewed an almost identical scene once before. Except that time it had been an Asian boy. He remembered Morrissey standing then, as Habib was standing now, trying to offer comfort to a father for whom such comfort was impossible. Morrissey's eyes, dark slate at the best of times, were today more like burnt-out coal, seeing yet not seeing the man before him, and when he left the hospital Habib's heart was heavy.

There was nothing for it but to get the elders out on the streets and make the youths see reason. Purposefully he turned his car towards the home of the Mullah, and began at the top.

LUCY WAS supposed to rest each afternoon between two-thirty and three-thirty, but most days the time was spent watching television, or staring out of the window weighing up her options. It seemed a long time since she had been at St Ursula's, wishing the rain would stop so she could get back out onto the streets again and pick up where she had left off. She let her mind explore something else. How long had it been since she thought about Rollo?

The construct she had carefully built was hazy, face and voice hard to conjure. A bit of the Irish, she reminded herself. Soft words and a lilt that made her smile. Smiling was important when you were having a baby. She remembered reading that somewhere, in a magazine. Said babies born to smiley mothers did better that than ones who weren't. She cut that thought off short and went back to rebuilding Rollo. Dark hair, longish and sort of curly. Not greasy, though. Rollo never let it get greasy 'cos he knew she hated it.

Her father had greasy hair.

Jeans and a leather jacket—a bit like hers 'cept his was bigger and more zips, like bikers wore. Looked good in it too, he did. Like he could look after her. When she found him. Or he found her. She sat cross-legged on the bed. A female fat Buddha, eyes closed, building images, because images were better than what came when you had none left.

She was still sitting in the same position when Diana Carpenter walked in without bothering to knock.

'Lucy, Mr Fielding is here, and he thinks it's time he had a look at you so we know how the baby is coming on.'

'What for?' said Lucy. ''S'all right, is the baby. Been kicking like hell all day today. Doing it again now. Want to feel?'

'No,' said Carpenter briskly. 'I want you to come with me.'

'Never said yet I was going to have it here, did I?' said Lucy stubbornly. 'An' if I'm not having it here, it's got nothing to do with Mr Nosy Fielding, has it?'

Carpenter's face closed up. Lucy kept her eyes locked a couple of seconds longer then broke contact.

''S'not as if there was anything wrong with me,' she muttered.

'I'll ask Father Donnelly if he can take you back,' said Carpenter, words spaced into ice shards, and walked towards the door.

'I'm not going back there,' said Lucy. 'No chance.'

'The streets then,' said Carpenter disinterestedly, her fingers on the door handle. 'If you choose not to remain here your welfare is no longer my responsibility.'

'Didn't say I wanted to leave, did I?'

'Staying here and accepting antenatal care are part of the same package. I made that plain when you arrived.'

'So?'

'Do you know how much you would have to pay for a private consultation with Mr Fielding, as a private patient?' What did it matter, thought Lucy resentfully, when she wasn't ever likely to be doing it. 'One hundred guineas.'

'Aren't any guineas anymore, it'd be a hundred and ten pounds. And I wouldn't be daft enough to do it,' Lucy said matter-of-factly. 'Not when there's the Health Service.'

Carpenter pulled the door open. 'I want you out of here first thing tomorrow morning.'

'What'll he do if I see him?' said Lucy. 'I don't like being poked about.'

Satisfied, Diana Carpenter turned, and let her face relax. 'A routine examination and blood tests. If you've changed your mind come with me and find out for yourself. You know the alternative.'

Unwillingly Lucy got up from the bed and followed the woman out of the door. 'I'm not giving it up, you know,' she said. 'It's mine. And I'm not giving it up.'

Carpenter shrugged. 'I don't remember that you were offered a choice, Lucy,' she said briskly, and moved away down the stairs.

THAT HE WORE the same aftershave as a rapist caused discomfort, and Smythe drove away from the Fitton house without looking at Rosie. After half a mile she said mildly, 'Kim didn't say she thought it was you, just that you wore the same stuff.'

'Stuff?' said Smythe, insult added to injury when he thought of the cost. 'Stuff? You know how much Armani costs?'

'I can guess,' said Rosie. She twitched her nose in his direction. 'Pretty distinctive. Not much chance of her making a mistake, is there?'

'Not much.'

Smythe's mind juggled with discarding the near-full bottle he'd not long opened against the cost to his wallet of changing brands. His wallet won hands down.

Rosie said, 'Who sells it?'

'Boots.'

'That's all?'

'Far as I know. Might be somewhere else I suppose.' He flicked his indicator and turned left into the yard. 'Why?'

'Just wondered.'

Still occupied with the injustices of life, Smythe was

halfway out of the car before the significance of what she'd asked reached his brain. 'Something I plan to check up on before closing time,' he said, as if he'd been intending to do that all along.

'Thought it might be,' said Rosie with a look that let him know she was bluff-proof. 'Must be telepathy.'

DONNELLY HAD BEEN conscious of his groin in a vague, uncomfortable way, for most of the day. An unmistakable sign he needed Molly's services again. Mid-afternoon the urgency peaked. Three times he dialled her number, and three times her answerphone kicked in with a taped thank-you for calling she was busy right now message. His mind twisted itself in tortuous fantasy around the contents of her cupboard, drawing out a fine sweat on his skin.

At his fourth try Molly answered, eyes rolling towards the ceiling when she heard his voice. 'It's been a busy day,' she said. 'Saturdays always are, told you before, money burns a hole in pockets. Not that I'm grumbling, like, more money I have the better.'

He digested that.

'I could manage a bonus,' he said grudgingly.

'Another twenty.'

'Ten.'

'Fifteen.'

Like haggling in a bazaar. The word fifteen stuck in Donnelly's throat.

''Course, if you're not all that bothered, give me a call in a day or so,' Molly said. 'Monday or Tuesday. Should be quiet by then.'

'Fifteen,' said Donnelly. 'Right now?'

'If you make it fast,' said Molly, and put the phone down.

'TURN OFF HERE,' said Darren as the Knottingly exit came up. Skeeter hauled on the wheel and almost sideswiped a

Sierra taking the same exit. The car driver sound a strident horn and put his foot down. 'Oh, right,' said Darren. 'Just what we need—a bleedin' accident.'

'Weren't my fault,' said Skeeter. 'What you expect when you don't say turn until I'm right on it?'

'I don't expect lip, so bloody button it.'

They came off the slip road onto the roundabout in the right-hand lane. 'First exit,' snarled Darren. Skeeter eyed the front end of a tanker looming up in his nearside mirror and didn't even try. 'I said...'

'I'm going round,' said Skeeter. 'Unless you want to argue with him.' He jerked a thumb at the side window. Darren eyed the tanker and shut up as they did a full circuit to get back to the exit he wanted. Skeeter notched up a small victory without knowing why.

Half an hour later Darren had swapped the white Transit for a red Honda with sliding side-doors and a blunt nose. Skeeter transferred their belongings from one to the other stoically. Didn't matter what Darren traded in for, not if it had four wheels and got him home.

LUCY WASN'T all that thrilled with her first sight of Fielding, though she recognised him as the kind of man most women would find attractive. It was something in his eyes that put her off. Chilly—and nosy with it the way he ran his eyes up and down her, like he was weighing her out in a butcher's.

And she didn't like his voice, either, although she couldn't have explained why. Like warm margarine, and it made her uncomfortable. She half turned, looking for the door, but Di Carpenter was standing there, her eyes not much warmer than Fielding's. His voice was brisker the second time he told her to sit down, and her legs moved her forward from old habits of obedience. Her father's image wavered over Fielding's face. She wrapped her hands around the chair's side frame and gripped it tight.

'That's better. Now tell me how many months you've been pregnant.'

Lucy shrugged. 'Seven I s'pose. Dunno.'

'And where's the father?'

She shrugged again. 'Doesn't know I'm having it. What's it matter?' Instead of answering he looked down at the form in front of him, rereading Carpenter's small writing. Lucy shifted uneasily, trying to remember what she'd said that first time about Rollo and other stuff.

'Mrs Carpenter's explained about the examination?'

'S'pose so.'

'I'll take that as a yes. You need to get undressed.' He waved a hand. 'Behind the screen there. Put the gown on and lie on the couch.'

'I don't see...'

'I don't have time to play games. Undress and get on the couch.'

Lucy loosed her hold on the chair and got up unwillingly. 'What you going to do?'

Fielding fixed his eyes on Carpenter. 'I thought you'd told her.'

'I told her about the examination, not the process. It didn't seem necessary at the time.'

Lucy looked from one to the other. Fielding turned his eyes to her. 'I'll be taking blood samples and examining you internally. You know what that means?'

'Yeah—you want to feel me up.'

'Crude, but accurate,' he said without emotion. 'It's necessary, not exciting. The couch is over there,' he waved a dismissive hand and broke eye contact. A cold, hard pebble of ice seemed to sink through Lucy's body, the baby kicking as it passed. She went behind the screen and undressed, then sat on the edge of the couch, waiting for him to come.

TWENTY-TWO

LUCY WAS BACK in her room, relieved of pushing round the tea trolley and told to rest. After five minutes spent lying on her bed feeling sorry for herself because of the indignities of Fielding's probing and bony fingers, boredom reasserted itself. She turned on the television and found two channels occupied with sport, flicked to another and found jungle-weary men ducking bullets. Desperate, she tried the final station and found racing from Kempton Park.

She swung her legs from the bed in disgust and went to her only other link with the world, the window that occupied so much of her time.

In the field that abutted The Cedars grounds, a dozen black and white Fresians were moving together, not pausing to graze as they went. She looked at the sky, searching for rain clouds and found none. Down at the field's bottom the cows stopped, still clumped together and uneasy. One lifted its head and lowed, the sound coming back to her faintly.

Still puzzled, her eyes went back to that part of the field they had left, where the tall hawthorne hedge ran solidly in a barrier. Just as they had done before, her eyes picked up a whisper of pink that when she focused closely was no longer there, and despite the warmth of the room she shivered.

SMYTHE FOUND HIMSELF wishing he'd remembered the old adage of never volunteer—that way he'd have been saved the sight of Barrett's smug grin.

'You remember where you were that morning, I suppose,' said Barrett. 'Better get it on record before someone asks questions. Might be you'll need to produce some body fluids too.'

'Ha ha,' Smythe said stiffly. 'That's a joke?'

'Think about it,' said Barrett. 'Think what a clever brief could do in court.'

'I wouldn't be in court. Not my case.'

'You could be called if it came out in evidence.'

'If it does I'll comply—if it doesn't my body fluids stay where they are.'

Barrett's grin broadened. 'Scared you might run out?'

'I can recognise a wind-up. I thought I'd get round the stockists before closing time, find out how much is sold locally. It's probably a lot, but if I get some comparison figures for other brands it'll give us percentages to work on.'

'Get on with it then, it's time we saw some movement.'

Smythe turned on his heel, dreaming a familiar dream that one day the dice would fall his way and leave Barrett looking a fool. Door half open, he turned and looked back. 'I'll get a computer check done. Might be a known sex offender wears the stuff.'

'Good thought,' said Barrett blandly. 'Get a few more and you might make a detective.'

THE VOLVO had turned and pulled in near the kerb, automatic transmission idling quietly, its driver's eyes intent on Molly's front door. When Donnelly came out pink and satisfied he gave no more than a cursory look up and down the street before stepping off the pavement. To his right the Volvo's engine note rose, but even with the accelerator foot-flattened to the floor, the sound wasn't enough to bring inquisitive eyes to windows fast enough to see the big car hit Donnelly full on. First the solid connection of the bull-bar, then the front of the bonnet, tossing him as a black bull tosses a matador, a limp and bloody rag doll coming fast to earth, smacking onto tarmac and not moving.

By the time Molly, still holding the door open, had got her wits together, the car had turned a corner and gone out of her sight. She didn't go to Donnelly's aid. Above the sickness at the pit of her stomach and the shock of what she'd seen, self-preservation rose strongly. She closed the door and dialled 999, impatient to shower and rid herself of Donnelly's odour. Not until she'd done that and dressed in everyday clothes did she look at the street again. Another car had stopped by then, half slewed across the road, its driver and four of her neighbours staring down at Donnelly in morbid fascination.

Molly wondered dispassionately if the priest were dead, only half surprised that the idea gave her more pleasure than pain, and that thought still in her head when the first police car arrived with an ambulance bare seconds behind.

GROUPS OF YOUTHS were gathering again and Habib was getting desperate. His pleadings had got ten elders out, touring trouble spots, talking to sullen-faced young men and trying to persuade them to move on. A few did, but the majority simply listened with stony faces, or called the elders old men afraid to stand up for their rights. Not even the Mullah could persuade the hard core of protestors to budge.

Outside the police station the jeering crowd had hardly changed in number since the trouble began, and as one youth tired, another seemed magically to appear to take his place.

Osgodby went out to face them again, flanked by a pair of wary-looking PCs, and tried to enter into conversation with the front-runners. It was a waste of time that gained nothing except an egg spattering against his left shoulder.

He eyed the protesters sourly, and not for the first time

speculated on whether or not the youths would still be there without reporters and camera crew to spur them on to greater efforts.

Before seven, riot police were on the streets again, facing off the hostile groups but keeping their distance, none of them wanting to be first to spark another night of trouble.

On Brook Street a pair of thirteen-year-olds playing an opportunist card smashed the window of an electrical store, running off with two video recorders, but getting no more than a hundred yards before a Panda car cut off their progress.

Morrissey, on his way back to Mike's bedside after a four-hour break, scarcely gave any of it a glance.

BARRETT HAD DINED on warmed-up Cornish pastie, oven chips and baked beans, standard bachelor fare for him unless he called in at the takeaway on his way home. He was still pushing a piece of bread around the plate, mopping up juices when the phone rang, and sent him back to work. By then it was coming up nine o'clock and some of the town centre streets had been closed to traffic, making his route to the police yard circuitous.

The crowd outside the front doors had grown, one window was broken, and metal security grids had been lowered inside the ground-floor windows. While he waited for the seldom-used gate to be opened, ungentle fists pounded the roof of his car.

When the gate slid back he drove inside fast, fuming at the thought of dents in his bodywork.

Rosie was on her own at the information desk, not apprehensive exactly, but wary as the noises outside alternately peaked and ebbed. The look she gave Barrett was distracted.

'I didn't know whether to call you on it or not,' she said.

'But if I'd let it go and there was a connection I'd have been in lumber, wouldn't I?'

'A pile of it,' said Barrett and didn't grin. 'Where's the file?'

'Upstairs. I put it on your desk. Everybody thinks it was a hit and run.'

He nodded and took the stairs with more energy than he had available, out of breath when he got to the top. That both disconcerted him and made him aware that the midriff he'd rid himself of a year ago, was creeping back.

Sighing, he let himself thump into his desk chair and began to read the reports of Donnelly's death. Hit and run, nothing else it could be, and the reports of both Panda crew and accident investigation officer confirming it.

No question to be raised about cause, but a lot to be answered on who, and why. He glanced at Morrissey's desk. To see it empty wasn't a new experience, but the sound of the chanting crowd drifting in through the part-open window brought the reason for its present bareness vividly to mind. He brought his eyes back to the reports and stared at them moodily.

Without Donnelly's tenuous link to the Mandy Sheard murder, would this particular hit and run demand more of his attention than any other road death—or would it have been left to uniform to track down what were probably joy riders?

What would Morrissey do?

Barrett's mind fumbled possibilities. Last thing he could afford to be seen doing was chasing duff hares.

Even so...

He sighed, then made his decision. Impossible to let the man's death lie torpid without digging deeper into Donnelly's background and the affairs of St Ursula's, especially when the one eye-witness said the car had accelerated into Donnelly, rather than tried to avoid him.

Not tonight though, with every ambulant officer out on the streets. He put the folder in his drawer and turned the key.

Across the landing in the big CID room, Woods was keeping lone vigil, mind engrossed in Sonic Hedgehog and near jumping a mile when Barrett came up behind him and asked unkindly if Woods's paperwork were up to date. The DC took his thumbs off the buttons and put the electronic game away.

'What do you do on night shift?' Woods said cockily. 'Bring a bird in? What you here for, anyway, something up?'

'Donnelly, St Ursula's, Lucy Walton and The Cedars Nursing Home, plus profiles of the people who run it. Anything you can find, on my desk when I come in tomorrow morning. Should save you being bored.'

Woods looked stricken and Barrett got a glow of satisfaction. Time the cocky little blighter learned who was boss.

SKEETER WAS BACK HOME in the bosom of his family, his mother glad to see him, his father as non-committal as ever in even acknowledging him as his own. He eyed the pile of belongings distastefully. 'You planning on stopping then?'

'Course he is, don't ask daft questions,' said Skeeter's mother. 'Be nice to have him here, what with our Gavin being locked up.'

'Locked up?' said Skeeter, going slack-mouthed again.

'Still talks like a bloody parrot,' said his father, and walked away.

'He got mixed up with them two from Quebec Street. They was larking around and this old age pensioner got knifed.'

'Shit,' said Skeeter, and wondered if he'd have been better off staying with Darren.

THE THREE NIGHTS of unrest had affected Willie's trade too, small-time dealers who usually came around nightly stayed away, street-corner and shop-doorway peddling turned hazardous by roaming youths and alert police. Eddie fared better: he'd moved his girls a half-mile out of town and managed to increase trade by doing it. Being Eddie, he managed to convince himself it was an astute business decision and not sheer necessity that brought about his extra profits.

Around ten o'clock Saturday night he sent Sam around to Willie's place, with what he hoped would be enough money to ensure an easy transaction. The money was tempting. Willie looked at it and thought about how it would make up for a few lost sales. Almost he reached out to pluck it from Sam's fingers. Almost. Only then his stubbornness set in.

'If I say Eddie comes to collect for himself, than he comes to collect for himself,' he said, and slammed the door in Sam's face again. Sam lifted his foot and tried kicking it in, but Willie shoved home the security bolts, and with those in place the door was too thick and solid to give way.

'He'll not be pleased,' Sam yelled at the door. 'Not pleased at all. You going to end up like that bloody stereo.'

'Piss off,' Willie yelled back. 'He wants the goods he can fetch 'em, he knows the rules.'

'You're dead, mate,' said Sam, with venomous hope that Eddie would see it the same way.

DARREN HAD RENTED a bedsit over a newsagent's shop on Park Street, the room L-shaped, with a bed in the short leg and the rest of its meagre furnishings in the long. Across the short landing a micro-sized bathroom threatened claustrophobia every time he went in.

Saturday night he kept away from the town centre and went into the Crown, looking to pull a skirt, hair slicked, and a good dose of fancy aftershave to show he didn't skimp on price. When the redhead sashayed up he'd thought he was into a good thing. With a leer that passed for a smile he bought her a drink and went into his chat-up routine. From the look on her face she swallowed it whole.

A second drink and a bit of surreptitious hands-on under the table told him the time was right. He told her what he fancied, and she told him her price.

Incensed he wouldn't be getting the freebie he'd expected, he called her a bloody whore, and knocked her glass over as he left. The word she screamed after him stayed with him all the way to the Rose and Thistle.

He drew a blank there too.

At two o'clock on Sunday morning, spilling out onto the pavement with the rest of the crowd from Romeo's and still on his own, he began to recognise that there'd been hidden advantages in dragging Skeeter around. He stuffed his hands into his pockets and started back to Park Street.

Passing the now dark and shuttered Crown he met a prostitute who'd given up for the night and was heading home. Flat-eyed, he took in the short red leather skirt and skimpy scoop-necked top and wondered where she stashed her takings.

Five busy minutes later, in the Crown's side alley, his hand tight on the woman's neck, and her bruised eyes dark and wide in the moonlight, he found out.

TWENTY-THREE

LUCY DREAMED she was ten and back at home, then Mandy appeared and Lucy got out of bed, almost close enough to reach out and touch when Mandy turned away and went out the door. Puzzled, Lucy followed, the linoleum cold as it always had been in the old terrace house. Across the landing, the door to her stepfather's room stretched and took on gigantic proportions. A familiar fear came back, that it might open and she'd be pulled into the big bed that smelled of stale sweat and spilled seed. Then door and fear vanished and she was back in The Cedars, with Mandy disappearing through the connecting door that separated the attic corridor into two halves.

When the dream fragmented Lucy opened her eyes expecting to be in bed, but instead found herself close to the door she'd been dreaming about. She reached a tentative hand to touch the solidity of wood.

Shivering and confused Lucy padded back to her room and crawled under the duvet, the pillow clasped in her arms for comfort until she fell asleep again.

DAWN HAD COME EARLY, the sky changing from midnight velvet into morning blue silk, and Morrissey had watched it change through the tall hospital window, standing there, hands in pant's pockets and stiff from sitting.

When a thrush sang he closed his ears. Time enough to take in such celebration of life if and when he learned he would still have a son.

Memories hung heavy in his head. A year ago the bed Mike now lay in had held another boy whose father had paced and sworn and bargained for with a non-existent God.

Like bargaining with smoke.

He shifted restlessly, a long line of grieving faces passing through his mind like ghosts at a festival of death. They were all looking, staring at him, as they felt the impact of his words fragment their lives. He could not remember all the doors he'd knocked on, or count how many hopes and dreams and prayers he'd ended. But with Mike in the bed behind him he really knew, felt for the first time, the pain of the mothers, fathers, sons, daughters, after the shock of his coming wore off.

Eyes sore from lack of sleep, he watched a porter wheel a covered trolley down the mortuary path. One of the hospital cats fled from its coming, streaking across the grass as if the devil were after it.

Except if there were no God there was no place for a devil either.

Despite the heat of the room his bones felt chilled. The thrush began to sing again, louder this time, nothing tentative about its song. A flock of starlings rose from a group of tall trees, circled once, then went in search of food. The thrush sang on, and this time he couldn't close it out of his mind. God's work and the devil's work. How was he supposed to separate them?

Evil existed. He'd felt it. Been close to it, eyeball to eyeball, seen it looking out of a killer's eyes, recognised it in the death rictus of innocents and felt rage at its power.

Exhausted, he turned from the window and went back to the bed. When he took up Mike's hand again his heart broke open, and stumbling over the strangeness of the words, he began to pray.

BARRETT KNEW from bitter experience that a day which began unpromisingly tended to get worse as it aged, and

Sunday had begun with a flat tyre on his way in. A bad enough omen on its own without finding Osgodby waiting for him when he got there. Unheard of on a Sunday morning.

'No slur on your ability,' Osgodby said uncomfortably, 'but I'm not top of the tree. The message that's come down is I borrow an inspector if the DCI is gone more than a week. A DS as senior officer with all this going on doesn't wash. We're not there yet—this is advance warning.'

'Appreciated, sir,' Barrett said stiffly.

'I know what you're thinking—you're thinking you've got your inspector's exams behind you so what's the problem. Right?'

'Something on those lines, sir.'

'Chief Inspector Morrissey reminded me of the same thing a week or so back. I passed his views on to the CC.'

Gratification stirred. 'Thank you, sir.'

'You thought of applying for anything outside the division?'

'I've thought about it, but that's as far as it's gone.' He shifted his weight, one foot to the other and back again. 'I suppose I'm not ready to move on yet, sir.'

'Feels like home.'

'I suppose so. Yes.'

'Happy to stay at sergeant's rank.'

'No, sir. Not for long.'

'So what's the solution?'

'I haven't found it yet.'

'But you're looking?'

Uneasily, wondering where it was all leading, Barrett said, 'Yes, sir.'

'I'll let the CC know that.'

Barrett's neck grew hot. He debated whether or not he was being invited to move on. Subtly. Uncertainty kept him silent.

'Nothing to add?'

'Only about the cases.'

'You've got movement?'

'Might be some—a bit tenuous though. I need a warrant countersigning to find out.'

'For what?'

Barrett heard wariness and felt a rise of resentment. 'To go through Donnelly's office at St Ursula's,' he told Osgodby bluntly. 'And no, before you ask I'm not sure there's a connection, but it's the closest we've got to one so far. Sir.'

'I suppose you've tried asking the man direct questions?' Osgodby said, sarcasm surfacing. 'Warrants need justifying. If this is a stab in the dark I'd be hard put to get you one.'

'I think Mandy Sheard stayed at the refuge before her death. Nothing concrete. More a feeling he's been holding something back… Held something back,' Barret corrected.

'Clarify that,' said Osgodby. 'Out with it.'

'Donnelly was killed in a hit and run, yesterday, and like the DCI, I don't believe in coincidences.'

'Witnesses?'

'One. According to her the car picked up speed before it hit. Male driver, no passengers.' Barrett shifted his feet again, uneasy in the Chief Superintendent's presence. 'I want to get a couple of uniforms out there this morning, sir. We need to knock on doors and see if anybody's being shy.'

'And the warrant? I seem to remember you went through his files once already.'

'I went through what he *said* were his files. There's no guarantee he hadn't moved the one I was looking for to another drawer—or anywhere else for that matter, sir.'

'Let me think about it a bit. Get your house-to-house going and then come back up.'

'Sir,' said Barrett, trying to free the word from resentment but not quite succeeding. Osgodby watched him go and thought about Beckett's empty desk—and how well Barrett might fill the chair.

LUCY COULDN'T DECIDE if she'd had a particularly bad dream during the night, or if she really had got out of bed and walked along the corridor. Wasn't as if she'd ever sleep-walked before in her life—except that time when she was ten. And there'd been a reason for that—not that her mother believed her. Or wanted to. She tried to cram the memory back into its box but it kept crowding out again, along with the words like wicked, and liar, and other things that trailed behind like dirty strings.

'You breathe one word outside this house and I'll flay your backside. What your dad will say when I tell him, I don't know.' Lucy shivered. What her dad had done was put her in the coal bunker, soon as her mother had gone out to play bingo.

She remembered the dark, and the sharp edges of coke, and the spiders who lived in there crawling across her legs, and her screaming that if he let her out she'd never never tell again.

Bastard!

She brushed her teeth, scrubbing them hard, rinsing her mouth again and again to rid herself of a metallic taste that was only imagination, until finally, hunger got the better of her and she left the toothbrush alone and went out onto the landing. The door she'd dreamed of was to the right of the staircase, along a stump of corridor. Until then it hadn't excited her curiosity—logic told her it led into the other half of the house, and having seen no one but Mrs C use it, she'd accepted it led to her private apartment.

She went three steps down, then came back up and went

to the door, touching it with her fingers as she had in her dream. If it *was* a dream.

The wood felt familiar.

She put her ear up close and listened carefully. A faint rattle of crockery came back. There, that proved it. Mrs C's place. Chiding herself for foolishness, she came away and went in search of breakfast.

TED ALWAYS GOT his milk float round the council estate as fast as he could. Not that the estate itself bothered him, or the people, but dogs were a different matter. Dogs didn't like him and he wasn't over fond of them. If he got his round done fast he could be on the last street before any got let out—and that's what kept his feet moving.

He was coming up at a fast trot to thirty-three Denton, when Skeeter, used to getting up early at the fairground, let himself out of his parent's house, and the quick, pale-eyed look he gave Ted held nothing, no curiosity, no interest, no recognition, but for Ted, recognition startled his bones.

As did the uneasy realisation that he'd never told the police about the Transit that near ran him off the road the morning Kim Fitton was raped.

WHEN BARRETT GOT downstairs Rosie was on duty in the front office again, trying to keep busy but feeling bored. He put his head in the door as he went by and said, 'Thanks for the call.' Her face brightened.

'Any good?'

'Worth coming in for. It was good thinking on your part.'

Pink crept up her neck. 'There was something else I noticed, too. I think he might have just been leaving the witness's house.'

Barrett moved into the office and perched one buttock on a table, fascinated by the slow-creeping pink tide.

'Wouldn't she have said?'

'Not if she was worried about getting in trouble. Molly's a working girl.'

Barrett kept his eyes on her, thoughtfully. 'You sure about that?'

'There was a rumpus eighteen months ago that got called in as a domestic. Willis and I were closest. I pulled the file if you want it?'

'Awkward client?'

'She'd had a right going over. It's all in the file.'

He held out his hand.

'Top drawer, cabinet to your right,' she said without moving. He grinned and found it for himself.

'What about follow-ups?'

'No point. She refused to say who he was—probably accepts it as a job hazard, she's been at it a long time.'

'I'll borrow this,' said Barrett, raising the file. 'And thanks.'

'Any time,' said Rosie as he went out the door, and added, 'Once a dogsbody always a dogsbody,' under her breath.

JULIE WADDLE had taken a long time to drag herself home after her meeting with Darren in the alley, and it had been an effort to climb into the bath and soak away some of her pain. When Eddie came round later that morning to get his share of the take, her face stood testimony to the fact she'd had a rough night. He eyed the bruises and swelling, then said roughly, 'You been to the police?'

'Oh, yeah,' she mumbled, grimacing at the jaw movement. 'I'd do that wouldn't I? Get banged up for soliciting after taking this lot. What do you think I am—stupid?'

'Lucky,' said Eddie. 'Who was it?'

'How the hell do I know? He didn't leave his card.'

'Not a regular.'

'Never seen him before. Sodding lunatic! Look what he did.' She lifted her chin and turned her head so he saw Darren's throttling fingermarks, then opened her peignoir to show the purpling contusions that had been his parting gift.

'You got a good look at him though,' said Eddie. 'I mean you'd know him if you saw him again.'

'Too right,' she closed the robe up and felt in its pocket for cigarettes. 'Not that I want to.'

'So tell me what he looks like,' said Eddie, 'because I want to see him real bad.'

SINCE PAULA WILLIAMSON went home the three single rooms on the short corridor had remained empty, but Sunday morning when Lucy took her trolley around there was a new name on the patient list. Jane Allen, and when she knocked on the door and took in a jug of iced water the face that looked up at her from the easy chair was that of the woman she'd seen in the waiting room a week ago. And it looked just as sour as it had then. Lucy set the fresh water-jug down and picked up the old.

'Next time you knock—wait until I say you can come in. One of the benefits of paying through the nose is supposed to be privacy. Remember that.' Like pure acid.

Lucy went out without speaking—the effort almost choking her. Boiling with unsaid words she gave the trolley a savage shove. It skittered ahead of her and careened into the bottom door, glasses and jugs rattling like breaking windows.

Lucy picked up speed and set the trolley to rights again, mopping spilled water and feeling sheepish. Good job the end room was empty.

She turned the knob to have a quick look inside, found it locked and flattened her ear against it, listening. Silence. Sighing, she delivered the last two jugs and went back to the kitchen. Mrs C was in there, reading the *Sun* and drinking coffee. When the trolley rolled in she lifted her eyes and turned them on Lucy.

'Finished?'

'Yeah. Don't think much to that new patient. Who's she think she is? Lady Muck?'

Carpenter turned her attention back to the newspaper without answering. Lucy started to manoeuvre past then stopped again.

'Does she know what her baby's going to be as well, like Mrs Williamson did?'

'Why do you want to know?'

'No reason,' said Lucy, giving the trolley another shove. 'Just wondered.'

TWENTY-FOUR

WHEN LUCY went back upstairs hot and sticky, intent on ridding herself of the damp uniform dress, the communicating door was ajar. It was a temptation she couldn't leave unexplored. Hand on its knob she pushed the door, cheek pressed against the jamb as the gap widened and let her see the corridor beyond. Two doors in the right-hand wall, a third facing and half open so she could see flowers on a round table. Vaguely disappointed, she puzzled over what it was she'd expected to see.

Just went to Mrs C's place like she'd thought it would. She turned away and caught a flash of pink from her eye corner, but when she looked again the corridor was empty, and no pink in sight.

BARRETT, pessimism returned, expected to be refused the warrant, but Osgodby surprised him and came through with it, grumbling all the while about the difficulties of doing such things on a Sunday. Barrett, tail up like a squirrel, headed for St Ursula's with Smythe and tried to find someone who'd admit they were in charge. The nearest he came was a tight-curled woman named Christine Brookbank, who stared at him uneasily and denied she was in charge of anything.

'Well if you're not, who is?' he said tightly, running out of patience as fast as he was running out of ways to ask the same question. He fingered the leather key case that had been found in Donnelly's pocket, and now resided in his own, and fought with an urge to walk past the woman and open up the office for himself. 'Don't tell me he had no deputy. Somebody must have run the place when he took holidays.'

'He was very dedicated,' she said. 'It's hard to explain. Oh dear! I don't know what we're going to do now, none of us on the committee have time to take St Ursula's on. *I* certainly haven't.' She stopped talking and looked at him as if she'd forgotten why he was there. Light dawned. 'His office,' she said. 'That's what you want, isn't it? His office! Let me see if I can find the keys.' Then the lost look came back and she started to turn away.

'I'll try these,' Barrett said, sliding Donnelly's bunch out of the clear plastic envelope he'd carried them in and walking past her. She half turned but didn't try to stop his progress.

'Funny set-up,' said Smythe. 'If the rest of the committee are like her, he'll have had it all his own way. I doubt she'd have noticed if he'd been running a brothel.'

'Be a good cover for one,' said Barrett, 'but he wouldn't have needed to go to Molly's then, would he?'

'Might have got tired of home-brew,' said Smythe cheerfully. 'Thought he'd spice it up a bit. What's a priest doing into that sort of stuff anyway?'

Barrett tried another key. 'What sort of stuff?'

'S&M. Kinky stuff. Molly's speciality.'

Barrett scowled at the keys then transferred the look to Smythe. 'If she's running a disorderly house…'

'She's solo, the johns come word of mouth. I remember her from when I was on the beat. She stood…'

'I know. Woolworth's corner. I've heard. Sure she hasn't got a pimp?'

'Never had one then, and I can't see her starting now when she's old bones,' he said as Barrett found the right key. He followed the DS into the office and shut the door behind them. 'You think she was in on it?'

'In on what?' said Barrett. 'We haven't established there's anything to be in on, have we?'

Smythe gave a half-shrug. 'Thought that's why we're here.'

'We're here to find a tie-in with Mandy Sheard,' said Barrett moving to the four-drawer file cabinet. 'I'm not convinced she never stayed here. Molly can wait. Let's get on with it shall we, it's Sunday and I'd like to get home before midnight.'

So would he, thought Smythe who had a hot date, and did as he was told.

SKEETER KEPT remembering the way Ted had looked at him, funny, like they knew each other, not a friendly look but more like Skeeter'd nicked a bottle of milk and Ted wanted paying for it. He hadn't. Or at least—not in a bit. It nagged him through his walk, and it nagged him through breakfast.

'How long you had that milkman, Ma?' he said through a loosely full mouth. Wet crumbs spattered on his plate. Some hit the tablecloth.

'I dunno. Years. What for?'

'Nuthin', just gave me a funny look is all.'

She watched yellow egg-dribble carry a crumb down his chin and said nothing. Skeeter had been getting funny looks since he was born.

'Like I owed him something.'

'What you and that Darren been getting up to?'

'Nuthin'—if we had done I'd know what was matter, wouldn't I? Anyway, he hasn't been round here has he, not for a long time.'

'And good riddance to bad rubbish. Don't know why you ever started going round with him, nasty piece like that.'

Skeeter thought about telling her that putting up with somebody you didn't like was better than being pasted round the walls. Half opened his mouth ready to do it until he looked at his father, remembered a few homecomings, and decided his mother knew enough about it already.

'Thought I might go see Gary,' he said.

'What for?' his father growled. 'Dunno what I done to get you two. Slack Alice and a bleedin' thug.' He eyed his wife malevolently and she avoided his eyes.

'Save me going then, if you go,' she told Skeeter. 'Tell him I'll be up next visiting.'

'Yeah,' said Skeeter. 'I'll tell him he's bloody daft as well, getting caught.'

TED BLESSED the fact it was Sunday and near to no traffic on Malminster's roads. Milk floats and sidewinds from heavy sixteen-wheelers weren't a happy mix. He left the float outside the police station and pushed in through the heavy doors. Rosie was glad to see him come in. Sunday mornings behind the desk were too quiet for her liking, even a complaint about kids pinching milk would be better than nothing. Ted said, 'It's about that rape on Maple Drive, three weeks back, I've remembered something.'

Rosie flicked through her memory. 'You reported it, didn't you?' she said. 'I remember you coming in to make a statement. There isn't anybody available in CID, can you make do with me?'

'Any day,' said Ted, gallantly. 'You're better looking than he was.' Rosie let herself smile, and went to find someone to look after the desk. When she came back a couple of minutes later he was busy reading anti-crime posters on the noticeboard. 'Amazing what some folks get up to, isn't it?' he said.

'We get used to it,' said Rosie. 'Do you want to come through here?' She opened the door to the outside interview room and let Ted go in first. 'There's no tape recorder in here so I'll take what you have to say down by hand, then type it up for you to sign. Is that all right?'

'Whatever you say, love. Might be nothing but a load of rubbish anyway.' He sat himself on one of the hard chairs, then got back up again until Rosie sat down. 'Nearly forgot me manners for a minute there,' he said. 'Sorry.'

Rosie smiled again, and didn't tell him that manners usually got left on the other side of the door.

'Suppose you tell me exactly what it is you've remembered,' she said. 'I'm sure it must be important or you wouldn't have felt a need to come.' His fingers, curled in and bunched on the table, relaxed.

'It was this Transit, you see,' he said. 'I'd forgot about it. Nearly ran me off the road. Then I saw him again this morning and it brought it all back.'

'Saw who?' said Rosie, pen poised.

'Him that was driving it. Nearly as close as I am to you we was, and it brought it all back, blooming maniac. And I can tell you something else about him as well,' he said triumphantly. 'I can tell you where he lives.'

WHEN LUCY CAME OUT of her room in her clean uniform dress, the connecting door was still part open. Curiosity fought reluctance and won. If Mrs C came she'd tell her it was open and she wondered where it went. Honest truth, so what was wrong with that? She took a hold of the knob and opened the door fully. No one came running to stop her, the corridor beyond stayed quiet. She took a couple of steps with slow caution then threw such consideration to the wind, moving at her usual rush until she reached the first of the two doors.

Behind it was a room much like her own save for the fact that it had an internal door, set in the left-hand wall and inviting inspection. The bit now well between her teeth, Lucy looked.

A bathroom.

So what had she expected? she asked herself. Dracula's bleedin' coffin? If Mrs C kept that hanging round it'd be down the cellar, not up here. This'd be where her friends got to sleep when they came visiting. Satisfied with her own explanation she closed both doors behind her and headed for the next.

That was different. Lucy stood in the doorway and stared. The bed in here was one of the high, hospital beds like she'd seen in the delivery room downstairs, with slots for the metal poles with their dangling straps that she tried to avoid thinking about. Over on the right-hand wall a baby's incubator stood empty and lined up next to it a wheeled stand held two stainless steel bowls. This room, too, had a door in the left wall which, like the other, opened into a bathroom, the only difference being that his one held a sluice sink. Lucy shivered without knowing why, closed the door and turned back towards the corridor. The other room might be for Mrs C's friends but this one wasn't and its discovery bothered her.

Only reason she could see why they'd want a room like this up in the attics was if Mrs C and her boss didn't want anyone to know who was in here. Wasn't no other explanation was there?

Formica-topped drawers and cupboards stretched either side of the bathroom door. Lucy explored their contents and found only dressing packs, sanitary towels, clean linen and babies napkins that she supposed would be found in any such room. The innocence of content didn't reassure her. She was looking out of the window when Diana Carpenter came into the room behind her and said, 'What the hell are you doing in here, Lucy?' in a voice that could have fried an onion. Jumping as her stomach curled and the baby kicked, Lucy turned around and faced the other woman.

'The door was open,' she said. 'I thought I'd have a look what was down here. Thought it just went to your place.'

'It does. Except for this room and the one before it. You've already been in there I suppose?'

'Thought it was probably for your friends. When they come to stop—you know?'

'It is.'

Lucy eyed the closed face.

'This one isn't though—couldn't decide about this.'

'What did you think it might be for?'

'Dunno.' Lucy shrugged. 'Was trying to work it out when you come in.'

'It's very close to your own room isn't it, Lucy?'

'Yes.'

'Do you remember my telling you that if you decided to have your baby here I'd be delivering it?'

'Yeah—and I said I hadn't made my mind up. Still haven't. Got plenty of time yet.'

'This is where the baby would be born. We can't use the private patients' rooms, or tie up the downstairs delivery rooms, so we chose to provide this instead. Other babies have been born in here, yours wouldn't be the first.'

'How many?'

'That isn't your business.'

'Don't suppose it is,' said Lucy and moved away from the window. Carpenter backed up against the door, blocking Lucy's way out.

'It's time I took the dinner things out.'

'Lunch,' Carpenter corrected automatically.

'Whatever.'

'You have less time than you think to decide in,' said Carpenter. 'Mr Fielding thinks you're on the eight-month mark.'

'So?' Another shrug. 'Still gives me a month doesn't it?'

'Babies often come early.'

'Mine won't. Can I go now?'

'Decide before Wednesday, Lucy, or we'll have to make other arrangements.' Carpenter moved away from the door and opened it. Lucy started through, then stopped and said, 'Why Wednesday?'

'Because that's when Mr Fielding will want to see you again.'

'That's nice for him,' said Lucy, marching out. ''Cos I mightn't want to see *him* again at all!'

THE THING BARRETT noticed as he drove back to the station with Smythe was that Malminster's streets looked almost normal. There were still groups of youths, both Asian and white, hanging around in open areas and looking for action, but none of them appeared prepared to start it. Police in normal uniform patrolled uneasily in twos, but there was no heavy presence that might provoke reaction, and the vans that held reinforcements were parked discretely out of sight along side streets and back streets, their occupants broiling in oven interiors.

Even the crowd outside the station's front door had thinned, although that had more to do with a loss of media interest than a wish for peace. Like football hooligans, Barrett thought. Turn the spotlight away and they drift off to other mischief. Like dropping concrete blocks from motorway bridges.

Osgodby, standing at an upstairs front window, had been having much the same thoughts, although his had drifted to Morrissey, and the random carelessness with which fate chose its victims. When he saw Barrett turn into the yard he moved away, and was sitting in Morrissey's desk chair waiting to be briefed when the DS came into the office. They eyed each other with mutual suspicion.

'Find what you expected to find then?' asked Osgodby.

'Not exactly, sir,' said Barrett. 'But it's been helpful.'

He eyed Rosie's report in the middle of his desk and put his briefcase down deliberately on top of it.

'Plan on telling me, then?'

'He seems to have paid more into his bank account than I would have expected, given his job,' Barrett said. 'It's something I need to look into tomorrow. If the amounts he paid in were in cash it'll be a waste of time, but if there's any cheques involved it might help find the source.'

'Even priests get paid,' said the Chief Superintendent dryly.

'Not in these amounts,' said Barrett, and handed him a pass-book. Osgodby's eyebrows went up. 'As you say, not exactly pocket money, is it? Any thoughts?'

'Not yet,' Barrett admitted. 'Payment of some kind. I'd like to find out what and why.'

'Well, what motive could Donnelly have had to kill Sheard if that's what you're thinking? Priests drink, gamble and whore, but they don't kill.'

'Sir, I promise, as soon as I get a glimmer of what it is he's been up to, I'll brief you on it.'

'Make sure you do,' said the Chief Superintendent, pushing up from the chair and wondering if he could still get a round of golf in. 'I'd hate to find I'd sanctioned that warrant for nothing.'

'Yes, sir,' said Barrett glumly, knowing if it turned out that way he'd never be allowed to forget.

TWENTY-FIVE

DIANA CARPENTER watched Lucy walk away from her with a feeling of regret. For some reason the girl's determined will not to be told what to do had raised a reluctant liking. Not something she could afford, or that Fielding would accept. Lucy would have to toe the line one way or another, and whichever way it went, the outcome would be the same.

By the time Lucy reached the connecting door Carpenter was already half turned away, snapping her head back in Lucy's direction only when her brain threw up a vivid hallucination that two people in pink were leaving the corridor, not one. For a second Carpenter caught herself holding her breath at the reality of the red-haired woman who followed Lucy so closely. But when she blinked the image was gone, and the only pink garment in sight was Lucy's uniform.

Her right hand found the comforting shape of a Benson & Hedges pack in her pocket, and she lit up, inhaling deeply, eyes still fixed on the connecting door. Whatever reason her brain might have had for playing tricks, one thing she was quite sure of—ghosts had no existence outside of fiction.

WITH OSGODBY out of the room, Barrett shifted his briefcase and started skimming Rosie's report, wandering with it over to the big wall map of Malminster as he read, tracing the route a Transit might have taken to get from the Fitton house to the junction where Ted and his milk float had near come to grief. It wasn't a direct route, but that meant nothing, a rapist with half a brain would know not to park outside the home of his victim.

The weight of Donnelly's keys in his pocket reminded him he still wanted to talk to Molly, and he was loathe to delegate either that or the Transit follow-up to Smythe. If Copeland hadn't been seconded on the blasted course this week…

If Morrissey were here…

If they weren't an inspector short…

If, if, if.

Irritably he recognised his hunger, and that Smythe was already in the canteen stuffing his face. Two years ago it would have been him, responsibility ended when he got within sniffing range of fried food. Expectantly his nostrils twitched and widened. Despite the heat of the day the thought of a bacon butty sent saliva flooding his mouth.

There were advantages to being low in the ranks. He remembered Beckett's perforated ulcer, and Morrissey's long-running battle with acidity, wondering gloomily if his own digestion would go the same way.

He sighed and went downstairs, stopping by the duty room to ask if he could borrow Rosie again, and then briefing Smythe in the canteen on what questions to ask Molly. Smythe grinned. 'I can think of a few more I might ask while I'm in there. Want me to tell you the answers when I come back?'

'WPC Quinn will be there,' Barrett said, attempting to damp down Smythe's imagination. 'I doubt she'd be over-thrilled at hearing male fantasies first-hand.'

'Why not?' said Smythe. 'She's started a few.'

'When you're ready,' Barrett said coldly. 'And don't even think about going home until you've been debriefed. I doubt you'll learn anything new, but there's always that chance.' He lifted his butty in both hands and bit savagely.

One day Smythe would really come unstuck, and the DS couldn't wait for it to happen.

SKEETER GOT to the secure unit just as they were letting visitors in, and felt his neck stiffen as the door slammed shut behind him. He supposed Gary was hearing doors shut all the time now. The thought came that if Darren ever got caught for the stuff he'd been up to, he'd take Skeeter down with him, and he tried to imagine what it would be like to be locked up in prison for a long time. Lurid film clips ran through his head and mixed with Darren's fumbled attempt at buggery in the back of the Transit. His stomach bunched and his knees went loose at the thought that in a shared prison cell there'd be no escape.

And then he remembered sex offenders were kept separate from other prisoners, because of what the regular inmates did to them. Darren'd be kept separate, but not him, he'd be left to take his chances. Resentment at what he'd been dragged into boiled up. Then he found Gary had a room to himself, not a cell but a room, and seemed to think the place was a holiday home. It wasn't fair. Before he could stop it the stuff about Darren raping the women churned up out of him, along with the post office they'd robbed on the way home. Gary listened with wide eyes. He'd never have thought Skeeter had it in him.

'You don't tell anybody,' Skeeter told him uneasily, realising he'd probably made the biggest mistake of his life.

'Course not,' said Gary. 'What you think I am? An informer? Mum'd half kill me if I did that.'

'And I'd finish it,' Skeeter warned darkly.

''S'all right,' said Gary. 'Shan't say nothing, wouldn't get me out of here so what's the point?'

Skeeter digested that but didn't answer. 'Mum wants to know if you've got everything you need.'

'Could do with some cigs.'

'When'd you start smoking?'

'Since I come in here.'

'I'll tell her,' Skeeter said. 'Anything else?'

'No. It's all right in here. Better than home.'

'It won't be if you get convicted,' said Skeeter. 'If you go to trial you'll be sixteen by then. Not treated special any more.'

'You're joking,' said Gary.

'Don't kid yourself,' said Skeeter, and got up. 'I'm going now. I'll tell Mum what you want.' He turned away and walked out without another look, unaware that he'd just started Gary's mind moving down a road that would do Skeeter no good at all.

MUZ'S EYES were hollowing out. He'd been harangued by just about every elder in the community for starting off the trouble for no good reason other than a guilty conscience. 'Why did you not do this the legal way?' Habib had demanded. 'Is it too much trouble to ask for a licence?'

Muz hadn't answered him. How was he supposed to explain that to do something illegally added spice? Habib wouldn't even know what he was talking about.

So he'd been up for almost two days solid, pumping out music that he interspersed with his pleas for everyone to go home, and now the town was getting quieter, his friends told him so. Last night no one had broken any windows, and no cars had been set alight. The thought of how much the cost of everything would come to when totalled brought him out in a cold sweat. He wondered if Habib's angry insistence that Muz could be charged with inciting a riot was the truth. The worry of that possibility was an added burden. If he went to jail his family would die of shame.

He went to the window and stretched as much as his arm would allow, watching Sam pound Willie's front door.

Willie didn't come.

Sam booted it, the noise reverberating in the dry heat, and when it still stayed shut he heeled out a path edging brick and hefted it ready to throw. Muz shoved the window to its full extent and leaned out.

'I call the police!'

Sam dropped the brick and ran for the car.

When both he and it had turned the top corner and were off the street, Willie opened the door and with both thumbs in the air grinned up at Muz. Muz thumbed him back and moved away from the window. The rights and wrongs weren't his business. Enough that this time it had been him keeping trouble off the street, and not starting it.

WHEN SKEETER handed his pass in, Barrett and Woods were waiting for him, and he found himself being given a free and unexpected ride back to Malminster. 'How'd you know where I was?' he complained. 'And what do you want me for anyway? It's not me what'd done nothing, it's our Gary.'

Barrett ignored Skeeter's faulty grammar, enough they had him in the car and no trouble. 'Your father told us,' he said. 'We went looking for you at home.' Skeeter's face closed up at that, and he stayed quiet until they turned into the police yard and Woods cut the engine. Then he said uneasily, 'What you want to ask me questions about? You're supposed to tell me that. I don't have to go in there if I don't want, not if I'm not arrested or nothing.'

'You want I should arrest you?' Woods asked helpfully.

'That a sodding joke? What I'm saying is, you've got to tell me what it's about, I've got rights, you know, same as everybody else, and I haven't done nothing.' He got out of the car and started edging towards the gate. Woods planted himself in the way.

Barrett said, 'Traffic offences for a start. Dangerous driving. Do you own, or have you driven recently, a white Transit van?'

Skeeter's stomach slid a little.

'Don't own a van or anything else,' he said.

'But you have driven a white Transit?'

'Might of done. Depends when.'

'We'll need to go inside for me to tell you that,' said Barrett. 'That's where all the details are. If you don't mind helping us out, that is. We shan't keep you any longer than we have to.' Like twenty years if the semen matched.

Skeeter dithered, saliva gathering on his bottom lip again. If he said no, it'd get their backs up, and if they banged him up he might never get out. His eyes shifted from one to the other before, reluctantly, and without saying anything else, he began to walk towards the back door. Woods grinned and brought up the rear. Made him wonder sometimes how any of them thought they'd get away with it. Not enough brain power to light a sodding torch.

Skeeter shoved his hands as far as they'd go into his jeans' pockets, and slouched as he walked with them unwillingly. Woods said, 'Which room are we heading for?'

'Two,' said Barrett. 'Be handier. Get a couple of teas in and have a chat. I need to find Sommerby.'

'Who's he?' said Skeeter, stopping dead.

Woods grinned. 'Nobody you know. Just a medic.'

'Who needs him?'

'Routine check, that he's on call. You want tea or coffee.'

'Two minutes,' said Barrett, and turned off into the charge room.

'Dunno what I'm getting myself into here, do I?' Skeeter said. 'S'pose I don't want to cooperate no more.'

'We'll have to have a rethink on where we're at then, won't we?' said Woods as they reached the interview room.

He waved Skeeter inside. 'In you go then. Make yourself comfy. You want tea or coffee?'

'Tea and two sugars,' Skeeter said resentfully. 'How long you going to keep me hanging around?'

'No longer than it takes,' said Woods unhelpfully, and left him to worry while he took a slow walk to the vending machine at the end of the corridor. He'd only just got back when Barrett arrived, file in hand and looking satisfied.

'You can go back and get me one now,' he told Woods. 'Coffee, black, and make it quick this time.' He sat himself facing Skeeter and squared the file folder neatly on the table. 'Want to tell me about this white Transit then,' he invited. 'And who it belongs to?'

Skeeter sucked at his tea and the liquid burned his lip. Tea slopped onto his jeans and he put the cup down, spilling more in the process, and rubbing at the wet patches. Barrett nudged the tissue box in his direction.

'Ta.'

'The white Transit,' said Barrett.

'I don't know. Honest. I just pick up these odd driving jobs—you know—here and there. Don't always ask for names and stuff.'

'Pick up jobs where?'

'Pubs and stuff, usually.'

'From people you haven't seen before.'

'Sometimes.'

'Doing what?'

'You know—moving things round. Furniture and stuff. Cheaper than getting a removal firm.'

'And cash in hand,' said Barrett as Woods came back.

'It'd have to be wouldn't it? If I didn't get money then and there I'd never get it at all,' Skeeter said self-righteously, feeling pleased with himself and his new-found powers of invention.

'So you'd remember what job you'd done even if you don't recall the punter's name,' Barrett pushed.

'Dunno,' said Skeeter, grabbing his tea again.

Barrett opened the file in front of him. 'May 14. You were driving a white Transit on the Forrest estate, at excessive speed. Do you remember that day?'

'No. Don't remember driving fast either. Who says I did?'

'A milkman making deliveries claims you almost ran him off the road.'

Skeeter's mind cleared and things fell into place. The funny look he'd got from the milkman when he came out of his mum's place magically explained itself. He relaxed.

'Don't remember being there, must have been somebody else. I mean if I'd hit a milk float I'd remember, wouldn't I?'

'But you didn't hit it, did you? The Transit swerved.'

'That's all right then. What's his problem?'

'I want to know where you were coming from, and where you were going.'

'I told you—I don't remember. Look there's a lot of Transits, I said that already.'

'So you did,' agreed Barrett. 'But you've been identified. Stiff-fingering him etched your face in his mind.'

Skeeter sat back, glowered and said nothing.

'Remember that, do you?'

'Gave me a shock coming out of a side street like that. Was his fault, not mine.'

'So you admit you drove the van?'

'Yeah. Didn't do nothing wrong though, did I? Was my right of way.'

'They'll put that on your coffin,' said Woods helpfully.

Skeeter glowered again.

'Where were you coming from?' said Barrett.

'I was taking a short cut.'

'From where to where?'

'I remember now,' Skeeter invented. 'I picked the van up at the Cock & Bottle, and I was going to Carlton Street.'

'What for?' said Woods.

'A meet in the car park.'

'Go on.'

'To pick some stuff up—only he never showed.'

'That right? What sort of stuff?'

'A fridge and stuff.'

'Wait a long time, did you?'

'Long enough.'

'Then what?'

'I took the van back.'

'To the Cock & Bottle?'

'Yeah. Didn't get paid though, did I? Waste of time.'

'Hard,' said Barrett unsympathetically. 'Especially since it means you've no witnesses.'

'To what?'

'To when you got the van, and why the big hurry. Like you were putting some distance between you and another place.'

'I wasn't,' said Skeeter, staring into the empty plastic cup.

'Like Maple Drive.'

Skeeter's heart sank. 'Don't know it.'

'There was a rape there, that morning.'

'Nothing to do with me. I wouldn't do that.'

'You won't mind providing us with a specimen then, will you?'

'What sort of specimen?' Skeeter said suspiciously. 'Fingerprints?'

'Semen,' said Woods. 'In a little bottle. You know how to wank don't you?'

Skeeter's bottom lip dropped completely. He brushed away saliva with his sleeve.

Barrett said, 'The police surgeon would explain the procedure. Refusal to provide a specimen would prompt us to draw certain conclusions, at which point we'd be forced to obtain authority to demand the specimen be given.'

Skeeter's mind scuttled like a startled rabbit. He hadn't been there. Couldn't pin it on him. No way. Not even fingerprints. Certainty overcame panic.

'Yeah,' he said. 'All right. Wasn't me. Where's the bottle?'

MARGARET MORRISSEY had experienced almost every emotion it was possible to experience since Mike had been injured, and now numbness seemed to have taken over. She felt empty, like a shell of somebody else sitting by the side of Mike's bed. The inertness of his hand held fast in hers almost convinced her it wasn't Mike at all lying there, that this was just a waking nightmare and when she woke from it Mike would be at home, rushing around, eager for whatever activity was foremost in his mind. Occasionally tiredness drove her into a half-doze and reality blurred even more, so that when she roused herself it was hard to distinguish between those things woven by imagination, and what might have really happened in the room. Like Mike's fingers tightening on her own. She snapped her eyes open and sat up, looking across the bed at Morrissey and finding an echoing hope.

SMYTHE'S AFTERNOON had been less successful than Barrett's. It wasn't so much that Molly had been unwilling to answer questions, more that the answers she gave were tailored to satisfy but not enlighten. Rosie had felt the same thing, but was less irked by it than was Smythe—for one thing she had no pressing need to make up for past faults. They were ready to leave when she threw in one last question.

'What was his preference then, how did he get his kicks?'

Molly grinned widely. 'Official question or personal curiosity?' Rosie grinned back.

'A bit of both.'

Smythe's interest perked up again.

'He had this baby fixation,' Molly said. 'Liked to dress up—you know—the whole parcel. Diaper, bonnet, comforter, frilly rompers, the lot. You want to see his potty?'

'You're joking,' said Rosie.

'God's truth. Liked his potty did Lenny, especially when it came to cleaning up and powdering.' She looked at Smythe, running her eyes over him measuringly. 'Ever wondered why women don't get into that sort of stuff?'

'They do,' Smythe said. 'They make a living from it.'

'Oo—aren't we quick off the mark?' said Molly with a quick jiggle of her boobs. She turned back to Rosie. 'You want my opinion he was an oily little bastard but his money was the same as anybody else's. It's business. Another couple of years and I'm out of it.'

'What then?'

'A bed and breakfast, little one at Scarborough. I'd be good at it.' When Smythe opened his mouth experience made her round on him before he got any words out. 'I said bed and breakfast, not brothel. Put it back in your pocket.' His mouth closed and temper fuelled up.

'Why do you think Donnelly wanted to play babies?' said Rosie before he thought of a comeback.

'You think I'm a psychiatrist too?' She studied Rosie's face. 'Learn not to be so innocent,' she advised. 'You'll only get hurt. Donnelly's problem was his ma dumped him. Anybody else and I'd have felt sorry, but with him I think she must have been bloody psychic. Either way, he hated her guts.'

'Dumped him when?'

'At birth. Dumped outside a women's refuge.' She watched Rosie's face take on understanding, and nodded. 'That's what I thought too but I didn't ask, and he didn't say.'

'Funny coincidence though,' said Rosie.

'Great minds.'

Smythe opened the outside door and dry heat met him. His armpits wept.

'If you think of anything else,' said Rosie as she stepped over the threshold.

'I'll ask for you,' said Molly.

'We-ll.' Rosie looked at Smythe's retreating back. 'It should really be CID.'

'If the world was as it should be,' said Molly, 'I wouldn't be doing this job, would I?' Impulsively Rosie touched the woman's shoulder before she followed Smythe.

'Nothing,' said Smythe as she got in the car. 'Except a wasted afternoon.'

'Yes,' said Rosie. 'Nothing.'

LUCY WASN'T THINKING of anything much as she took the tea trolley round at three-thirty, and when she got to Jane Allen's room she gave her usual brief knock and went in, forgetting her instructions to wait for permission. The room was empty, but she could hear the shower running fast in the bathroom and her nose picked up the scent of expensive shower gel. She put the tray on the low table and was turning to leave when she saw the harness dumped carelessly on the bed. Never having seen anything like it before, Lucy moved across to take a look. Two long padded straps to go over the shoulders, fastening to a buckled strap around the waist. Another strap at hip height. And all of them fastened to a weighted foam pad that when Lucy held it at the right angle could only be one thing.

She put the harness back as she had found it and only then belatedly remembered she wasn't supposed to be in there at all.

Tray in her hands, Lucy was halfway to the door when the shower noise stopped and made her heart jump. Her feet moved faster. The click of the bathroom lock came as she closed the corridor door safely behind her.

'NOTHING?' said Barrett.

'Nothing,' said Smythe. 'Doesn't know what make of car, can't remember if it was dark blue or black, didn't see what the driver looked like. I told her if it was a drunk driver we needed to get him off the streets before he did it again, but she just looked gormless and said nothing. She could be holding back.'

'She knows where to find you if she changes her mind.'

'She knows,' said Smythe. 'But she won't.'

'You did ask specifically if it looked deliberate?'

'I asked. She said how was she supposed to know.'

'Which of course you explained.'

'It didn't make any difference.'

'Waste of time, then.'

'Yes.'

Rosie listened silently and wondered why it was that males and females had such poor communication systems. Barrett watched her staring past his head and wondered if she was thinking about work or that night's date.

'PC Quinn?' he said. 'Did you think Molly was jerking us around?'

'I don't know about that,' Rosie said. 'I think she was worried, and I can't blame her. I don't suppose she gets much chance to screen clients, so she's hardly going to want to put herself up as a witness, is she?'

'She's the only one we've got,' said Barrett. 'Do you think she's likely to change her mind?'

'No,' said Rosie. 'No, I don't.'

'Anything else?'

Rosie looked at Smythe and felt uncomfortable. 'Only about Donnelly's background, but I don't see how it helps.'

'Tell me,' Barrett invited. 'Then I can judge.'

Smythe swallowed a snort. The DS had worked with Morrissey so long he was beginning to sound like him. He waited for Rosie to make a fool of herself with the baby talk. Rosie cleared her throat and told Barrett the whole sequence.

'It struck me as odd,' she finished. 'Donnelly's fixation on babies, his being dumped at a refuge, Mandy's closeness to giving birth, and little Lucy Walton. Probably coincidence, I suppose.'

'Definitely coincidence,' said Smythe, with certainty given by the wish to be right.

Barrett looked from one to the other, and thought how much better it would be if Smythe wore the uniform and Rosie were in CID.

TWENTY-SIX

LUCY HAD BORROWED a Mills & Boon romance from the cook, and sat on the small easy chair in her room, feet up on the bed, reading. From time to time she lowered the book, closed her eyes, and tried to imagine what it would be like to be pursued by two men of such looks and lustiness. She also tried to think of herself with black curls, green eyes, and freckles, and failed miserably on all counts. It didn't deter her for long, a second after she sighed herself out of disappointment she was back in the book, and so absorbed she didn't notice midnight come and go until the noise disturbed her. A woman's voice, sounding very close, and saying just the one word, 'No,' but the word itself loud and verging on panic.

Except that the heroine in the romance had just said the same thing, and Lucy couldn't decide if she'd really heard a voice anywhere but in her own head.

She put the book down and went out onto the landing, peering over the bannister rail and listening hard. Silence. On her way back to her room she turned down the stump of corridor and set her ear against the communicating door. Quite clearly she heard Fielding's voice say, 'God! It's cold in here,' but couldn't decipher Carpenter's reply. Her imagination, fuelled by the romance, went into overdrive, and after a few seconds of unbroken silence, she went back to her room with her head full of images of Carpenter and Fielding shagging in the spare room.

THE GIRL HAD ARRIVED in Fielding's car just before midnight, and was already in labour. Carpenter had come down from her apartment and helped get her up the stairs, and into the delivery room that Lucy had discovered earlier.

'This is what I call cutting it a bit fine,' she said tight-lipped, struggling to get the girl into a short gown. 'Why did they leave her 'til she was this advanced?'

He shrugged. 'Mistake. They happen.'

'And if she'd dropped it in the car?'

Fielding looked at her flatly and didn't respond.

Another contraction came and the girl grabbed Carpenter's arm, knuckles white. Carpenter's lips compressed even further, but she didn't move away.

Fielding eyed her, busy with a drip. 'You'd have fitted well in Sparta,' he said without smiling.

'Just get the sedation going,' said Carpenter. 'Before the whole damn place wakes up.'

DARREN HAD DRIVEN into Leeds in search of better night-life, and in a Country & Western pub had found a willing partner for the kind of games he liked to play in the back of his van. At two a.m. when he drove back into Malminster, his mind was still firmly crotch-centred, but without a strong enough urge to do anything about it except detour along Maple Drive on his way back to his bedsit. Outside the Fitton house he slowed and looked at the darkened windows. Memories came and strengthened libido to the extent that he had to shift on the seat to get himself comfortable. By the time he reached his bedsit and let himself in the door to his room, the itch to pay Kim Fitton a return visit had grown strong roots.

WHEN LUCY LOOKED at the clock it was three-thirty, and already there was a faint hint of dawn in the colour of the sky. She lay still for a couple of minutes, wondering what had wakened her, then heard it again. A baby crying. Only last time she'd thought that, it had turned out to be cats.

She strained her ears, heard it again, couldn't make up her mind which it was, and like the first time, padded barefoot down the attic stairs, listening for the sound to be repeated, but all she heard was the faint sound of snoring. Must be cats then, she decided. Out round the back somewhere, under the bushes.

She turned and started back to her room, but then the baby kicked and acid regurgitated in her throat. When she swallowed on it her stomach rolled and the memory of a half-packet of Jammy Dodgers sent her downstairs again, this time to the kitchen.

Enough early light came through the window for Lucy to home in on the biscuits without needing to turn on the long fluorescents, and she sat on a kitchen chair, the packet open on her lap and her feet up, sighing when craved sweetness reached her tongue. Four biscuits down she raided the fridge for milk and liberated a chicken drumstick left over from the previous day, enjoying the feeling that she shouldn't be there. She was grinning to herself as she got rid of the evidence. One in the eye for Mrs C. Stingy old cow!

She was back in the attic and half in bed when wheels crunched on gravel. Not fast and noisy like when the bread man came round, but slow, and the gravel only spitting, like whoever it was wanted to be quiet. Ever curious, Lucy backed out from under the sheet and went to peer through the window, balancing precariously with a foot on either arm of the easy chair so she could get a better view. From the angle she was at, she could see the black van but couldn't make out the name on its side. the back doors were wide open and Lucy felt a faint twinge of disappointment.

If it was only a delivery it wasn't much point spying.

She was shifting backwards, ready to step down, when she heard Mrs C., the words indistinct but the voice unmistakable, and in her eagerness to see what was happening her foot slipped so she almost fell, scaring herself enough that her heart picked up speed and tried to burst through her chest. The child shifted and twitched in response and she rested her free hand on her abdomen and leaned into the window recess again.

Fielding and the driver were at the back of the van, hidden by the open doors. Lucy couldn't see what they were doing, but Mrs C stood a couple of feet away, watching. The dull clang of a heavy weight hitting the van's metal floor reached Lucy through the open window. She watched the van leave faster than it had come, careless of the gravel as if the noise it made no longer mattered. As it swung around the corner she strained to read the words on its side, catching only 'PETS' and no more. Carpets, she decided with a sense of disappointment. That's what it was all about. Kind that fell off lorries. Lowering herself from the window, more carefully this time, she padded back to bed and curled up under the sheet.

Funny, though, she thought as she cuddled the pillow and closed her eyes, 'cos that last night she thought she'd heard cats there'd been wheels on the gravel then, too, and she'd forgotten all about it until now. She wondered if it had been the same van or something else, and then decided it wasn't worth thinking about because she'd never know one way or the other.

KEN FITTON was up at five-thirty, and in the kitchen by six, his travelling bag and holdall waiting by the front door. He didn't try to go into Kim's bedroom, she still insisted on having the dog in there every night, and he and Julius still shared a common distaste for each other's company. If she woke, she woke, and if she didn't he'd leave a note to tell her where he'd gone. That he could have told her the previous day about his business trip gave him no guilt.

She didn't need him anyway. Not now she was married to the blasted Rottweiler.

His plate was empty, coffee cup nearly so when she came in, eyes still heavy with sleep. Julius came with her, ignoring him and heading for the back door. Kim opened it and let the dog out before she came to the table. He muttered good morning in a disconnected kind of way and kept his eyes on the morning paper.

'Business trip?'

'Didn't I tell you?'

'I probably wasn't listening,' she said, and went to fill the kettle. It irritated him, the way she managed to turn things to her own advantage. Blunt his words and sharpen her own.

Except when she'd been raped. She hadn't turned that around. He eyed her with speculative heat. Kim put a teabag in the pot, turned, and read his face.

Without rush, but with her ears alive for a scrape of chair, she went to open the back door.

BARRETT GOT TO his desk early, his mind still occupied with Donnelly. The thought plagued him constantly that the priest's death was linked with Mandy's, and that the key was buried in the police reports. Systematically he read both files again, and when he came no closer to the answer, slammed the manilla folders closed in irritation and glared at Morrissey's chair. That the DCI would be able to put his finger on it without difficulty was a knowledge that added to Barrett's frustration. From his top drawer he took the bank statements and cash book Smythe had found in Donnelly's room, and laid them out on the desk, staring at the number of irregular but large deposits that had been paid into his account. They weren't enough to make Donnelly rich, but they were enough to need explaining.

Except the man was no longer around to do it.

Why the hell had he put nothing but CF in his cashbook. Carried forward to what?

When he dumped both items on Smythe's desk the DC looked at them with sinking heart and a fair idea of what came next.

'Donnelly's bank,' Barrett said. 'Get yourself down there and find out how these deposits were made. Cash or cheque.'

'And then what?' said Smythe, hunting for an envelope. 'Pick Skeeter up again?'

'For what?' said Barrett, with impatience. 'We've been through this already. Forget Skeeter. If he'd done the rape he wouldn't have given a specimen so fast. It's enough we know where he is and who he is, for now.' He tapped the cashbook. 'Fast as you like. I'm at The Cedars talking to Lucy Walton if there's anything urgent.'

Smythe opened his mouth, then thought better of it, and nodded. Up to the DS what he did. Only thing any of them had done so far was run in circles. He watched Barrett walk out the door and got up from his chair disgruntedly. Not his problem if he got sent on another wild goose chase.

THIS TIME when Lucy took round the fresh water jugs she remembered to knock on Jane Allen's door, surprised when she got an instant answer, and more surprised still when she went into the room and saw a crib at the bottom of the bed. Jane lay back against the pillows, looking wan.

'Whose is it?' Lucy said, bending to get a closer look.

'Whose do you think?' Jane said curtly. 'Mine. And don't breathe all over him?'

'Oh yes? Born last night I suppose.'

'Should be obvious,' said Jane. 'And since I'm tired and

sore, get the hell out of here and don't ask stupid questions.'

'Stupid questions my foot!' Lucy flared. 'I saw the...' She stopped there and turned around, moving towards the door.

'Saw what?' Jane said from behind her.

'Nothing,' said Lucy over her shoulder. 'Just didn't think you was that far on is all.'

This time there was no answer, and she got to the corridor without having to look in the woman's face. Just as well, she told herself, since the woman was lying in her teeth.

When she got the trolley back to the ground floor, Barrett's voice was plain and tetchy in reception. Lucy grinned to herself. Lenore never made it easy for him. She parked the trolley up against the wall and strolled round the corner, hands in her pockets as usual.

'You wanting me?'

Barrett's frown deepened. 'I thought you said she wasn't here?' he said to Lenore. Lucy watched the woman's face darken. Silly old cow.

'Well I am here,' she said. 'So what you want?'

'More questions,' said Barrett. 'Is the day room empty?'

'Shouldn't think so. Why'n't we go in the garden, I could do with a bit of air.'

Lenore said, 'You'll go nowhere until Mrs Carpenter knows about it,' and glaring at Barrett added, 'This is a nursing home—not a police station.' He eyed her flatly.

'What you can tell Mrs Carpenter is I don't want to be interrupted. Understood?' Lucy looked at him with new respect. A voice like that could sizzle a sausage.

Lenore flounced past towards the office. Barrett got rid of his frown and gave Lucy a smile. 'Lead the way,' he said. 'Do we go out the front, or is there a quicker route?'

'We'll go out the back,' said Lucy 'now the bag isn't here to stop us.' She led him back round the corner, down the passage, and through the kitchen. The cook stopped mixing crumble and stared at them. Barrett gave her a polite nod. Lucy said cheerfully, 'It's all right Joanie, we're just going out the back for a bit of a snog,' and snorted when the other woman's eyes measured up Barrett for suitability.

He speeded his passage across the room.

'Funny that,' said Lucy when they got outside. 'You should have seen your face.'

'Should I?' said Barrett with more severity then he felt, and made for a garden seat out of eavesdropping distance from the windows.

'So what you want now?' said Lucy, sitting with her legs out, and akimbo. 'There isn't nothing else I know about Mandy—I told you that.'

'It isn't about Mandy,' said Barrett. 'It's about St Ursula's. Tell me about it, how it runs and how you got there.'

'Thought you knew that. It was your lot picked me up, I was dossing in a doorway out of the rain, wasn't I, and one of your Pandas saw me. Next thing I know they've dumped me there. At St Ursula's I mean.'

'Tell me about it. What was it like?'

'All right I s'pose,' said Lucy. 'Didn't think much to Holy Joe, though. What do you want to know for?'

'How many staff besides Father Donnelly?'

'Didn't have none, the women do it all. He used to put a list up, you know, who does what.' She turned her head and looked at Barrett. 'I told him to get stuffed,' she said defiantly. 'Didn't want to be there in the first place.'

'How did he react?'

'Didn't like it. I'd have gone if it hadn't been raining. It's just...you know...' Her hands moved to her rounded belly.

'I know,' said Barrett.

'Think that's why he got me a job here, 'cos I wouldn't do anything there.'

'Did he find jobs for the other women?'

'Don't think so. Him and Mrs C said it was 'cos of the baby, so I could have it here, if I wanted. Don't know if I do.'

'Looks all right,' said Barrett, glancing back at the home.

'Yeah,' said Lucy, in a tone that meant the opposite.

'Too much of a battleaxe for you?'

'Mrs C? No. I can handle her. Don't like him though. Slimy, like Holy Joe.'

'Who's him?' Barrett asked ungrammatically.

'Doctor Fielding. Toffee-nose. Does it for charity and he can stuff it. I don't need charity, I can go and have it on the Health.' She shrugged. 'Anyway, you should see the women. More money than brains.'

'The patients, you mean?'

'He calls them *clients,* says patients are for hospitals.' She shrugged. 'He's having it off with Mrs C, on the side. Bet you didn't know that.' She pointed up at the attic windows. 'My room's up there same as her apartment. That window with pink curtains, that's mine. What do you want to know about St Ursula's for? Haven't told me yet.'

Barrett grinned. 'I get to ask the questions—you get to answer them. What would have happened if you'd told Father Donnelly you didn't want to come here?'

'What he said, was, he didn't have room at the hostel anymore 'cos he wanted a bed for somebody else. Straight choice, come here or sleep rough.' She leaned forward, hands resting on the wooden seat on either side of her, and stared down at the grass. 'Was when there was all that rain—you know? I mean, if it hadn't been pissing down I'd have told him to shove it. Said it was regulations I could only stop three nights.' She lifted her head and looked at Barrett. 'I didn't believe him, mind. Thought it was just he wanted me out 'cos I answered him back. Gets him mad.' She grinned in recollection.

'You weren't sorry to go then?' Barrett held his face straight. 'Anything wrong with the hostel *except* Father Donnelly?'

'Don't suppose. The women were better than this lot.'

Barrett studied the back of the nursing home, saw Diana Carpenter's face staring back at him from her office window, and made no acknowledgement. 'You seem to be looked after well enough,' he said. 'Has Father Donnelly dropped by since you left the hostel?'

'What? Here? To see me?'

'Or anybody else?'

'Haven't seen him if he has. Why?'

'Call it curiosity,' said Barrett.

'Yeah, I know all about police curiosity,' Lucy said. 'What's he been up to? Hand in the till?'

'Nothing,' Barrett said firmly.

'He'd phone anyway, wouldn't he?'

'Is that how he found a place for you?'

'Dunno.' Lucy shrugged. 'I got called into his office, and there's Mrs C, sitting in the easy chair. Told you that before, didn't I?' she added suspiciously.

'Did you?' Barrett said innocently. 'Probably didn't make a note of it.'

'Yeah, that's what I thought,' she said unbelievingly, leaning back and folding her arms. 'It's 'cos of Mandy. That's what you're asking for, and you said it wasn't.'

'There's a possibility Mandy might be connected,' said Barrett. 'No more than that at this stage.'

'I dreamed about her,' Lucy said abruptly. 'I followed

her from my room to Mrs C's apartment, and when she went in, I woke up outside the door to it. Weird.'

'Dreams are. I'd better let you get back to work,' said Barrett, and started to get up.

'And then there was the van last night,' said Lucy. 'That was weird too.'

He sat down again, and looked at her with new-found patience. 'I'm listening.'

'Well,' said Lucy. 'It was the cats woke me up...'

TWENTY-SEVEN

BARRETT AND LUCY were almost at the kitchen door when Diana Carpenter began to turn from the window, then her eye corner picked up a third figure, coming from the tall bushes just behind them. As she swung back, her eyes met Barrett's and moved on, but there was no third figure visible, only Lucy and the detective sergeant, coming back into the Home.

'CASH,' said Smythe, as Barrett looked at him expectantly. 'No cheques, no banker's drafts, just lump sums paid in over the counter. The manager's frozen the account until heirs show up. I did get the name of Donnelly's solicitors though—Gibson and Dunn on Wood Street. Should help us track down who inherits, but that's about all.' The look on Smythe's face was a plain I-told-you-so.

'You'd better get down there then,' said Barrett. 'Ask who the next of kin is, and get a look at his will while you're at it.' Smythe didn't argue, the look of resignation as he headed back to the door said it all.

Barrett settled back at his desk, his mind re-examining the conversation he'd had with Lucy. It hadn't moved him on in the investigation of either Donnelly's death or Mandy Sheard's, and yet there was still the uneasy feeling at the back of his mind that it should have. Just as Rosie's comments hung there too, waiting expectantly for him to grasp a connection. The replay of Lucy's words stopped when he got to the van. What the hell was a van doing at the nursing home at that time of day? He riffled back through Mandy

Sheard's file to Bernie Parks's statement. Don't know what colour the van was. Dark, that's all I could see.

That was a connection. Tenuous, maybe non-existent even, but there until it was proved not to be. Something to occupy Woods. His spirit lifted. Any movement was better than none.

He was still briefing Woods when he heard the telephone ring in his own office and broke off conversation to take it on Woods' extension. His spirits lifted again. Find one crack and another appeared, but what in blue blazes could Gary Westcott know about the rape of Kim Fitton?

LUCY HAD PUSHED the water trolley back into the kitchen and was unloading its contents when Diana Carpenter came looking for her. 'In my office,' she said brusquely. 'There are some things we have to get straight.' Lucy carried on unloading.

'Five minutes,' she said. 'Got to do this first.'

'Now!'

Lucy's hands stilled. 'What's it about?'

'Decisions,' said Carpenter, and held the door, waiting for Lucy to go through, while the eyes of cook and kitchen help swivelled towards her, interestedly.

'What decisions?' said Lucy as she stepped out to keep up with Carpenter.

'About whether you stay or go. It's time to decide that.'

'You said tomorrow,' said Lucy. Carpenter shrugged.

'What difference is there in one day? Whatever decision you would have arrived at tomorrow, can just as easily be reached today.'

'If you say so.' Lucy's shoulders hunched resentfully. When they reached Carpenter's office, Lucy went in first because the other woman gave her no choice. Fielding was sitting in the desk chair, flat-eyed and expressionless. 'You didn't say he'd be here,' said Lucy.

'Sit down,' said Carpenter. 'Mr Fielding wants to talk to you about your blood tests, that's why he's here. And I want to talk to you about this morning's police visit. What did he want this time? Mandy again?'

'I don't have to tell you what he wanted,' said Lucy. 'It was me he came to see.'

'On the nursing home's property,' said Carpenter acidly. 'That makes it my business too.'

'Better ask *him* about it then, hadn't you?' Lucy came back. 'Wasn't anything to do with you.'

Carpenter's eyes flickered. 'In working hours, and on this property, it has a lot to do with me. Was it about the Mandy woman again?'

'No, it wasn't,' said Lucy sulkily. 'It was about St Ursula's, and whether I liked it there. I told him it was all right 'cept for the priest.'

'Father Donnelly,' corrected Carpenter.

'Suit yourself.'

'That's all you talked about?'

'Yeah. What else is there?'

Fielding said impatiently, 'Can we get on, I have work to do. You can discuss that with Lucy later. At the moment I need to talk with her.' Carpenter's lips tightened, but she said nothing else. Lucy didn't bother to hide her grin.

'The blood tests show you're anaemic, Lucy,' said Fielding. 'They also show mineral imbalance—probably due to poor diet. If you want to improve your baby's chances of survival, now is the time to accept treatment.'

'What kind of treatment?' said Lucy, arms crossing over her abdomen again. The child inside her kicked reassuringly.

'Injections to remedy the deficiency.' His finger rapped the lid on a kidney dish. 'The first one is here. It will go in your buttock.'

'Backside, you mean,' said Lucy.

Fielding shrugged. 'Less elegant, but the same meaning.'

'If I let you do that it means I'm stopping, I suppose.' Fielding inclined his head. Lucy looked at Carpenter, whose eyes were fixed on Fielding. Instinctive protectiveness for her baby vied with dislike of the other two people in the room.

Wasn't fair Lucy told herself. Making her decide. Like blackmail.

'I s'pose, I'll have to,' she said, and nodded at the examination couch. 'Want me up there I expect.' Her eyes met Fielding's and she made one last, defiant quip. 'Skirt up and pants down I suppose. That how you like it?'

THE ONLY overnight incidents in Malminster had been two broken shop windows, and with that in mind Osgodby ordered the release of Arshad Majid. When he walked out of the front door the desultory group of protesters, still mounting a demonstration, gave a weak cheer and proclaimed victory.

When Barrett drove out of the police yard five minutes later, the street was empty. The whole thing had been useless, he thought. The riot, the damage, the waste, and most of all the fact that Mike Morrissey was still hovering in the thin grey area between life and living death. He wondered what he himself would choose if he were faced with the prospect of prolonged coma or extinction, and then admitted that his real concern was which Morrissey and his wife would choose for their son if it became obvious that the decision was theirs, and had to be made.

No one should have to decide that.

Deliberately he moved his thoughts back to Gary. The only link Barrett could see between Gary and the Fitton rape was Skeeter, and Barrett had let Skeeter go. He squirmed a little about having made that decision. If Skeeter turned out to be the culprit, Osgodby would want

To know why they'd had him in custody, and then set him free.

And it would be Barrett's head on the block, no one else to blame it on. The thought was still with him as he turned into the small car park at the secure unit. An empty spot, shaded by the high wall, promised not to turn the car into an oven, and he pulled into it, trying to convince himself its being there was an omen, and failing abysmally.

Gary showed no sign of such internal worry when he came into the room where Barrett was waiting. 'Wondered if it'd be you that came,' he said. 'Or that other one with the fancy hairdo. You're higher up than him, aren't you?'

'What did you want to tell me?' said Barrett, deliberately ignoring Gary's question.

'Never said I wanted to tell you nothing,' said Gary. 'I said I wanted to talk to somebody about a rape. Talking isn't telling—is it?' His voice rose on the final two words, making it a statement, not a question.

'Sit down,' said Barrett, sniffing the possibility of a wasted journey. 'And get on with it. Why did you ask to talk with a police officer?'

''Cos I want to swap information. I tell you who done the rape, and you get me out of here. You can do that, I know. One of the lads told me.' Gary eyed Barrett warily. 'Or aren't you high enough up the tree? Wasn't me killed the old man, you know. Don't see why I should go to jail for it, I'd have stopped him if I'd known. Honest.'

Barrett had heard the same words used before, and felt the same degree of disbelief. 'First you give the information,' he said. 'Then if it's worth anything, we put a good word in for you when the case comes to court.'

'I want more than that,' said Gary. 'I want to know I won't get sent to jail.'

'Look at it this way,' Barrett said unkindly, 'if you don't tell me, jail is something you can bank on.'

'That's a threat,' said Gary. 'You're not allowed to do that.'

'Suit yourself,' said Barrett, and started to push up from the table.

'What sort of good word?' the youth asked sullenly.

'The court will be informed that you have given us valuable assistance in solving another case, and that will be taken into consideration when sentence is passed,' Barrett replied formally. 'That's as much as we can do.'

'Thought you could let me off,' Gary said sullenly. 'It's what happens on TV.'

'Too many American movies, that's your trouble,' Barrett told him. 'This is England, and there's no plea bargaining.' He watched the other's bravado collapse. The resemblance between Gary and Skeeter became more apparent as it did. 'You can't lose anything,' the DS pushed, 'but you might have something to gain. Give me a name.'

Shoulders slumped, eyes fixed on the table, and not on Barrett, Gary said, 'Darren Minter. Our Skeet's mate.'

IT WAS COMING UP to three o'clock when Barrett got back to his office, a mug of coffee with two chip butties balanced on top in his hand, and stomach churning out juices in anticipation. He unloaded them on his desk and went in search of Smythe. The look he got was resentful. Barrett ignored it.

'You got the next-of-kin?'

'Yes, it's...'

'And who inherits?'

'Yes, it's...'

'Then borrow a body from uniform and pick up Skeeter. If he's not home, find him.'

'What if he won't come?'

'Tell him he's no choice,' said Barrett, and headed back

to the butties. Halfway there when Smythe asked plaintively, 'What's the charge?'

'Aiding and abetting a rape,' the DS said over his shoulder. 'Give him something to think about on his way in.'

COMPUTERS WERE USEFUL, something Woods had long acknowledged. The transfer of information from the DVLR had taken minutes where once it would have taken days, and back then, even after they'd got the stuff, he'd have had to physically check out every van on the list to find any with the combination of letters PETS on their side. He grinned at the thought of how much footwork he'd been saved. By two-thirty he'd checked out six carpet firms, Snippets the Stationers, and a local brass band that called itself Trumpets Voluntary.

It was a quarter to three when he drew up outside the pets' crematorium, making himself fourth in a line of parked cars. The van was around the back, out of sight from the road, but when Woods stuck his face up to the wrought-iron gate he could just see the tail end of it. He eyed the padlock on the inside of the gate with annoyance, and walked back to the front door.

In the reception area two elderly couples sat, the women moist-eyed, the men with them looking uncomfortable. Woods found himself quietening his footsteps on the tiled floor. The woman behind the counter gave him a look of practised sympathy, and asked if he'd come about his pet. Woods had his hand halfway to his pocket when he saw the ring she was wearing and changed his mind.

'Yes,' he invented rapidly. 'A dog. He won't last long though.' Dropping his voice on the last two words and feeling pleased with himself.

The look of sympathy heightened. 'It's close?'

'Oh, yes,' said Woods, his eyes slipping to the silver and turquoise on her finger. 'It's close.'

She gave him a brochure and two leaflets. 'You can read these if you like. They're about the crematorium.'

Woods gave them a quick flick. 'Can I get a look at where it's done?'

Her eyebrows went up. He could almost see thoughts trying to surface. 'That'd be up to Charlie.'

'Charlie who?'

Her eyes flashed to the waiting couples and her voice lowered. 'He operates the incinerator.' She put her hand on the telephone. 'You sure you want to see?'

'I like the ring,' said Woods. 'Nice. Unusual.'

'A present,' she said, giving it a twist so it was straight. 'From Charlie.'

'You and him an item then?'

'Sort of.' She picked up the receiver.

'Don't bother,' said Woods. 'I'll come back when you're not busy.' Halfway to the door when she reminded him about the brochure. 'When I come back,' he said, and kept on walking.

LUCY WOKE UP in bed, but it wasn't her bed, and she couldn't remember how she'd got there. Her head felt fuzzy like she was thinking through layers of cotton wool, and her limbs were heavy and languid. She blinked up at the ceiling, with its circular light, and tried to remember what had happened, her hands moving to the roundness of her abdomen for reassurance.

The room took on significance. It was the one she'd found yesterday when she'd snooped down the corridor behind the connection door. The delivery room. Lucy felt a prickle of unease, then a warm rush of fear following it.

Wasn't time for her baby yet, and she didn't want it born here anyway. Not anymore she didn't, she wanted it born in a proper hospital. Hands pushing against the mattress she made herself sit up, eyebrows screwing as the room shimmered and moved. When it stilled she remembered the couch in Carpenter's office, and Fielding's hand, stretching the skin of her buttock before the needle sank in.

She was halfway to the door, walking like a drunken child, when it opened and let Fielding and Carpenter in, and all she gained from fighting not to be returned to the bed, was a clump of Carpenter's hair.

'YOU SURE it's the same ring?' asked Barrett, unable to believe two cases could be cracking on the same day.

'No,' said Woods, doing a racing gear change as he took a corner. 'What I said is it fits the description, plus there's a dark blue VW van round the back. It's not like I can go ask Mandy Sheard if it's hers.'

Barrett gave him a cold eye. 'Shame you didn't ask how long she'd had it.' This time Woods stayed silent, turning onto the industrial estate and driving through the warren of near-identical roads until he got to the crematorium again. A belch of smoke came out of the squat chimney at the back as he pulled into the kerb. Only one car was parked there now, a red K registered Metro that could have done with a wash. Barrett climbed out and eyed the arrow-shaped sign that invited him to explore the Garden of Rest.

'Let's see if he pulls a receipt out of his wallet, then,' he said pessimistically. Woods eyed him, but for once kept quiet.

The receptionist was away from her desk. Woods had his hand on the brass bell when a lavatory cistern emptied behind a door marked Toilets, and he changed his mind. A couple of minutes later she came out, and recognised him.

'Come back for the brochure,' she said, pasting on the sympathetic smile again. Barrett showed her his warrant card.

'Detective Sergeant Barrett and Detective Constable

Woods, Malminster CID. Do you mind showing me the turquoise ring you're wearing?'

She looked from one to the other. 'What's it about?'

'It answers the description of a ring we've been looking for,' said Woods.

'Well it isn't it,' she said hotly. 'I told you—it was a present.'

'If you wouldn't mind,' said Barrett. She eyed them both and flushed, then pulled off the ring and put it in Barrett's outstretched hand. To his eyes, it looked exactly as Lucy had described. 'Where did you get it?'

'I've already told *him* that.' She nodded at Woods. 'Charlie gave it to me.'

'Charlie who?'

'Foster. He's out the back.'

'He'd have a receipt for it?'

'I suppose.'

'We'll go ask him then, shall we?'

She looked at them, indecisively.

'Through this door, is it?' Woods said, moving away.

'Let me go first.' Almost running to get in front, taking them through a storage room into the bleakness of barren concrete where the incinerator still gave off a haze of heat. Foster, in a pair of brown cotton overalls, was standing in front of an overworked electric fan, arms, chest and face running with sweat.

'It's the police, Charlie,' she said before Barrett got his mouth open. 'About that ring.' Barrett showed his warrant card again.

'I need to know where you bought the silver ring you gave to...?' He looked at the woman enquiringly. 'Haven't asked you that yet, have we?'

'Rita Smailes,' she said, face set.

'...To Rita,' Barrett finished.

'Depends what you want to know for,' said Foster. 'Why should I have to tell you?'

'The ring is identical to one we've been looking for, that's why. Can you answer the question please?'

'I bought it in a pub.'

'What pub?'

'George.'

'Who from?'

'Stranger.'

'But you'd remember what he looked like.'

'Not a clue, I was half-pissed.'

'Did anybody else see the transaction?'

'How the hell would I know?'

'Can you tell us where you were on the twenty-second of March between midnight and four a.m.?'

'In bed,' said Foster. 'That it?'

'Did you know a woman by the name of Mandy Sheard?'

'I know a lot of women. I don't always ask their names. If you've finished, I've got work to do.'

'Where were you this morning at four a.m.?'

This time Foster's eyes flickered. Barrett felt himself relax. Not a wild goose chase after all.

'In bed,' said Foster. 'Where else would I be at that time? I get up at six.'

'Who else has access to your van?'

'Nobody. It's parked here all night, behind locked gates.'

'More than one key to the gate?'

'One in the office, one I keep.'

'Impossible for anybody else to get the van out, then.'

'That's because nobody did. It was there all night, and there when I got here this morning.'

'A bit earlier than usual?' suggested Woods.

'No. Can I get on now? I've asked once already.'

'I'd like you to come back to Malminster police station with us, so we can question you further,' Barrett said.

'Charlie…?' said Rita, uncertainly.

'Shut up,' he said. 'Last thing I ever give *you.*' Her flush this time was deeper.

'We'll be as quick as we can,' said Barrett.

'I don't have time now. I'll come down later.'

'Now,' Barrett insisted. 'Otherwise you'll be cautioned and taken there anyway.'

Foster picked a T-shirt up from the metal table the fan stood on. Grubby beige with a split under the left arm. 'You'll have to finish off by yourself tonight, Rita,' he said, giving her a hostile look. 'Mind you don't burn your fucking fingers.'

TWENTY-EIGHT

LUCY COULDN'T wake herself up, she kept drifting into and out of deep sleep without any ability to control the process. Sometimes when she roused she was conscious of only light beyond her eyelids, and other times they would half-open and let her see the room. The dreams she had as she drifted up and down through the layers of sleep were always the same. Mandy, urging her to get up and run away.

WHEN BARRET WALKED into The Cedars he had the ring in his pocket, packaged as all such things had to be, in a regulation plastic envelope. Foster, detained for questioning, cooled his heels in Malminster police station waiting on Barrett's return. The ring was unusual with its long, turquoise stone, and filigree mount, and the stamped in 1960 silver hallmark meant a duplicate wouldn't be easy to find—even if one existed.

Whether it had been Mandy's was a different question and one that only Lucy could answer.

Except that when he asked for her he was told she wasn't there. 'I'll get Mrs Carpenter,' Lenore said when he voiced his disbelief. 'You can ask her instead.' Sailing off with her nose in the air and leaving him alone.

Barrett asked himself if he was any more likely to believe Diana Carpenter than her receptionist, and got back a negative, knowing he wouldn't be able to prove it one way or the other unless Lucy put in an appearance as she had done the last time. He positioned himself under the fan again and waited. When she finally came, Carpenter's vexed look was even more pronounced than usual.

'I don't know where she is,' she said flatly before he could ask. 'The girl simply said she didn't want to have her baby here and walked out. Look in shop doorways—that's your best bet.'

'Walked out when?' said Barrett.

'Soon after you left.'

'And you didn't think to notify me?'

'Why should I?'

'A sixteen-year-old with her baby almost due, who's been assisting the police in an investigation of the murder of an equally pregnant woman, and you need to ask me that?'

'This isn't a prison, and I'm not Lucy's guardian, she's always been free to leave or not to leave as she wished. I've told you that before.'

'And I told you before that if she left I wanted to know about it when it happened. That was an instruction—not a request. I also remember being told once before that Lucy wasn't here when she was.'

'That was in Lucy's own interest.'

'Why should this be any different?'

'The girl isn't here, Detective Sergeant. I can't put it more plainly than that. If you want her, you'll have to find her, although she could be anywhere by now. She's still wearing her uniform dress, flatly refused to take it off and told me to take it out of the wages I owed her.'

'You gave her money?' Barrett said.

'Twenty pounds, plus the dress.'

'Low wages.'

'Add food, lodging, and obstetric care, and you'll find it wasn't low at all. Is that all you need to know? Can I get on with my work now?'

'If Lucy comes back I want to know as soon as it happens, and not an hour or two later. Understood?'

'Imprinted in my mind,' Diana Carpenter said dryly. I

hope she appreciates your interest. Now may I return to my office?'

'Be my guest,' said Barrett, and walked away himself, annoyed that he hadn't stressed to Lucy the importance of letting him know where she was. She might not have taken any notice of his instruction, but at least he would have the knowledge that he'd covered all possibilities as well as he could. Now he had a suspect and no one to identify the only piece of evidence he had. He cursed quietly as he started up his car, turning left out of the drive, heading back towards Malminster, seeing The Cedars' cook at the bus stop and passing it before he realised it was her.

When he pulled into the kerb fifty yards away and looked in the rear-view mirror, her head was angled towards him. He shifted the stick into reverse and backed up. She moved away from the kerb, out of arm's reach and he grinned to himself. It was always the ones with the least to worry about who took the greatest precautions. He got out on his side and let her get a look at him.

'It's Joan, isn't it? From The Cedars? Detective Sergeant Barrett, Malminster CID, you saw me with Lucy, earlier today.'

Her face cleared. 'Oh yes. I remember.'

'If you're waiting for the Malminster bus, I can give you a lift.'

Doubt creased her face, then she shrugged and came to the car. 'Can't be any hotter than waiting,' she said. 'Been murder in that kitchen with all this heat.' He made an understanding noise and got back in himself. 'You been to see her again, then?' she said as he pulled away from the kerb. 'She's not in any trouble is she? Nice girl, Lucy, except for...you know what.' Her face turned to look at him, then away again.

'No, she isn't in any trouble,' said Barrett. 'Not with us, but I don't know what she'll get herself into now she's out on her own.' He cut his speed, and took his eyes off the road to look at her as he said that. She looked startled.

'Out on her own? You saying she's left? No, she wouldn't do that, not without having said goodbye she wouldn't. Who told you she had?'

'Mrs Carpenter.'

'Oh.'

'Right after I left this morning apparently.'

'She did the water jugs after that,' Joan said. 'I remember. She brought the trolley back in the kitchen and Mrs C didn't give her time to empty it before she came looking for her.'

'What for?'

'Said she wanted to see her in her office, because there was things they had to get straight. It'd be about the baby.' She gave him a sideways glance. 'Lucy had been mucking her around a bit. Wouldn't tell Mrs C if she was going to have it there or not. I told her she should. I'd have looked after her.'

'Did you tell Lucy that?'

'Yes, 'course I did. Funny business. Where's she gone?'

'I was hoping you could tell me that.'

'I don't know. She didn't know anybody round here, and she wouldn't have gone home.'

'Why not?'

'She just wouldn't,' said Joan stubbornly.

Barrett drove slowly, telling himself it wouldn't hurt Foster to wait. 'What about the baby's father?' he said. 'She mentioned someone called Rollo. Lucy could have gone to him, if she'd found out where he was?'

'No!'

'Sounds as if you know that for sure.'

She stayed silent for a minute, then said. 'You think she's in trouble, don't you?'

'I think she could get *into* trouble,' Barrett conceded. 'If we don't find her.'

'Oh.'

They were almost at the roundabout at the top of Middlebrook Road before she said, 'There wasn't any Rollo, you know, she made him up so she could make out he was the father.'

'She didn't get pregnant on her own,' said Barrett as he waited for a gap in the traffic.

'No, you're right, she didn't,' said Joan. 'She told me about that too. It was her father done it. Dirty old sod!'

CARPENTER HAD BEEN doodling on the scribble-pad while Fielding talked, and he'd watched the moving pen with a displeased eye. When he paused, the pen stilled and she looked up. 'We'll start the induction this afternoon,' he said. 'Get it over with.'

She set the pen down, carefully. 'It's too risky.'

'The danger is acceptable.'

'I don't think so. Lucy put herself out of bounds when she talked to the police about the Sheard woman. And that was an even bigger mistake.'

'Unavoidable.'

Carpenter didn't reply.

Anger twisted Fielding's face. 'It had to be done, don't forget your own involvement.'

'My involvement didn't include leaving her in a ditch when she should have been dealt with like the rest,' she snapped. 'It put us all in danger.'

'That mistake was Foster's. When I got there it was too late, she was already dead.'

'There were two of you—enough to get her in the back of the van. If you'd done that we wouldn't have problems now.'

'Foster panicked.'

'Just Foster?'

His anger grew. 'Careful, Diana, you're not unexpendable.'

'The police don't believe Lucy isn't here. It was written all over the detective sergeant's face.'

'By tomorrow it won't matter if he believes it or not. Let Foster know we need him again. Do it now!' he flared as she made no move.

Stiff-fingered, she punched in the crematorium's number and sat, set-faced, listening to the continuing emptiness of its ring.

WHEN BARRET GOT BACK to the police station, Skeeter and Foster were in adjoining cells while Smythe and Woods exchanged moans about enforced overtime in the CID room upstairs. The exchange stopped short when the DS walked in.

'I'd rather be at home too,' he said shortly, letting them know he'd heard. 'So let's get on with it. Skeeter first. The longer Foster cools his heels the better.' Smythe perked up. 'Don't get too hopeful,' Barrett said. 'Depending on what we get out of him, you could be here for a while yet.' Woods smirked. 'Same applies to you,' Barrett reminded. 'We haven't even started on Foster. Paperwork done?'

Woods said nothing, just pulled the necessary stationery out of his desk drawer and got busy. Barrett hid his grin and headed back downstairs, Smythe in tow.

Facing them across the interview room table, Skeeter looked like he couldn't make up his mind whether to relax or panic. 'I wasn't there,' he said. 'Told you that already.'

'Wasn't where?' said Barrett mildly. 'Haven't asked you anything yet, have we?'

'Same thing you pulled me in for yesterday, that's why I'm here isn't it? Weren't me.'

'Maybe not,' said Barrett. 'But you do know who did it,

which makes for a charge of aiding and abetting—if you don't cooperate and give us a name.'

'Can't,' said Skeeter, lip drooping again. 'Dunno.'

'Enjoy your visit with Gary did you?'

Skeeter stared, unease flooding his belly in a rush of heat as he remembered what he'd talked about. 'What's it got to do with Gary?'

'He sent a message out today,' said Barrett. 'Asking me to go and see him, so he could cut a deal. Of course I had to tell him we don't do that kind of thing.'

'That's all right then,' said Skeeter, feeling happier.

'I told him all we could do was put in a good word for him when he came to trial. He settled for that.'

'Who is it you go around with?' said Smythe. 'Who's your best mate? Got one, have you?' Skeeter's eyes went from one to the other like a trapped rabbit. 'What's his name, Skeeter? Can't hurt to tell us that, can it?'

'Our Gary makes these things up,' Skeeter tried. 'Always has. Wouldn't know the truth if he fell over it, what he wants is to get hisself off, is all.'

'We can always go and ask your dad,' said Smythe. 'Or your mother. They'd know who you go about with, wouldn't they?'

Too right, thought Skeeter. And they'd both be happy to say. He asked himself if it was any use keeping quiet, and went cold when he remembered the stuff Darren had got him mixed up in while they were out of Malminster.

Like that post office.

His stomach crawled. He couldn't say he hadn't been there that time. And then there was the other stuff. He clamped his mouth and stayed quiet.

'Aiding and abetting it is then,' said Barrett, pushing up from the table. 'Might even manage a conspiracy charge as well.' He turned his head and looked at Smythe. 'Charge him and get him back in the cells, we don't have time to play.'

'I weren't mixed up in it,' Skeeter said. 'I weren't. Look, our Gary's telling lies, like I said, he's always doing it. Likes getting me into bother.'

'He's managed it this time then, hasn't he?' said Barrett, and took a step towards the door.

'Can I go if I tell you his name?'

'We know his name,' Barrett said, sitting down again. 'It's Darren Minter. What we don't know is where to find him.'

'But you're going to tell us that, aren't you?' said Smythe. 'Because you want to be helpful.'

'I don't know where he is,' said Skeeter desperately. 'I haven't seen him since we got back.'

'Got back from where, Skeeter?' Barrett asked as light dawned. 'Where is it you've been hiding?'

EDDIE HAD BEGUN to see Willie's intransigence as a threat to his manhood. He was losing face with every encounter and it stuck in his throat. Three times over the weekend he'd sent Sam back there, and each time Willie had stayed safe and made mockery from behind his door. Enough was enough. Willie needed a lesson that Eddie couldn't wait to teach, and the only thing still to decide was the size of it. Big enough to hurt in all the right places. And if that didn't work…

There were times when Eddie caught himself hoping it wouldn't, savouring the knowledge that he had friends who'd enjoy helping Willie move house on a permanent basis. *Very* permanent.

SKEETER WAS BACK in his cell, working on ways he could get even with his brother, while Smythe followed up new leads and knew that by the time he got home it would be too late to do anything more pleasurable than eat, watch an hour's TV, and go to bed. He could think of better things to do.

Woods was in the same frame of mind. The smell of Foster's sweat was rank. Dried-on stuff earned at the crematorium overlaid by new and damp. It hung on the dry air in the interview room like an all-pervading miasma as Foster stuck to his story of buying the ring in a pub.

'I don't know what he looked like because I was half-pissed,' he said for the umpteenth time. 'Keep asking the same sodding question, you'll get the same sodding answer. I'd have thought you'd have cottoned on to that by now.'

'Change it then,' said Barrett. 'Your van was seen at The Cedars nursing home in the early hours of this morning. What were you doing there?'

'Nothing. I was home in bed.'

'It was also seen by a witness in Parson's Lane the night Mandy Sheard was killed...'

'Not possible. I weren't there, and nobody else has a key.'

'...and you can offer no satisfactory alibi for either occasion,' finished Barrett. 'I'll ask you again. Do you have any witnesses who will vouch for where you were at either of those times?'

'I'll have to look in me diary and see who I slept with,' Foster said sarcastically. 'It weren't my van. How many more times?'

'Then you'll not object to an identity parade?' said Barrett, blandly. 'Since there's obviously nothing for you to worry about.'

'An identity parade for what?'

'To give witnesses an opportunity of identifying you as the man they saw. If you're telling the truth they won't be able to do that, will they?'

'Unless you tell 'em who to point at,' sad Foster. 'It's been done.'

'Not in this division.'

'No?' said Foster. 'In a pig's ear it hasn't. Stuff it. I'm not saying nothing else. You can't hold me. I want to go.'

'Interview suspended at seven-o-two p.m.,' said Barrett for the benefit of the interview tape. 'Get him back in the cells.' As he walked out a uniformed constable moved in and took his place.

'You heard,' said Woods. 'On your feet, Foster, you're going back downstairs.'

'You can't hold me,' Foster said. 'It isn't legal.'

'News to me,' said Woods, pocketing the recording tape. 'We can hold you for a long time yet—unless you turn into Houdini.' He held the door. 'After you.'

WHEN FIELDING SLID the canula into the back of her hand, Lucy woke up again, and tried to pull away. 'Hold her,' he snapped as blood flowed back from the vein and spilled over his fingers.

To Lucy, both Fielding and Carpenter were blurry figures who might or might not be real, and she tried desperately to make herself focus, and understand what was happening before sedative flowed into her and she fell asleep again, still not knowing.

At the side of her while she slept the glucose and saline drip Fielding had set up carried pitocin into her bloodstream, and within an hour, the muscles of her uterus had begun, tentatively, to prepare themselves for labour.

TWENTY-NINE

BARRETT WAS BACK in his office, disgruntled that a couple of hours in the cells hadn't encouraged Foster to be more forthcoming. Gut instinct told him that the van Lucy had seen and the van Foster drove, were one and the same. He was less sure about it being that which Bernie Parks and his girlfriend had noticed on Parson's Lane, but the possibility was there. When he slid the ring out of the packet onto the palm of his hand the metal's coldness surprised him, almost icy as he slipped it onto the first joint of his little finger and wandered over to the wall map, still thinking of connections.

MIKE HAD BEEN OFF the respirator and breathing without help for twenty-four hours, and Morrissey was beginning to believe that death had relaxed its hold. The increasingly cheerful face worn by Honeyman, the consultant, seemed to confirm it; he no longer talked in terms of percentages, although he still refused to be pinned down to estimates of recovery. All he would say was that he was satisfied.

For Margaret that was enough, and she refused even to contemplate that there might be a backward slide that would put Mike on the respirator again.

Morrissey wished he could pretend to the same kind of confidence but knew it wasn't in his nature.

Katie had reacted differently to them both once the initial shock had worn off. Breezing in every few hours to castigate Mike for his laziness in not waking up, and telling him the minutiae of what she had done and seen since the last time she had been there. Occasionally Margaret thought she caught the brief flicker of a half-formed smile on her son's face as his sister prattled like a never-ending talk-machine, but she never mentioned that, except once to her husband whose forced attempt at agreement and harrowed face kept her silent from then on.

BARRETT HAD BEGUN to clear his desk for the day, irritated that the idea lurking at the back of his mind still refused to become concrete. Rosie Quinn had talked about babies being a common link, and Smythe had got on a smug grin like she didn't know what she was talking about, but Barrett hadn't been so sure—and that's when the idea had first started to niggle like an irritant zit under his skin. Mandy's baby, Lucy's baby, Donnelly's dressing up, the women's refuge and The Cedars probably full of the things, enough to start a shop and...

When he saw where that thought might lead his mind shied away from it, then the policeman in him reasserted itself and he went back to the wall map, cursing himself that the proximity of The Cedars to Parson's Lane had never penetrated before. A prickle of sweat broke and trickled down his chest. His mind built an ugly scenario into which Foster and Donnelly would slot neatly into place—so neatly that for the first time he could remember, Barrett wanted somebody to prove him wrong.

CARPENTER was jumpy nervous, more so than she'd ever been since she became involved with Fielding. Every instinct she possessed screamed that this time he'd made a mistake, and her nervousness threatened to tip over into panic. Three times she'd gone into the room where Lucy lay to turn off the medication pump, and three times left it alone from fear of Fielding's reaction. The fourth time she checked on the girl, the pitocin had already begun its work. A faint contraction line wavered on the monitor readout, like a reedy wave testing out the shore before the rush of a tide.

Even if she stopped the pump now it would probably be too late; all it could do would be to slow Lucy's labour down, not end it. And the longer it took, the greater the danger.

Damn Fielding!

And where the hell was Foster?

WOODS WAS ALMOST at the first landing and on his way home when Barrett's voice stopped him in his tracks. He turned around, intent to point out his shift had finished hours ago and enough was enough. Then he saw the expression on Barrett's face and thought better of it. It was a look he'd seen Morrissey wear plenty of times, but never Barrett.

'What's up?' he said 'Something happened?'

'What's happened is it's time we had a talk with Foster again,' said Barrett testily. 'Get him into an interview room and encourage him to think we're backing off. Think you can do that?' His stomach rumbled with emptiness again and the sound carried down the stairs to Woods.

'We could get a butty apiece first,' Woods suggested brightly. 'Wouldn't take long.'

'Foster!' snapped Barrett, with a strength of voice that made Woods pick up speed. 'If it isn't too much trouble.'

Not when he asked like that it wasn't, thought Woods, getting himself out of range. Sounded almost like he knew what he was doing for once.

Barrett's stomach trumpeted again as he collected the papers he needed from his desk and followed Woods down the stairs. His hesitation as his foot left the bottom step was brief. He turned left instead of right, and headed for the canteen. It'd do both Woods and Foster good to wait for him. Get Woods well up on his toes and with any luck bring out a bit of nervousness in Foster. The faint niggle of conscience that came he sat on, hard, but still felt impelled to swallow down the butty he asked for faster than he'd ever swallowed one before.

The tactic didn't work.

When he got to the interview room Woods was the one looking restless while Foster sat with arms folded and feet up on a spare chair. Barrett kept his face expressionless as he sat next to Woods and said curtly, 'Put the tape in and let's get it over with.'

''Bout time,' said Foster. 'You ever heard of being sued for wrongful arrest?'

'It doesn't keep me awake at night.'

Woods set up the recorder. Foster put his head back and laughed. 'It'll make no difference,' he said. 'Whether you've got it on or off. I've nothing to say.'

'Let's see if I can persuade you to change your mind then,' said Barrett as he put the ring, in its packet, on the table in front of him. 'Nice ring. How much did you pay for it?'

Foster shrugged.

'A fiver? Ten?'

Another shrug.

'Nothing incriminating in telling us how much you paid for it,' Barrett said. 'Unless you didn't.'

'A fiver,' said Foster grudgingly. 'What do you expect me to pay for silver?'

'If I told you the ring came off a dead woman's hand it would shock you?'

'Might.'

'We found the woman's body in a storm drain.'

Foster went back to shrugging.

'Shall I tell you what I think happened? I think you drove down Parson's Lane late one night, and either by accident or deliberate intent knocked down a woman. After it had happened you got out of your van and shoved her into the field ditch, and when she tried to get out you held her face in the mud until she suffocated. And then, before you gave her a final push into the ditch bottom, you stole this ring.'

'You're bloody mad,' said Foster. 'I wasn't there.'

'The only thing I don't know,' said Barrett. 'Is why she had to be killed. What was it that she'd seen to make it necessary to stop her?' Foster folded his arms again and stared past Barrett's head. 'Where were you coming from?' Barrett insisted. 'When you hit her? Wouldn't have been The Cedars would it—where you were this morning?'

Foster's silence returned.

'I hope you've been well paid,' said Barrett, 'and invested what you've had wisely. It's going to be a long time before you get to spend any of it.' He watched the scowl on Foster's face deepen and went on chattily, 'It's surprising how much information can be got from ashes, especially when they contain bone fragments and pieces of teeth. Forensics is a pretty exact science these days—good for us, but not good for villains. Would it worry you to know ashes from the Garden of Rest are on their way for testing right now?'

Woods had his eyes fixed on Barrett, trying to piece together what was being said and making neither head nor tail of it. What dead dogs might have to do with Mandy Sheard was beyond him, then he shifted his eyes from the Detective Sergeant to Foster, and saw fear in the gathering muscles. He eased back in his chair, ready to move, and saw Barrett do the same.

'You know what we're going to find among those bone fragments, don't you?' said Barrett. 'And the only hope you have of getting out of a cell before you're senile is to tell us about your part in it.'

'I want a brief.'

'You have that right.'

'We've done talking then,' said Foster, and started to get up.

'It might go easier in court if you were frank with us,' said Barrett, trying for something concrete. 'What do you have to lose when we know all about it anyway?'

'Bluff,' said Foster. 'That's what you're doing. Must think I was born sodding yesterday. You've got bugger all. Soon as a brief gets here I walk.'

'Oh, yes,' said Barrett with soft distaste. 'You walk all right, I'll guarantee that, brief or no brief. From here to a magistrate's court, and after that straight to a remand centre.' He picked up the ring packet and closed the file.

Foster sat back down on his chair, doubt and dark in his eyes. 'You've got nothing to charge me with.'

'There's murder,' said Barrett. 'That'll do—for a start.'

JULIE DIDN'T FEEL like going out looking for trade, but she didn't feel like saying no to Eddie either. She was sore enough without being worked over by him. At eight o'clock, with an extra thick layer of make-up, she was in the public bar of the Crown, sipping at a tonic and lemon and sizing up the trade. At half-past Eddie came by to make sure she'd done as she was told. When he saw she had, he bought her a gin to show approval. 'If mad John shows up,' he said. 'Him what worked you over. Use the phone. All right? Me and the lads is wanting a word.'

'All right,' said Julie, tipping what was left of the tonic into the gin before she swallowed it down.

More than all right.

Best idea she'd heard in weeks.

IT HAD TAKEN a lot of wrangling for Barrett to get a blessing of any kind from Osgodby, whose first reaction to the Detective Sergeant's theory had been incredulity and a blanket *no!* Impatiently Barrett went over the same ground again while the Chief Superintendent, annoyed and resentful at having been dragged away from dinner, put as many obstacles in the way as he could find. Barrett's ears grew tired of hearing such phrases as *'respected member of the community.'*

When Osgodby finally gave way it was from wearing down more than conviction. 'Kid gloves,' he warned. 'I don't like being leaned on from either side, and I'm nowhere near convinced.'

'If I take Woods and two uniforms,' said Barrett, 'I can't see that'll make us look heavy handed.'

'I've played golf with the man,' Osgodby complained, as if such activity made unlawful behaviour impossible. 'Get it wrong, and I'm the one who'll have to do the explaining.'

'I don't plan on getting it wrong, sir,' said Barrett stiffly. 'Carl Fielding. CF. The initials are in Donnelly's cashbook against each large credit.'

'Unless they mean carried forward,' snapped Osgodby.

'Yes, sir,' said Barrett, thinking agreement might be quicker than dispute. 'But if I'm right, Lucy Walton is still at The Cedars and at risk.'

'Then you'd best stop wasting time,' Osgodby growled, 'and get on with it.'

Which is what he'd been wanting to do for the past hour, thought Barrett as he closed the door behind him with a solid snap. And his neck in the noose if he got there an hour too late.

LUCY STIRRED but didn't open her eyes as Fielding's fingers probed her relaxing cervix, exploring its rim. 'Another hour,' he said, taking the glove off, satisfied. 'Two at the most.' Carpenter didn't reply, unease still shifting in her gut.

Foster still wasn't answering the phone.

As if the thought communicated itself he said, 'Got hold of Foster yet?'

'No,' she said shortly. 'What happens if I can't? That isn't something we've discussed, is it? Carl Fielding's plans never go wrong.'

'You need a rest,' he said as he washed his hands. 'Edginess doesn't suit. A couple of weeks in the Seychelles should do it.'

'And you're not edgy enough. The McKechnie woman is barely here, there's no time to make it look like she's given birth before this one delivers.'

'So we do it straight after,' he said carelessly. 'What's the difference?'

'You're breaking your own rules.' Her voice rose. 'As if it no longer mattered.' He dried his hands and stared at her. 'As if you planned to be far away when trouble broke.'

'I'm going to talk to Myra McKechnie,' he said evenly, and walked out.

She had her hand on the driver, deliberately slowing down the pitocin rate again, when she heard the cars draw up. Barrett's brakes showy on the gravel.

With a sense of nightmare fulfilment she went out of the room and along the corridor to the attic stairs, looking back towards Lucy's room just once and seeing the blur of pink that seemed forever on the edge of her vision. When she reached the bottom landing Fielding was in the reception area, hands gesticulating, voice angry. As Carpenter hesitated Barrett cut across Fielding's flow, voice hard and dismissive.

'It's over. We've had Charlie Foster in custody since late afternoon and I have to tell you he's cooperated fully. We know what you pay him to do. Where's Lucy?'

'She's upstairs,' said Carpenter, coming down the last flight. 'But you'll need an ambulance, she's in labour.'

Fielding moved on her, fist raised. Woods intercepted, twisting the arm up behind Fielding's back until the man grimaced with pain. Carpenter watched dispassionately, and wondered why she felt only relief, and not fear.

THIRTY

LUCY WAS STILL DREAMING, drifting up and down through differing depths of consciousness. When she dreamed it was still of Mandy, shaking her awake and trying to make her get up. But Lucy didn't want to get up, she was too drowsy, and too comfortable, except for ripples of pain that made her grunt and move.

When Barrett found her a contraction had just ended, and sweat shone on her face. Relieved she was still alive he stayed in the room until the ambulance crew came and took her away. As they loaded her into the ambulance Lucy's dream changed. Mandy was no longer shaking her and telling her to get up, she was hugging a baby and smiling, and Lucy smiled too, because she didn't want to get up at all.

AT TEN O'CLOCK when Darren came into the Crown, Julie had already serviced two quickies around the back and was chatting up another likely. When she saw Darren she put her glass down and turned her back, sliding a hand up the undecided punter's thigh, telling him to hang around, she had to go somewhere. His shoulders jerked and his drink slopped. Having made sure he'd still be there when she got back, Julie went to the phone and called Eddie. 'Make it quick,' she said, 'I've got a john lined up and I wouldn't want you to lose money, would I?' Putting the receiver down fast before he'd time to wonder if she was being sarcastic.

It wasn't more than two minutes before she saw Tony come in with his bristle hair-cut, not as big as Sam but brighter and meaner. Eddie must have had him hanging around outside, waiting. Or counting punters. One of his tricks that, trying to catch his girls short-changing. Tony caught her eye and jerked his head. Julie stabbed a finger at the bar, where Darren, unaware, was putting on his Mr Nice act and chatting up the barmaid.

Must be a new girl, thought Julie, or she'd have cottoned on. Tony shoved in on the conversation, heavy enough to make Darren move a bit, and got a scowl in reply.

'You got a problem?' said Tony. Darren looked at the set of him and decided better of it.

'What about it?' said the punter. 'We on then?'

'In a bit,' Julie said, not wanting to miss anything. 'I fancy another drink. Thirsty work—if you know what I mean.' The punter thought he did and bought her another gin and tonic that she made last until Eddie and Sam came in five minutes later, Eddie shoving in on the opposite side of Darren to Tony, Sam standing like a mountain behind. She downed her glass then and went over, tapping Darren on the shoulder. 'Remember me?' she said as he turned round. He did, she saw it in his eyes. Saw something else, too, that he wanted to do it again, and that made her cold as well as angry. 'Have a drink,' she said, picking up Tony's beer and pouring it down the front of Darren's jeans.

'Nah, look what you've done,' said Tony, shoving Darren. 'Spilled me bleedin' drink.'

'Wasn't me, it were that frigging c...' his breath whooshed out as Tony's fist sank into his belly.

'Out,' said the landlord. 'Come on—all of you. Out, before I call the police.'

'You hear that?' said Eddie in Darren's ear. 'You're not welcome any more. Give him a hand lads, before he gets in any more trouble.'

Hurting already, and still gasping, Darren didn't stand a chance.

CARPENTER HAD GIVEN a full statement, bitter that Fielding hadn't listened to her advice, but Fielding himself had refused to admit anything, reiterating, 'I have nothing to say,' to whatever question was asked.

Barrett's mind had taken on numbness as the enormity of evil that he'd uncovered fully penetrated. Another day's delay and Lucy's name would have been added to the tally.

According to Carpenter, there were bodies in the cellar and more in the grounds. They'd have to start digging at first light, before the media got wind of it. Eight or nine she'd said, the first year. After that Foster had got rid of them instead. That sickened him—the knowledge that the girls who'd gone through the incinerator would never be identified, and he cursed Fielding for never even having bothered to keep record of their names, giving them less value than was given to breeding bitches.

It was close on eleven when he climbed the stairs to the Chief Superintendent's office, his mind arranging and rearranging what he had to say, wishing that Morrissey was there to do the talking instead of him. Osgodby listened, then silently got out the whisky bottle and poured two glasses. One he pushed across the desk to Barrett. 'It's called for,' he said. 'Drink it. When the press get hold of this they'll have a field day.'

Barrett picked up the glass and stared at it as if had come from Mars. Being handed a whisky by Osgodby had never entered his calculations. Grumbles—yes. Complaints that he should have had the brains to work it out before—yes. But whisky, no. Whisky was tantamount to being given a slap on the back, and unheard of for the lowly rank of sergeant.

He tried to forget that he didn't actually like the stuff, and swallowed, feeling it burn a warmly scented path to his stomach. 'Kind of you, sir,' he said. 'Thanks.'

'What's happening now then?'

'Smythe and Copeland are at The Cedars taking statements from the women, and from the staff. There's one agency nurse and an orderly there—I don't think they knew what was going on.'

'But we're sure, aren't we? No chance it's a jealous woman telling lies?'

'I'm sure, sir. Carpenter claims Fielding's run the nursing home as a baby farm for three years now, and made a mint out of rich women. Donnelly trawled the county with his dog collar, getting hostel workers to steer girls Fielding's way—and when they did the babies were sold and the girls disposed of.' He sighed. 'The hostel workers weren't in on it, and I don't fancy having to tell them the truth.'

'How many are we looking at?' Osgodby asked heavily. 'What are the numbers?'

'A lot,' said Barrett, tight-voiced. 'More than twenty. We'll need to check every hostel in the county.' He seared his throat again. This time the spirit felt better as it slid down.

Osgodby sucked in air that whistled over his tongue, moving his hand towards the bottle and then thinking better of it.

'You've done some good work on this, Neil. It'll be noticed.'

Barrett perked up, basked, then deflated.

He didn't see he'd done good at all. All he saw was that Lucy had come close to being another job for Foster, and that made him sick to his stomach.

LUCY WOKE UP in the maternity hospital and felt afraid, then she found out where she was and fell asleep again. When her baby was born at four o'clock on Tuesday morning, she was still drowsy, but felt a quick spark of joy as the child slid wetly from her body. A boy, like she'd known it would be all along. When they gave him to her, towel wrapped, she hugged him close, and with her lips close to his frowning face she began to reinvent his father. 'He's nice,' she said, softly, so only he could hear. 'You'll like him. Call him Rollo, they do, and he makes me laugh. And he loves me, that's nicest of all. He really, really loves me...'

DARREN HAD GOT OFF lucky and knew it, touching places where the boot had gone in, swearing when pain stabbed and thinking he'd have had a right kicking if that Kwik-Shift van hadn't pulled in behind the Crown when it did. Sodding hospital case he'd be now, 'stead of just sore. Then he thought about Julie and the beer and felt like wrecking something. Didn't matter what.

Women sucked. Slags every one.

He saw the yellow Punto in the car park when he went to buy a six-pack at the supermarket next morning, and felt a quick lift. When he peered inside, seats and dashboard were empty. Didn't have to be her car of course, could be anybody's. He tried the doors, nonchalant, like he'd just got out and was checking, unsurprised they were locked, then crossed to the supermarket at a trot, walking past the aisle ends until he saw her, standing by the meat counter, and felt heat rise in him.

Pictures formed in his head. Best shag he'd had, that. Best for her, too, he bet. She'd be panting for it next time.

Next time...

He turned on his heel and went out the exit, crossing the wide and busy main road against the traffic in his hurry to get to the van, anxious to be waiting for her when she got home, the pulse in his groin like a hammer-beat.

BY TEN O'CLOCK, three bodies had been uncovered in the cellar at The Cedars. Barrett had been called when the first was unearthed and had knelt, grim-faced, eyeing the body's position, stepping back out of the way for the photographer to move around, squatting, leaning, seeking angles. Warmsby came in twenty minutes later, face flat and emotionless as he climbed into coveralls and gloves and got to work. When he'd given the go-ahead for the body to be moved, he asked Barrett the same question Osgodby had asked—how many—and Barrett could only shake his head and give Warmsby the same response.

When the third corpse was discovered Osgodby went to The Cedars to see for himself, knowing the inevitable press conference would put Malminster on the national news, and in the public eye.

It wasn't a thought he enjoyed.

DARREN PARKED on Ash Mount, walking round the corner onto Maple Drive. As he lay in wait for the Punto, half-hidden behind a boxy laurel, he rehearsed his moves.

This'd teach her old man to take better care. Women like that needed regular attention.

He heard a car engine and gathered himself, started to relax when it stopped nearby then tensed again as a different engine note came nearer. This time it was the yellow Punto, pulling up on the drive just like the last time and Kim getting out to open the boot. He eyed the short denim skirt and bare legs and used his imagination.

When she shut the boot and moved towards the front door, Darren began to move too, pulling on the monkey mask as he unwound from his squat, rushing her through the door like he had the first time.

Round the corner on Ash Mount where the first car engine had stopped, a Panda driver called control to say he'd found the van they were looking for. The order to get themselves round to the Fitton house fast came at the same time as Darren took Kim to the hall floor, kick-closing the door behind him.

This time it was a bad move.

The Rottweiler's rush from the kitchen knocked Darren off Kim and turned him onto his back like a stranded beetle. Panicking, his foot connected with the dog's jaw and incensed it further. It ducked in low under the flailing feet to sink its teeth into the most conveniently central place it could find.

Darren's scream reached the Panda crew before they were even halfway out of the car.

BARRETT WAS halfway up the stairs to his office when Smythe came clattering down looking happy, and told him the news about Darren. 'We'd best tell Skeeter the good news too then, hadn't we?' Barrett said, and started back down again.

When he came into the interview room, Skeeter looked dejected. Instinct told him he wasn't there because they'd decided to let him go. Then Barrett told him about Darren and his face moved convulsively between mirth and misery, until he ended up slack-jawed and watery-eyed.

'If there's anything else you'd like to tell us, now's the time,' said Barrett.

'Like what?'

'Like anything else you'd like to be taken into consideration when you go to court accused of aiding and abetting rape.'

'I never! Told you that. I was in the van.'

'But you knew about it.'

'Not then I didn't. Not till after. Told you that.'

'Well suppose instead you tell us exactly where you both were while you were out of Malminster, so we can check if you were both good boys.'

Skeeter blinked, screwed his face up, and rubbed at it with his sleeve. The sleeve came away wet. 'There was this post office,' he said, 'when we was coming home…'

MORRISSEY HAD GONE HOME for a change of clothing and a shower, revelling in the spray of water on a body that felt aged beyond belief. He had asked himself many questions about his relationship with his son while Mike had been in hospital, and still couldn't understand how they had become so wary of each other. Perhaps it happened in all father-son relationships—the day the father stopped being superhero. In his case because he'd failed to protect Katie.

But she had forgiven him that, long ago. Why hadn't Mike?

The answer lay heavy in his heart.

Because he hadn't talked about it, hadn't explained his own fear, had stayed aloof and stiff because that was his nature. He turned off the water and towelled himself dry, in a hurry suddenly to get back to his son, driven by an instinct of urgency and throwing on whatever clothes came first to hand.

When he walked into Mike's cubicle and Margaret's face turned to him he saw that she was crying, and his soul sank in agony. Then he saw the smile behind the tears, and beyond her Mike's open eyes, and the agony went as his heart rejoiced. Grinning insanely he went to kiss his son.

EDDIE HAD HAD ENOUGH. He was losing face. It was time Willie got taught a permanent lesson. At six o'clock Tuesday night he went round in the car with Sam driving, soft-voiced through Willie's letterbox, telling him he'd brought the money himself and was ready to deal. After a bit of to-ing and fro-ing Willie opened the door. It was a mistake. Sam's big hand pushed him backwards until he and Eddie were inside and the door shut on inquisitive neighbours.

'You an' me got business,' said Eddie. 'Like I'm going to teach you some respect. Nobody tries to make a fool out of Eddie Gunn and gets away with it.' He looked at Sam. 'Give him a hand downstairs—he wants to show us his kitchen.' Sam took hold of Willie, lifted him bodily, and helped him go down the cellar steps the quick way. When Willie hit the bottom he thought he'd broken everything he had, but then surprised himself by getting up before Sam came to help him do that as well.

He backed away and the big man grinned at him, flexing his hands. Eddie picked up a block of resin and sniffed at it. 'Doing well, are you?'

'I get by,' said Willie, and edged round the other side of the table. Sam edged round too, from the other end, and Willie stopped in his tracks.

'How much do you clear in a week, then?' said Eddie.

'I don't keep accounts.'

'Not the right answer,' Eddie said, shaking his head. 'I think you like making things difficult for yourself.'

Willie looked from one to the other, feeling like a filling in a sandwich. 'I dunno,' he said. 'Depends what you mean by clear.' Sam edged closer and Willie backed up. 'Costs a lot you know. Resin. I got to pay the price.'

'You never learn, do you, that's your trouble,' said Eddie, getting out a thin panatella. Sam fished out his matches, flicking the brimstone with his thumb nail because it looked good. The head ignited and snapped off, cutting a blazing arc towards the open barrel of solvent. Willie started moving for the door fast and Eddie went with him. Neither of them got there in time.

Morrissey, driving Margaret home from the hospital, together for the first time in more than a week, heard the explosion and saw the quick flash of orange in the sky over the industrial park. Margaret saw it too and reached out to him. 'You're not…?'

'No,' he said, taking his eyes off the road to look at his wife. 'I'm not.'

A JAMES P. DANDY MYSTERY

BLOODY BONSAI

PETER ABRESCH

James P. Dandy—yes, that's Jim Dandy to those who can't resist the obvious joke—finds himself in a small Atlantic beach town for a course on the Japanese art of bonsai. Cranky and craving isolation, he doesn't expect to encounter a beautiful woman, a dead body, or the accusations of the local police.

Who jammed the pointed end of a bonsai tree into the chest of the sneaky little busboy? Sure, James had a minor argument with the creep over five dollars, but did that make him a killer?

Available September 1999 at your favorite retail outlet.

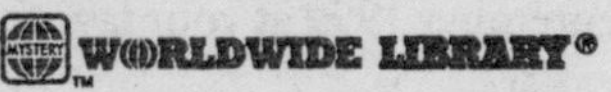

Visit us at: www.worldwidemystery.com WPA321